The X-Fil

Kevin J. Anderson's fir...
Zero and *Ruins*, The became international bestsellers.
He is also the author of the critically acclaimed novels
Blindfold, *Climbing Olympus* and (with co-author Doug
Beason) *Virtual Destruction*, *Ill Wind* and *Assemblers of
Infinity*. His work has been nominated for the Nebula
and Bram Stoker Awards.

THE
X-FILES

ANTIBODIES

KEVIN J. ANDERSON

Based on the characters created by
Chris Carter

HarperCollinsPublishers

Voyager
HarperCollins*Publishers*
77–85 Fulham Palace Road,
Hammersmith, London W6 8JB

The *Voyager* World Wide Web site address is
http://www.harpercollins.co.uk/voyager

This paperback edition 1998
1 3 5 7 9 8 6 4 2

First published in Great Britain by
Voyager 1997

ISBN 0 00 648252 X

Printed and bound in Great Britain by
Caledonian International Book Manufacturing Ltd, Glasgow

*To all the agents, investigators, scientists, and other
employees of the Federal Bureau of Investigation.
In conjunction with my writing research, I have met
several agents and seen the Bureau at work on real cases.
These people aren't all like Mulder and Scully, but they
are all proud of the professionalism and dedication they
bring to their jobs.*

ACKNOWLEDGMENTS

Writing a book like this is sometimes as involved as the deepest government conspiracy. For *Antibodies*, a few of the shadowy people lurking behind the scenes were: Kristine Kathryn Rusch, Chris Carter, Mary Astadourian, Jennifer Sebree, Frank Spotnitz, Caitlin Blasdell, John Silbersack, Dr. Robert V. Stannard at Adobe Pet Hospital, Tom Stutler, Jason C. Williams, Elton Elliot, Andrew Asch, Lil Mitchell, Catherine Ulatowski, Angela Kato, Sarah Jones, and (as always) my wife, Rebecca Moesta.

1

Late on a night filled with cold mist and still air, the alarm went off.

It was a crude security system hastily erected around the abandoned burn site, and Vernon Ruckman was the only guard stationed to monitor the night shift . . . but he got paid—and surprisingly well—to take care that no intruders got into the unstable ruins of the DyMar Laboratory on the outskirts of Portland, Oregon.

He drove his half-rusted Buick sedan up the wet gravel driveway. The bald tires crunched up the gentle rise where the cancer research facility had stood until a week and a half ago.

Vernon shifted into park, unbuckled his seatbelt, and got out to investigate. He had to be sharp, alert. He had to scope out the scene. He flicked on the beam of his official security flashlight—heavy enough to be used as a weapon—and shone it like a firehose of light into the blackened ruins that covered the site.

His employers hadn't given Vernon his own security vehicle, but they had provided him with a uniform, a badge,

1

and a loaded revolver. He had to display confidence and an intimidating appearance if he was to chase off rambunctious kids daring each other to go into the charred husk of the laboratory building. In the week and a half since the facility had been bombed, he had already chased a few trespassers away, teenagers who ran giggling into the night. Vernon had never managed to catch any of them.

This was no laughing matter. The DyMar ruins were unstable, set to be demolished in a few days. Already construction equipment, bulldozers, steam shovels, and little Bobcats were parked around large fuel storage tanks. A padlocked locker that contained blasting caps and explosives. Someone sure was in a hurry to erase the remains of the medical research facility.

In the meantime, this place was an accident waiting to happen. And Vernon Ruckman didn't want it to happen on *his* watch.

The brilliant flashlight beam carved an expanding cone through the mist and penetrated the labyrinth of tilted girders, charred wooden beams, and fallen roof timbers. DyMar Lab looked like an abandoned movie set for an old horror film, and Vernon could imagine celluloid monsters shambling out of the mist from where they had lurked in the ruins.

After the fire, a rented chain-link fence had been thrown up around the perimeter—and now Vernon saw that the gate hung partially open. With a soft exhale of breeze, the chain-link sang faintly, and the gate creaked; then the air fell still again, like a held breath.

He thought he heard movement inside the building, debris shifting, stone and wood stirring. Vernon swung the gate open wide enough for him to enter the premises. He paused to listen carefully, then proceeded with caution, just like the guidebook said to do. His left hand gripped the flashlight, while his right hovered above the heavy police revolver strapped to his hip.

He had handcuffs in a small case on his leather belt, and he thought he knew how to use them, but he had never managed to catch anyone yet. Being a nighttime security guard generally involved a lot of reading, mixed with a few false alarms (especially if you had a vivid imagination)—and not much else.

Vernon's girlfriend was a night owl, an English major and aspiring poet who spent most of the night waiting to be inspired by the muse, or else putting in a few hours at the round-the-clock coffee shop where she worked. Vernon had adjusted his own biological cycle to keep up with her, and this night-shift job had seemed the perfect solution, though he had been tired and groggy for the first week or so.

Now Vernon was wide awake as he entered the burned-out labyrinth.

Someone was indeed in there.

Old ashes crunched under his feet, splinters of broken glass and smashed concrete. Vernon remembered how this research facility had once looked, a high-tech place with unusual modern Northwestern architecture—a mixture of glossy futuristic glass and steel, and rich golden wood from the Oregon coastal forests.

The lab had burned quite well after the violent protest, the arson, and the explosion.

It wouldn't surprise him if this late-night intruder was something more than just kids—perhaps some member of the animal rights group that had claimed responsibility for the fire. Maybe it was an activist collecting souvenirs, war trophies of their bloody victory.

Vernon didn't know. He just sensed he had to be careful.

He stepped deeper inside, ducking his head to avoid a fallen wooden pole, black and warty with gray-white ashes where it had split in the intense heat. The floor of the main building seemed unstable, ready to tumble into the base-ment levels. Some of the walls had collapsed, partitions blackened, windows blasted out.

He heard someone moving stealthily. Vernon tilted the flashlight around, and white light stabbed into the shadows, making strange angles, black shapes that leapt at him and skittered along the walls. He had never been afraid of closed-in spaces, but now it seemed as if the whole place was ready to cave in on him.

Vernon paused, shone his light around. He heard the sound again, quiet rustling, a person intent on uncovering something in the wreckage. It came from the far corner, an enclosed office area with a partially slumped ceiling where the reinforced barricades had withstood most of the destruction.

He saw a shadow move there, tossing debris away, digging. Vernon swallowed hard and stepped forward. "You there! This is private property. No trespassing." He rested his hand on the butt of his revolver. Show no fear. He wouldn't let this intruder run from him.

Vernon directed his flashlight onto the figure. A large, broad-shouldered man stood up and turned toward him slowly. The intruder didn't run, didn't panic—and that made Vernon even more nervous. Oddly dressed, the man wore mismatched clothes, covered with soot; they looked like something stolen from a lost duffel bag or torn down from a clothesline.

"What are you doing here?" Vernon demanded. He flared the light into the man's face. The intruder was dirty, unkempt—and he didn't look at all well. *Great*, Vernon thought. A vagrant, rooting around in the ruins to find something he could salvage and sell. "There's nothing for you to take in here."

"Yes, there is," the man said. His voice was strangely strong and confident, and Vernon was taken aback.

"You're not supposed to be here," Vernon repeated, losing his nerve now.

"Yes I am," the man answered. "I'm authorized. I . . . worked at DyMar."

Vernon moved forward. This was entirely unexpected.

4

He continued to shine the flashlight, counting on its intimidation factor.

"My name is Dorman, Jeremy Dorman." The man fumbled in his shirt pocket, and Vernon grabbed for his revolver. "I'm just trying to show you my DyMar ID," Dorman said.

Vernon took another step closer, and in the glare of his powerful flashlight he could see that the intruder appeared sick, sweating. . . . "Looks like you need to go to a doctor."

"No. What I need . . . is in here," Dorman said, pointing. Vernon saw that the burly man had pulled away some of the rubble to reveal a hidden fire safe.

Dorman finally managed to pluck a bent and battered photo badge out of his shirt pocket—a DyMar Laboratory clearance badge. This man had worked here . . . but that didn't mean he could root around in the burned wreckage now.

"That means nothing to me," Vernon said. "I'm going to take you in, and if you really have authorization to be here, we'll get this all straightened out."

"No!" Dorman said, so violently that spittle sprayed from his lips. "You're wasting my time." For a moment, it looked as if the skin on his face shifted and blurred, then reset itself to normal. Vernon swallowed hard, but tried to maintain his stance.

Dorman ignored him and turned around.

Indignant, Vernon stepped forward and drew his weapon. "I don't think so, Mr. Dorman. Get up against the wall—right now." Vernon suddenly noticed the thick bulges underneath the man's grimy shirt. They seemed to move of their own accord, twitching.

Dorman looked at him with narrowed dark eyes. Vernon gestured with the revolver. With no sign of intimidation or respect, the man went to one of the intact concrete walls that was smeared and blackened from the fire. "I told you, you're wasting my time," Dorman growled. "I don't have much time."

"We'll take all the time we need," Vernon said.

With a sigh, Dorman spread his hands against the soot-blackened wall and waited. The skin on his hands was waxy, plastic-looking . . . runny somehow. Vernon wondered if the man had been exposed to some kind of toxic substance, acid or industrial waste. Despite the reassurance of his gun, Vernon didn't like this at all.

Out of the corner of his eye, he saw one of the bulges beneath Dorman's shirt squirm. "Stand still while I frisk you."

Dorman gritted his teeth and stared at the concrete wall in front of him, as if counting particles of ash. "I wouldn't do that," he said.

"Don't threaten me," Vernon answered quickly.

"Then don't touch me," Dorman retorted. In response, Vernon tucked the flashlight between his elbow and his side, then quickly patted the man down, frisking him with one hand.

Dorman's skin felt hot and strangely lumpy—and then Vernon's hand touched a wet, slick substance. He snatched his palm back quickly. "Gross!" he said. "What is this?" He looked down at his hand and saw that it was covered with a strange mucus, a slime.

Dorman's skin suddenly writhed and squirmed, almost as if an army of rats rushed along beneath the flesh. "You shouldn't have touched that." Dorman turned around and looked at him angrily.

"What is this stuff?" Vernon shoved the revolver back into his holster and, staring squeamishly at his hand, tried to wipe the slime off on his pants. He backed away, looking in horror at the unsettling movement throughout Dorman's body.

Suddenly his palm burned. It felt like acid eating deep into his flesh. "Hey!" He staggered backward, his heels skidding on the uneven rubble.

A burning, tingling sensation started at Vernon's hand,

as if miniature bubbles were racing up his wrist, tiny bullets firing through his nerves, into his arms, his shoulders, his chest.

Dorman lowered his arms and turned to watch. "I told you not to touch me," he said.

Vernon Ruckman felt all of his muscles lock up. Seizures wracked his body, a thousand tiny fireworks exploded in his head. He couldn't see anymore, other than bright psychedelic flashes, static in front of his vision. His arms and legs jittered, his muscles spasmed and convulsed.

From inside his head he heard bones breaking. His own bones.

He screamed as he fell backward, as if his entire body had turned into a minefield.

The flashlight, still glowing brightly, dropped to the ash-covered ground.

Dorman watched the still-twitching body of the guard for a few moments before turning his attention back to the half-exposed safe. The victim's skin rippled and bubbled as large red-black blotches appeared in the destroyed muscle tissue. The guard's flashlight illuminated a brilliant white fan across the ground, and Dorman could see swollen growths, pustules, tumors, lumps.

The usual.

Dorman ripped away the last of the wall frame and the powdery gypsum from the burned Sheetrock to expose the fire safe. He knew the combination well enough, and quickly spun through the numbers, listening to the cylinders click into position. With one meaty, numb hand, he pounded on the door to chip free some of the blackened paint that had caked in the cracks. He swung open the door.

But the safe was empty. Somebody had already taken the contents, the records, and the *stable* prototypes.

He whirled to look at the dead guard, as if Vernon Ruckman somehow had been involved with the theft. He winced as another spasm coursed through him. His last hope had been inside that safe. Or so he thought.

Dorman stood up, furious. Now what was he going to do? He looked down at his hand, and the skin on his palm shifted and changed, like a cellular thunderstorm. He shuddered as minor convulsions trooped through his muscle systems, but taking deep breaths, he managed to get his body under control again.

It was getting harder every day, but he vowed to keep doing whatever was necessary to stay alive. Dorman had always done what was necessary.

Sickened with despair, he wandered aimlessly around the wreckage of DyMar Laboratory. The computer equipment was entirely trashed, all of the lab supplies obliterated. He found a melted and broken desk, and from its placement he knew it had been David Kennessy's, the lead researcher.

"Damn you, David," Dorman muttered.

Using all his strength, he ripped open one of the top drawers, and in the debris there he found an old framed photograph—burned around the edges, the glass cracked—and stared at it. He peeled the photo out of the remnants of the frame.

David, dark-haired and dashing, smiled beside a strong-looking and pretty young woman with strawberry-blond hair and a towheaded boy. Sitting in front of them, tongue lolling out, was the Kennessys' black Labrador, always the dog . . . The family portrait had been taken when the boy was eleven years old—before the leukemia had struck him. *Patrice and Jody Kennessy.*

Dorman took the photo and stood up. He thought he knew where they might have gone, and he was sure he could find them. He *had* to. Now that the other records were gone, only the dog's blood held the answer he needed. He would gamble on where they might go, where Patrice might think to hide. She didn't even know the remarkable secret their family pet carried inside his body.

Dorman looked back to the guard's dead body. Paying no attention to the horrible blotches on his skin, he removed the guard's revolver and tucked it in his pants pocket. If it came down to a crisis situation, he might need the weapon in order to get his way.

Leaving the cooling, blotched corpse behind and taking the weapon and the photograph, Jeremy Dorman walked away from the burned DyMar Laboratory.

Inside of him, the biological time bomb kept ticking. He didn't have many days left.

2

The bear stood huge, five times the size of an all-star wrestler. Bronze-brown fur bristled from its cable-thick muscles—a Kodiak bear, a prize specimen. Its claws were spread as it leaned over to rip a salmon from the rocky stream, pristine and uninterrupted.

Mulder stared at the claws, the fangs, the sheer primal power.

He was glad the creature was simply stuffed and on display in the Hoover Building, but even still, he appreciated the glass barrier. Mounting this beast must have been a taxidermist's nightmare.

The prize hunting trophy had been confiscated in an FBI raid against a drug kingpin. The drug lord had spent over twenty thousand dollars for his own personal hunting expedition to Alaska, and then spent more money to have his prize kill mounted. When the FBI arrested the man, they had confiscated the gigantic bear according to RICO statutes—since the drug lord had funded the expedition with illicit drug money, the stuffed bear was forfeited to the federal government.

11

Not knowing what else to do with it, the FBI had put the monster on display beside other noteworthy confiscated items: a customized Harley-Davidson motorcycle, emerald and diamond necklaces, earrings, bracelets, bricks of solid gold.

Sometimes Mulder left his quiet and dim basement offices where he kept the X-Files just to come up and peruse the display case.

Looking at the powerful bear, Mulder continued to be preoccupied, perplexed by a recent and highly unusual death report he had received, an X-File that had come across his desk from a field agent in Oregon.

When a monster like this bear killed its prey, it left no doubt as to the cause of death. A bizarre disease raised many questions, though—especially a new and virulent disease found at the site of a medical research laboratory that had recently been destroyed by arson.

Unanswered questions had always intrigued Agent Fox Mulder.

He went back down in the elevator to his own offices, where he could sit and read the death report again. Then he would go meet Scully.

She stood between the thick, soundproofed Plexiglas partitions inside the FBI's practice firing range. Special Agent Dana Scully removed her handgun, a new Sig Sauer 9mm. She slapped in an expanded clip that carried fifteen bullets, an extra one in the chamber.

She entered the code at the computer keypad at her left; hydraulics hummed, and a cable trundled the black silhouetted "bad guy" target to a range of twenty yards. She locked it into place and reached up to grab a set of padded earphones. She snugged the hearing protection over her head, pressing down her red-gold hair.

Then she gripped her pistol, assuming a proper isosceles

firing stance, and aimed at her target. Squinting and focusing down the hairline, she squeezed the trigger in an unconscious reflex and popped off the first round. She paid no attention to where it struck, simply aimed and shot again, firing over and over. Expended casings flew into the air like metal popcorn, clinking and rattling on the cement floor. The smell of burned black powder filled her nostrils.

She thought of those shadowy men who had killed her sister Melissa, those who had repeatedly tried to silence or discredit Mulder and his admittedly unorthodox theories.

Scully had to stay calm, maintain her firing stance, maintain her edge. If she let her anger and frustration simmer through her, then her aim would be off.

She looked at the black silhouette of the target and saw only the featureless men who had entwined themselves so deeply in her life. Smallpox scars, nose implants, vaccination records, and mysterious disappearances—like her own—and the cancer that was almost certainly a result of what they had done to her while she had been abducted. She had no way to fight against the conspiracies, no target to shoot at. She had no choice but to keep searching. Scully gritted her teeth and shot again and again until the entire clip was expended.

Removing her ear protection, she punched the button to retrieve the yellowish paper target. FBI agents had to requalify at the Quantico firing range at least once every three months. Scully wasn't due for another four weeks yet, but still she liked to come early in the morning to practice. The range was empty then, and she could take her time.

Later in the day, tour groups would come through to watch demonstrations as a special agent forced into tour guide service showed off his marksmanship skills with the Sig Sauer, the M-16, and possibly a Thompson submachine gun. Scully wanted to be long finished here before the first groups of wide-eyed Boy Scouts or schoolteachers marched in behind the observation windows.

She retrieved the battered target, studying her skill, and was pleased to see how well her sixteen shots had clustered around the center of the silhouetted chest.

Quantico instructors taught agents not to think of their mark as a person but as a "target." She didn't aim for the heart or the head or the side. She aimed for the "center of mass." She didn't aim to shoot the bad guys—she simply "removed the target."

Drawing her weapon and firing upon a suspect was the last possible resort of a good agent, not the proper way to end an investigation unless all other methods failed. Besides, the paperwork was horrendous. Once a federal agent fired her weapon, she had to account for every single shell casing expended—sometimes a difficult task during a heated running firefight.

Scully yanked the paper target from its binder clip and left the gunshot-spattered piece of support cardboard hanging in place. She punched the computer controls to reset the target to its average point, and then looked up, startled to see her partner Mulder leaning against the wall in the observation gallery. She wondered how long he had been waiting for her.

"Good shooting, Scully," he said. He didn't ask whether she was simply doing target practice or somehow exorcising personal demons.

"Spying on me, Mulder?" she said lightly, trying to cover her surprise. After an awkward moment of silence she said, "All right, what is it?"

"A new case. And this one is going to capture your interest, no doubt about it." He smiled.

She replaced her safety goggles on the proper hook and followed him. Even if they weren't always believable, Mulder's discoveries were always interesting and unusual.

3

Khe Sanh Khoffee Shoppe
Washington, D.C.
Monday, 8:44 A.M.

As Mulder led her out of the Hoover Building, Scully wondered about the new case he had found almost as much as she dreaded the coffee shop where he planned to take her. Even his offhanded promise, "I'm buying," hadn't exactly won her over.

They walked together past the metal detector, out the door, and down the granite steps. At all corners of the big, box-like building, uniformed FBI security teams manned imposing-looking guard stations.

Mulder and Scully passed alongside the line of tourists that had already begun to form for the first FBI tour of the day. Though most of the pedestrians wore the formal business attire typical in the bureaucratic environment of Washington, D.C., the knowing looks told Scully that the tourists recognized them as obvious federal agents.

Other federal buildings stood tall around them, ornate and majestic—the architecture in downtown Washington had to compete with itself. Upstairs in many of these buildings were numerous consulting firms, law offices, and high-powered lobbyist organizations. The bottom levels contained cafes, delis, and newsstands.

Mulder held the glass door of the Khe Sanh Khoffee Shoppe. "Mulder, why do you want to take me here so often?" she asked, scanning the meager clientele inside. Many immigrant Korean families had opened similar businesses in the federal district—usually delicious cafeterias, coffee shops, and restaurants. But the proprietors of the Khe Sanh Khoffee Shoppe imitated mediocre American cuisine with a vengeance, with unfortunate results.

"I like the place," Mulder said with a shrug. "They serve coffee in those nice big Styrofoam cups."

Scully went inside without further argument. In her opinion, they had more important things to do . . . and she wasn't hungry.

Handwritten daily specials were listed on a white board propped on an easel near a large and dusty silk plant. A refrigerator filled with bottled water and soft drinks stood beside the cash register. An empty steam table occupied a large portion of the coffee shop; at lunchtime the proprietors served a cheap—and cheap-tasting—lunch buffet of various Americanized Oriental specialties.

Mulder set his briefcase on one of the cleared tables, then bolted for the cash register and coffee line as Scully took her seat. "Can I get you anything, Scully?" he called.

"Just coffee," she said, against her better judgment.

He raised his eyebrows. "They've got a great fried egg and hash browns breakfast special."

"Just coffee," she repeated.

Mulder came back with two large Styrofoam cups. Scully could smell the bitter aroma even before he set the cup in front of her. She held it in both hands, enjoying the warmth on her fingertips.

Getting down to business, Mulder snapped open his briefcase. "This one will interest you, I think." He withdrew a manila folder. "Portland, Oregon," he said. "This is DyMar Laboratory, a federally funded cancer research center."

He handed her a slick brochure showcasing a beautifully modern laboratory facility: a glass-and-steel framework trimmed with handsome wood decking, support beams, and hardwood floors. The reception areas were heavily decorated with glowing golden wood and potted plants, while the laboratory areas were clean, white, and sterile.

"Nice place," Scully said as she folded the pages together again. "I've read a lot about current cancer research, but I'm not aware of their work."

"DyMar tried to keep a low profile," Mulder said, "until recently."

"What changed?" Scully asked, setting the brochure down on the small table.

Mulder removed the next item, a black-and-white glossy photo of the same place. This time the building was destroyed, gutted by fire, barricaded by chain-link fences— an abandoned war zone.

"Presumably sabotage and arson," Mulder said. "The investigation is still pending. This happened a week and a half ago. A Portland newspaper received a letter from a protest group—Liberation Now—claiming responsibility for the destruction. But nobody's ever heard of them. They were supposedly animal rights activists upset at some of the research the lead scientist, Dr. David Kennessy, was performing. High-tech research, and a lot of it was classified."

"And the activists burned the place down?"

"Blew it up and burned it down, actually."

"That's rather extreme, Mulder—usually those groups are just content to make their statement and get some publicity." Scully stared down at the charred building.

"Exactly, Scully. Somebody really wanted to stop the experimentation."

"What was Kennessy's research that got the group so excited?"

"The information on that is very vague," Mulder said, his forehead creasing. His voice became troubled. "New cancer therapy techniques—really cutting-edge stuff—he and his brother Darin worked together for years, in an unlikely combination of approaches. David was the biologist and medical chemist, while Darin came to the field from a background in electrical engineering."

"Electrical engineering and cancer reseach?" Scully asked. "Those two don't usually go together. Was he developing a new treatment apparatus or diagnostic equipment?"

"Unknown," Mulder said. "Darin Kennessy apparently had a falling-out with his brother six months ago. He abandoned his work at DyMar and joined a fringe group of survivalists out in the Oregon wilderness. Needless to say, he isn't reachable by phone."

Scully looked again at the brochure, but found no mention of the specific team members. "So, did David Kennessy continue the work even without his brother?"

"Yes," Mulder said. "He and their junior research partner, Jeremy Dorman. I've tried to locate their records and reports to determine the exact nature of their investigations, but most of the documents have been removed from the files. As far as I know, Kennessy concentrated on obscure techniques that have never been previously used in cancer research."

Scully frowned. "Why would anyone be so upset about that? Did his research show any progress?"

Mulder gulped his coffee. "Well, apparently the members of the mob were outraged at some supposedly cruel and unapproved animal tests Kennessy had performed. No details, but I suppose the good doctor strayed a bit from the rules of the Geneva Convention." Mulder shrugged. "Most of the records were burned or destroyed, and it's hard to get any concrete information."

"Anyone hurt in the fire?" Scully asked.

"Kennessy and Dorman were both reported killed in the

18

blaze, though the investigators had trouble identifying—or even accounting for—all the body parts. Remember, the lab didn't just burn, it exploded. There must have been some kind of bombs planted. That group meant business, Scully."

"That's all interesting, Mulder, but I'm not sure why it's interesting to you."

"I'm getting to that."

Scully's brow furrowed as she looked down at the glossy print of the burned lab. She handed the photo back to Mulder.

At other tables, people in business suits hunched over, continuing their own conversations, oblivious to anyone listening in. Scully kept her senses alert out of habit as a federal investigator. A group of men from NASA sat at one table, discussing proposals and modifications to a new interplanetary probe, while other men at a different table talked in hushed tones about how best to cut the space program budget.

"Kennessy had apparently been threatened before," Mulder said, "but this group came out of nowhere and drew a big crowd. I've found no record of any organization called Liberation Now before the DyMar incident, until the *Portland Oregonian* received the letter claiming responsibility."

"Why would Kennessy have kept working under such conditions?" Scully picked up the colorful brochure and unfolded it again, skimming down the predictable propaganda statements about "new cancer breakthroughs," "remarkable treatment alternatives," and "a cure is just around the corner." She took a deep breath; the words struck a chord with her. Oncologists had been using those same phrases since the 1950s.

Mulder withdrew another photo of a boy eleven or twelve years old. The boy was smiling for the camera, but looked skeletal and weak, his face gaunt, his skin gray and papery, much of his hair gone.

"This is his twelve-year-old son Jody, terminally ill with

cancer—acute lymphoblastic leukemia. Kennessy was desperate to find a cure, and he certainly wasn't going to let a few protesters delay his work. Not for a minute."

She rested her chin in her hands. "I still don't see how an arson and property-destruction case would capture your interest."

Mulder removed the last photo from the folder. A man in a security guard's uniform lay sprawled in the burned debris, his face twisted in a mask of agony, his skin blotched and swollen with sinuous lumps, arms and legs bent at strange angles. He looked like a spider that had been dosed with bug spray.

"This man was found at the burned lab just last night," Mulder said. "Look at those symptoms. No one has figured it out yet."

Scully snatched the photo and looked intently at it. Her eyes showed her alarm. "He appears to be dead from some fast-acting and exceedingly virulent pathogen."

Mulder waited for her to absorb the gruesome details, then said, "I wonder if something in Kennessy's research could be responsible? Something that didn't entirely perish in the fire . . ."

Scully frowned slightly as she concentrated. "Well, we don't know what exactly the arsonists did before they destroyed the lab. Maybe they liberated some of the experimental animals . . . maybe something very dangerous got loose."

Mulder took another sip of his coffee, then retrieved the papers from the folder. He waited for her to draw her own conclusions.

Scully let her interest show plainly as she continued to study the photo. "Look at those tumors . . . How fast did the symptoms appear?"

"The victim was apparently normal and healthy when he reported to work a few hours earlier." He leaned forward intently. "What do you think this guard stumbled upon?"

Scully pursed her lips in concern. "I can't really say without seeing it myself. Is this man's body being held in quarantine?"

"Yes. I thought you might want to come with me to take a look."

Scully took her first sip of the coffee, and it did indeed taste as awful as she had feared. "Let's go, Mulder," she said, standing up from the table. She handed him back the colorful brochure with its optimistic proclamations.

Kennessy must have performed some radical and unorthodox tests on his lab animals, she thought. It was possible that after the violent destruction of the facility, and with this possible disease outbreak, some of the animals had escaped. And perhaps they carried something deadly.

4

State Highway 22
Coast Range, Oregon
Monday, 10:00 P.M.

The dog stopped in the middle of the road, distracted on his way to the forest. The ditch smelled damp and spicy with fallen leaves. Roadside reflectors poked out of the ditches beside gravel driveways and rural mailboxes. Unlike the rich spruce and cedar forest, the road smelled of vehicles, tires, hot engines, and belching exhaust.

The twin headlights of the approaching car looked like bright coins. The image fixated the dog, imprinting spots on his dark-adapted eyes. He could hear the car dominating the night noises of insects and stirring branches in the trees around him.

The car sounded loud. The car sounded angry.

The road was wet and dark, shrouded by thick trees. The kids were cranky after a long day of traveling . . . and at this point the impromptu vacation didn't seem like such a good idea after all.

The rugged and scenic coast was still a dozen miles away, and then it would be another unknown number of miles up the highway until they encountered one of the clustered tourist havens filled with cafes, art galleries, souvenir shops, and places to stay—each one called an "inn" or a "lodge," never a simple motel.

Ten miles back, they had driven past a lonely crossroads occupied by a gas station, a hamburger joint, and a run-down fifties-era motel with a pink neon "No" flickering next to the "Vacancy" sign.

"We should have planned this trip better," Sharon said beside him in the front seat.

"I believe you mentioned that already," Richard answered testily. "Once or twice."

In the backseat, Megan and Rory displayed their intense boredom in uncharacteristic ways. Rory was so restless he had switched off his Game Boy, and Megan was so tired she had stopped picking on her brother.

"There's nothing to do," Rory said.

"Dad, don't you know any other games?" Megan asked. "Were you ever bored as a kid?"

He forced a smile, then glanced up in the rearview mirror to see them sulking in the back seat of the Subaru Outback. Richard had rented the car for this vacation, impressed by its good wheels, good traction for those mountain roads. At the start of the long drive, he had felt like SuperDad.

"Well, my sister and I used to play a game called 'Silo.' We were in Illinois, where they've got lots of farms. You'd keep watch around the countryside and call out every time you saw a silo next to a barn. Whoever saw the most silos won the game." He tried to make it sound interesting, but even back then only the tedium of the Midwestern rural landscape had made Silo a viable form of entertainment.

"Doesn't do much good when it's dark out, Dad," Rory said.

"I don't think there are any silos or barns out here anyway," Megan chimed in.

The dark trees pressing close to the narrow highway rushed by, and his blazing headlights made tunnels in front of him. He kept driving, kept trying to think of ways to distract his kids. He vowed to make this a good vacation after all. Tomorrow they would go see the Devil's Churn, where waves from the ocean shot up like a geyser through a hole in the rock, and then they would head up to the Columbia River Gorge and see waterfall after waterfall.

Now, though, he just wanted to find a place to spend the night.

"Dog!" his wife cried. "A dog! Watch out!"

For a frozen instant, Richard thought she was playing some bizarre variant of the Silo game, but then he spotted the black four-legged form hesitating in the middle of the road, its liquid eyes like pools of quicksilver that reflected the headlights.

He slammed on the brakes, and the new tires on the rental Subaru skiied across the slick coating of fallen leaves. The car slewed, slowed, but continued forward like a locomotive, barely under control.

In the back, the kids screamed. The brakes and tires screamed even louder.

The dog tried to leap away at the last instant, but the Subaru bumper struck it with a horrible muffled thump. The black Lab flew onto the hood, into the windshield, then caromed off the side into the weed-filled ditch.

The car screeched to a halt, spewing wet gravel from the road's shoulder. "Jesus Christ!" Richard shouted, slamming the gearshift into park so quickly the entire vehicle rocked.

He grabbed at his seatbelt, fumbling, punching, struggling, until the buckle finally popped free of the catch. Megan and Rory huddled in stunned silence in the back, but Richard popped the door open and sprang out. He looked from side to side, belatedly thinking to check if another car or truck might be bearing down on them.

Nothing. No traffic, just the night. In the deep forest, even the nocturnal insects had fallen silent, as if watching.

He walked around the front of the car with a sick dread. He saw the dent in the bumper, a smashed headlight, a scrape in the hood of the rental car. He remembered too vividly the offhanded and cheerful manner in which he had declined insurance coverage from the rental agent. He stared down now, wondering how much the repairs would cost.

The back door opened a crack, and a very pale-looking Megan eased out. "Daddy? Is he all right?" She peered around, blinking in the darkness. "Is the dog going to be okay?"

He swallowed hard, then crunched around the front of the car into the wet weeds. "Just a second, honey. I'm still looking."

The dog lay sprawled and twitching, a big black Labrador with a smashed skull. He could see the skid marks where it had tumbled across the underbrush. It still moved, attempting to drag itself into the brambles toward a barbed-wire fence and denser foliage beyond. But its body was too broken to let it move.

The dog wheezed through broken ribs. Blood trickled from its black nose. Christ, why couldn't the thing have just been killed outright? A mercy.

"Better take him to a doctor," Rory said, startling him. He hadn't heard the boy climb out of the car. Sharon stood up at the passenger side. She looked at him wide-eyed, and he gave a slight shake of his head.

"I don't think a doctor will be able to help him, sport," he said to his son.

"We can't just leave him here," Megan said, indignant. "We gotta take him to a vet."

He looked down at the broken dog, the dented rental car, and felt absolutely helpless. His wife hung on the open door. "Richard, there's a blanket in the back. We can move the suitcases between the kids, clear a spot. We'll take the dog to the nearest veterinary clinic. The next town up the road should have one."

Richard looked at the kids, his wife, and the dog. He had absolutely no choice. Swallowing bile, knowing it would do no good, he went to get the blanket while Sharon worked to rearrange their suitcases.

The next reasonably sized town up the road, Lincoln City, turned out to be all the way to the coast. The lights had been doused except for dim illumination through window shades in back rooms where the locals watched TV. As he drove through town, desperately searching for an animal care clinic, he wondered why the inhabitants hadn't bothered to roll up the sidewalks with sundown.

Finally he saw an unlit painted sign, "Hughart's Family Veterinary Clinic," and he swerved into the empty parking lot. Megan and Rory both sniffled in the backseat; his wife sat tight-lipped and silent next to him up front.

Richard took the responsibility himself, climbing the cement steps and ringing the buzzer at the veterinarian's door. He vigorously rapped his knuckles on the window until finally a light flicked on in the foyer. When an old man peered at them through the glass, Richard shouted, "We've got a hurt dog in the car. We need your help."

The old veterinarian showed no surprise at all, as if he had expected nothing else. He unlocked the door as Richard gestured toward the Subaru. "We hit him back up the highway. I . . . I think it's pretty bad."

"We'll see what we can do," the vet said, going around to the rear of the car. Richard swung open the hatchback, and both Megan and Rory clambered out of their seats, intently interested, their eyes wide with hope. The vet took one look at the children, then met Richard's eyes, understanding exactly the undertones here.

In back, the dog lay bloody and mangled, somehow still

alive. To Richard's surprise, the black Lab seemed stronger than before, breathing more evenly, deeply asleep. The vet stared at it, and from the masked expression on the old man's face, Richard knew the dog had no hope of surviving.

"This isn't your dog?" the vet asked.

"No, sir," Richard answered. "No tags, either. Didn't see any."

Megan peered into the back to look. "Is he going to be all right, Mister?" she asked. "Are we coming back to visit him, Daddy?"

"We'll have to leave him here, honey," he answered. "This man will know what to do with the dog."

The vet smiled at her. "Of course he'll be all right," he said. "I've got some special kinds of bandages." He looked up at Richard. "If you could help me carry him in back to the surgery, I'll let you all be on your way."

Richard swallowed hard. The way the old man looked right into his heart, he knew the vet must see cases like this every week, hurt animals abandoned to his care.

Together the two men reached under the blanket, lifting the heavy dog. With a grunt, they began to shuffle-walk to the back door of the clinic. "He's *hot*," the vet said as they entered the swinging door. Leaving the dog on the operating table, the vet went around the room, flicking on lights.

Anxious to be away, Richard stepped to the door, thanking the old man profusely. He left one of his business cards on the reception table, hesitated, then thought better of it. He tucked the card back in his pocket and hurried out the front door.

He rushed back to the Subaru and swung himself inside. "He'll take care of everything," Richard said to no one in particular, then jammed the vehicle into gear. His hands felt grimy, dirty, covered with fur and a smear of the dog's blood.

The car drove off as Richard desperately tried to relocate the peace and joy of a family vacation. The night insects resumed their music in the forest.

5

Mercy Hospital
Portland, Oregon
Tuesday, 10:03 A.M.

 The middle of morning on a gray day. Early mist hanging above and through the air made the temperature clammy and colder than it should have been. The clouds and gloom would burn off by noon, giving a blessed few minutes of sunshine before the clouds and the rain rolled in again.

Typical morning, typical Portland.

Scully didn't suppose it made any difference if she and Mulder were going to spend the day in a hospital morgue anyway.

In the basement levels of the hospital, the quiet halls were like tombs. Scully had seen the same thing in many hospitals where she had performed autopsies or continued investigations on cold cadavers in refrigerator drawers. But though the places were by now familiar, she would never find them comforting.

Dr. Frank Quinton, Portland's medical examiner, was a bald man with a feathery fringe of white hair surrounding the back of his head. He had wire-rimmed glasses and a cherubic face.

Judging by his friendly, grandfatherly smile, Scully would have pegged him as a charming, good-natured man—but she could see a tired hardness behind his eyes. In his career as a coroner, Quinton must have seen too many teenagers pulled from wrecked cars, too many suicides and senseless accidents, too many examples of the quirky nature of death.

He warmly shook Scully's hand, and Mulder's. Mulder nodded at his partner, speaking to the coroner. "As I mentioned on the phone, sir, Agent Scully is a medical doctor herself, and she has had experience with many unusual deaths. Perhaps she can offer some suggestions."

The coroner beamed at her, and Scully couldn't help but smile back at the kind-faced man. "What is the status of the body now?"

"We used full disinfectants and have been keeping the body in cold storage to stop the spread of any biological agents," the ME said.

The morgue attendant held out a clipboard and smiled like a puppy dog next to Quinton. The assistant was young and scrawny, but already nearly as bald as the medical examiner. From the idolizing way he looked up at the ME, Scully guessed that Frank Quinton must be his mentor, that one day the morgue attendant wanted to be a medical examiner himself.

"He's in drawer 4E," the attendant said, though Scully was certain the coroner already knew where the guard's body was stored. The attendant hurried over to the bank of clean stainless-steel refrigerator drawers. Most, Scully knew, would contain people who had died of natural causes, heart attacks, or car accidents, surgical failures from the hospital, or old retirees fallen like dead leaves in nursing homes.

One drawer, though, had been marked with yellow tape and sealed with stickers displaying the clawed-circle "Bio-Hazard" label: 4E.

"Thank you, Edmund," the ME said as Mulder and Scully followed him to the morgue refrigerators.

"You've used appropriate quarantine conditions?" Scully asked.

Quinton looked over at her. "Luckily, the police were spooked enough by the appearance of the corpse that they took precautions, gloves, contamination wraps. Everything was burned in the hospital incinerator here." '

Edmund stopped in front of the stainless-steel drawer and peeled away the BioHazard sticker. A card on the front panel of the drawer labeled it "Restricted, Police Evidence."

After tugging on a sterile pair of rubber gloves, Edmund grabbed the drawer handle and yanked it open. "Here it is. We don't usually get anything as curious as this poor guy." He held open the drawer, and a gust of frosty air drifted out.

With both hands, Edmund dragged out the plastic-draped cadaver of the dead guard. Like a showroom model revealing a new sports car, the attendant drew back the sheet. He stood aside proudly to let the medical examiner, Scully, and Mulder push forward.

Mixed with the cold breath of the refrigerator, the smell of heavy, caustic disinfectants swirled in the air, stinging Scully's eyes and nostrils. She was unable to keep herself from bending over in fascination. She saw the splotches of coagulated blood beneath the guard's skin like blackened bruises, the lumpy, doughy growths that had sprouted like mushrooms inside his tissues.

"I've never seen tumors that could grow so fast," Scully said. "The limited rate of cellular reproduction should make such a rapid spread impossible." She bent down and observed a faint slimy covering on some patches of skin. Some kind of clear mucus . . . like slime.

"We're treating this as a high-contamination scenario. Our lab tests are expected back in another day or so from the CDC," Quinton said. "I'm doing my own analysis, under tight controls, but this is an unusual one. We can't just do it in-house."

Scully continued to study the body with the practiced eye of a physician analyzing the symptoms, the patterns, trying to imagine the pathology. The attendant offered her a box of latex gloves. She snapped on a pair, flexing her fingers, then she reached forward to touch the cadaver's skin. She expected it to be cold and hard with rigor—but instead the body felt warm, fresh, and flexible.

"When was this man brought in?" she asked.

"Sunday night," Quinton answered.

She could smell the frosty coldness from the refrigerator, felt it with her hand. "What's his body temperature? He's still warm," she said.

The medical examiner reached forward curiously, and laid his own gloved hand on the cadaver's bruised shoulder. The ME turned and looked sternly at the morgue attendant. "Edmund, are these refrigerators acting up again?"

The morgue attendant scrambled backward like a panicked squirrel, devastated that his mentor had spoken sternly to him. "Everything is working fine, sir. I had Maintenance check it just yesterday." He dashed over to study the gauges. "It says that the drawers are all at constant temperature."

"Feel his temperature for yourself," the ME snapped.

Edmund stuttered, "No, sir, I'll take your word for it. I'll get Maintenance down here right away."

"Do that," Quinton said. He peeled off his gloves and went over to a sink to scrub his hands thoroughly. Scully did the same.

"I hope those refrigerators don't fall apart on us again," Quinton muttered. "The last thing I need is for that guy to start to smell."

Scully looked again at the cadaver and tried to picture what Dymar's mysterious research might have produced. If something had gotten loose, they might have to deal with a lot more bodies just like this one. What had Darin Kennessy known, or suspected, that had led him to run and hide from the research entirely?

"Let's go, Mulder. We've got a lot of ground to cover." Scully dried her hands and brushed her red hair away from her face. "We need to find out what Kennessy was working on."

6

Kennessy Residence
Tigard, Oregon
Tuesday, 12:17 P.M.

The house looked like most of the others on the street—suburban normal, built in the seventies with aluminum siding, shake shingles, average lawn, average hedges, nothing to make it stand out among the other middle-class homes in a residential town on the outskirts of Portland.

"Somehow, I expected the home of a hotshot young cancer researcher to be more . . . impressive," Mulder said. "Maybe a white lab coat draped on the mailbox, test tubes lining the front walkway . . ."

"Researchers aren't that glamorous, Mulder. They don't spend their time playing golf and living in mansions. Besides," she added, "the Kennessy family had some rather extraordinary medical expenses beyond what insurance would cover."

According to records they had obtained, Jody Kennessy's leukemia and his ever-worsening spiral of last-ditch treatments had gobbled their savings and forced them into taking a second mortgage.

Together, Mulder and Scully walked up the driveway toward the front door. Wrought-iron railings lined the two steps up to the porch. A forlorn, waterlogged cactus looked out of place beside the downspout of the garage.

Mulder removed his notepad, and Scully brushed her hands down her jacket. The air was cool and damp, but her shiver came as much from her thoughts.

After seeing the guard's body and the gruesome results of the disease that had so rapidly struck him down, Scully knew they had to determine exactly what David Kennessy had been developing at the DyMar Laboratory. The available records had been destroyed in the fire, and Mulder had so far been unable to track down anyone in charge; he couldn't even pinpoint who had overseen DyMar's funding from the federal government.

The dead ends and false leads intrigued him, kept him hunting, while the medical questions engaged Scully's interest.

She wouldn't necessarily expect the wife of a researcher to know much about his work, but in this case there were extenuating circumstances. She and Mulder had decided their next step would be to talk to Kennessy's widow Patrice—an intelligent woman in her own right. In her heart, Scully also wanted to see Jody.

Mulder looked up at the house as he approached the front door. The garage door was closed, the drapes on the house windows drawn, everything quiet and dark. The fat Sunday *Portland Oregonian* lay in a protective plastic wrapper on the driveway, untouched. And it was Tuesday.

As Mulder reached for the doorbell, Scully instantly noticed the shattered latch. "Mulder . . . "

She bent to inspect the lock. It had been broken in, the wood splintered. She could see dents around the knob and the dead bolt, the torn-up jamb. Someone had crudely pressed the fragments back in place, a cosmetic cover-up that would fool casual passersby from the street.

Mulder pounded on the door. "Hello!" he shouted.

Scully stepped into a flowerbed to peer inside the window; through a gap in the drapes she saw overturned furniture in the main room, scattered debris on the floor.

"Mulder, we have sufficient cause to enter the premises."

He pushed harder, and the door swung easily open. "Federal agents," he called out—but the Kennessy home answered them only with a quiet, gasping echo of his call. Mulder and Scully stepped into the foyer, and both stopped simultaneously to stare at the disaster.

"Very subtle," Mulder said.

The home had been ransacked, furniture tipped over, upholstery slashed, stuffing pulled out. The baseboards had been pried away from the walls, the carpeting ripped up as the violent searchers dug down to the floorboards. Cabinets and cupboards hung open, bookshelves lay tipped over, with books and knickknacks strewn about.

"I don't think we're going to find anybody here," Scully said, hands on her hips.

"What we need to find is a housekeeper," Mulder answered.

They searched through the rooms anyway. Scully couldn't help wondering why anyone would have ransacked the place. Had the violent protest group struck at Kennessy's family as well, not satisfied with killing David Kennessy and Jeremy Dorman, not content with burning down the entire DyMar facility?

Had Patrice and Jody been here when the attack occurred?

Scully dreaded finding their bodies in the back room, gagged, beaten, or just shot to death where they stood.

But the house was empty.

"We'll have to get evidence technicians to search for blood traces," Scully said. "We'll need to seal off the site and get a team in here right away."

They entered Jody's room. The Sheetrock had been smashed open, presumably to let the searchers look between the studs in the walls. The boy's bed had been overturned, the mattress flayed of its sheets and fabric covering.

"This doesn't make any sense," Scully said. "Very violent . . . and very thorough."

Mulder picked up a smashed model of an alien space-ship from *Independence Day*. Scully could imagine how care-fully and lovingly the twelve-year-old boy must have assembled it.

"Just like the DyMar attack two weeks ago," Mulder said.

Mulder bent over to pick up a chunk of broken gypsum board, turning it in his fingers. Scully retrieved a fighter jet model that had been suspended by fish line from the ceiling but now lay with its plastic airfoils broken on the floor, its fuselage cracked so that someone could pry inside. Searching.

Scully stood, feeling cold. She thought of the young boy who had already received a death sentence as the cancer ravaged his body. Jody Kennessy had been through enough already, and now he had to endure whatever had happened here.

Scully turned around and walked into the kitchen, mind-ful of the drinking glasses shattered on the linoleum floor and on the Formica countertop. The searchers couldn't pos-sibly have been looking for anything inside the glass tum-blers. They had simply enjoyed the destruction.

Mulder bent down next to the refrigerator and looked at an orange plastic dog food bowl. He picked it up, turning it to show the name "Vader" written in magic marker across the front. The bowl was empty, the food crumbs hard and dry.

"Look at this, Scully," he said. "If something happened to Patrice and Jody Kennessy . . . then where is the dog?"

Scully frowned. "Maybe the same place they are." With a long, slow look at the devastation in the kitchen, Scully swallowed hard. "Looks like our search just got wider."

7

No one would ever find them in this cabin, isolated out in the wilderness of the Oregon coastal mountains. No one would help them, no one would rescue them.

Patrice and Jody Kennessy were alone, desperately trying to hold onto some semblance of normal life by the barest edges of their fingernails.

As far as Patrice was concerned, though, it wasn't working. Day after day of living in fear, jumping at shadows, hiding from mysterious noises . . . but they had no other choice for survival—and Patrice was determined that her son would survive this.

She went to the window of the small cabin and parted the dingy drapes to watch Jody bounce a tennis ball against the outside wall. He was in plain view, but within running distance of the thick forest that ringed the hollow. Each impact of the tennis ball sounded like gunshots aimed at her.

At one time the isolation of this plot of land had been a valuable asset, back when she had designed the place for her brother-in-law as a place for him to get away from

DyMar. *Darin was good at getting away,* she thought. Scattered empty patches on the steep hills in the distance showed where clear-cutting teams had removed acres and acres of hardwood a few years before, leaving stubbled rectangles like scabs on the mountainside.

This cabin was supposed to be a private vacation hideout for relaxation and solitude. Darin had deliberately refused to put in a phone, or a mailbox, and they had promised to keep the location secret. No one was supposed to know about this place. Now the isolation was like a fortress wall around them. No one knew where they were. No one would ever find them out here.

A small twin-engine plane buzzed overhead, aimless and barely seen in the sky; the drone faded as it passed out of sight.

Their plight kept Patrice on the verge of terror and paralysis each day. Jody, so brave that it choked her up every time she thought about it, had been through so much already—the pursuit, the attack on Dymar . . . and before that, the doctor's assessment—terminal cancer, leukemia, not long to live. It was like a downward-plunging guillotine blade heading for his neck.

After the original leukemia diagnosis, what greater threat could shadowy conspirators possibly use? What could outweigh the demon inside Jody's own twelve-year-old body? Any other ordeal must pale in comparison.

As the tennis ball bounced away from the cabin into the knee-high weeds, Jody chased after it in a vain attempt to amuse himself. Patrice moved to the edge of the window to keep him in view. Ever since the fire and the attack, Patrice took great care never to let him out of her sight.

The boy seemed so much healthier now. Patrice didn't dare to hope for the remission to continue. He should be in the hospital now, but she couldn't take him. She didn't dare.

Jody halfheartedly bounced the tennis ball again, then once more ran after it. He had passed a remarkable milestone—

their crisis situation had become *ordinary* after two weeks, and his boredom had overwhelmed his fear. He looked so young, so carefree, even after everything that had happened.

Twelve should have been a magic age for him, the verge of the teenage years, when concerns fostered by puberty achieved universal importance. But Jody was no longer a normal boy. The jury was still out as to whether he would survive this or not.

Patrice opened the screen door and, with a glance over her shoulder, stepped onto the porch, taking care to keep the worried expression off her face. Although by now, Jody would probably consider any look of concern normal for her.

The gray Oregon cloud cover had broken for its daily hour of sunshine. The meadow looked fresh from the previous night's rain showers, when the patter of raindrops had sounded like creeping footsteps outside the window. Patrice had lain awake for hours, staring at the ceiling. Now the tall pines and aspens cast afternoon shadows across the muddy driveway that led down from the rise, away from the distant highway.

Jody smacked the tennis ball too hard, and it sailed off to the driveway, struck a stone, and bounced into the thick meadow. With a shout of anger that finally betrayed his tension, Jody hurled his tennis racket after it, then stood fuming.

Impulsive, Patrice thought. Jody became more like his father every day.

"Hey, Jody!" she called, quelling most of the scolding tone. He fetched the racket and plodded toward her, his eyes toward the ground. He had been restless and moody all day. "What's wrong with you?"

Jody averted his eyes, turned instead to squint where the sunshine lit the dense pines. Far away, she could hear the deep drone of a heavily laden log truck growling down the highway on the other side of the tree barricade.

"It's Vader," he finally answered, and looked up at his mother for understanding. "He didn't come back yesterday, and I haven't seen him all morning."

Now Patrice understood, and she felt the relief wash over her. For a moment, she had been afraid he might have seen some stranger or heard something about them on the radio news.

"Just wait and see. Your dog'll be all right—he always is."

Vader and Jody were about the same age, and had been inseparable all their lives. Despite her worries, Patrice smiled at the thought of the smart and good-natured black Lab.

Eleven years before, she had thought the world was golden. Their one-year-old son sat in his diapers in the middle of the hardwood floor, scooting around. He had tossed aside his action figure companions and played with the dog instead. The boy knew "Ma" and "Da" and attempted to say "Vader," though the dog's name came out more like a strangled "drrrr!"

Patrice and David chuckled together as they watched the black Lab play with Jody. Vader romped back and forth, his paws slipping on the polished floor. Jody squealed with delight. Vader woofed and circled the baby, who tried to spin on his diaper on the floor.

Those had been peaceful times, bright times. Now, though, she hadn't had a moment's peace since the fateful night she had received a desperate call from her husband at his beseiged laboratory.

Up until then, learning that her son was dying of cancer had been the worst moment of her life.

"But what if Vader's lying hurt in a ditch somewhere, Mom?" Jody asked. She could see tears on the edges of her son's eyes as he fought hard against crying. "What if he's in a fur trap, or got shot by a hunter?"

Patrice shook her head, trying to comfort her son. "Vader will come home safe and sound. He always does."

Once again, Patrice felt the shudder. *Yes, he always did.*

8

Even through the thick fabric of her clumsy gloves, she could feel the slick softness of the corpse's inner cavity. Scully's movements were irritatingly sluggish and imprecise—but at least the heavy gear protected her from exposure to whatever had killed Vernon Ruckman.

The forced-air respirator pumped a cold, stale wind into her face. Her eyes were dry, burning. She wished she could just rub them, but enclosed in the anticontamination suit, Scully had no choice but to endure the discomfort until the autopsy of the dead security guard was complete.

Her tape recorder rested on a table, voice-activated, waiting for her to say in detail what she was seeing. This wasn't a typical autopsy, though. She could see dozens of baffling physical anomalies just on first glance, and the mystery and horrific manifestations of the symptoms grew more astonishing as she proceeded with her thorough inspection.

Still, the step-by-step postmortem procedure had been established for a reason. She remembered teaching it to students at Quantico, during the brief period when the X-Files had been closed and she and Mulder had been separated. Some of her students had already completed their training through the FBI Academy and become special agents like herself.

But she doubted any of them would ever work a case like this one.

At such times, falling back on a routine was the only way to keep her mind clear and focused.

First step. "Test," she said, and the red light of the voice-activated recorder winked on. She continued speaking in a normal voice, muffled through her transparent plastic faceplate.

"Subject's name, Vernon Ruckman. Age, thirty-two; weight, approximately one hundred eighty-five pounds. General external physical condition is good. He appears to have been quite healthy until this disease struck him down." Now he looked as if every cell in his body had gone haywire all at once.

She looked at the man's blotchy body, the dark red marks of tarlike blood pooled in pockets beneath his skin. The man's face had frozen in a contortion of agony, lips peeled back from his teeth.

"Fortunately, the people who found this body and the medical examiner established quarantine protocols immediately. No one handled this cadaver with unprotected hands." She suspected that this disease, whatever it was, might be exceedingly virulent.

"Outward symptoms, the blotches, the swellings under the skin, are reminiscent of the bubonic plague." But the Black Death, while killing about one-third of Europe when it raged through the population centers of the Middle Ages, had acted over the course of several days, even in its deadliest pneumonic form. "This man seems to have been struck down nearly instantaneously, however. I know of no disease short of a direct nerve toxin that can act with such extreme lethality."

Scully touched the skin on Ruckman's arms, which hung like loose folds of rubbery fabric draped on the bones. "The epidermis shows substantial slippage, as if the connective tissue to the muscles has been destroyed somehow.

"As for the muscle fiber itself . . ." She pushed against the meat of the body with her fingers, felt an unusual softness, a squishing. Her heart jumped. "Muscle fibers seem dissociated . . . almost *mealy*."

Part of the skin split open, and Scully drew back, surprised. A clear, whitish liquid oozed out, and she gingerly touched it with her gloved fingertips. The substance was sticky, thick and syrupy.

"I've found some sort of unusual . . . mucus-like substance coming from the skin of this man. It seems to have pooled and collected within the subcutaneous tissue. My manipulations have released it."

She touched her fingertips together, and the slime stuck, then dripped back down onto the body. "I don't understand this at all," Scully admitted to the tape recorder. She would probably delete that line in her report.

"Proceeding with the body cavity," she said, then drew the stainless-steel tray of saws, scalpels, spreaders, and forceps close to her side.

Taking great care with the scalpel so as not to puncture the fabric of her gloves, she cut into the man's body cavity and used a rib-spreader to open up the chest. It was hard work; sweat dripped down her forehead, tickling her eyebrows.

Looking at the mess of the guard's opened chest, she reached inside the wet cavity, fishing around with her protected fingers. Getting down to work, Scully began by taking an inventory, removing lungs, liver, heart, intestines, weighing each on a mass-balance.

"It's difficult to recognize the individual organs, due to the abundant presence"—perhaps *infestation* was a better word, she thought—"of tumors."

In and around the organs, Vernon Ruckman's lumps, growths, tumors spread like a nest of viperous worms, thick and insidious. As she watched, they moved, slipping and settling, with a discomforting *writhing* appearance.

But in a body this disturbed, this damaged, no doubt the simple process of autopsy would have caused a vigorous reaction, not to mention the possibility of contraction due to the temperature variations from the morgue refrigerator to the heated room.

Among the displayed organs, Scully found other large pockets of the mucus. Inside, under the lungs, she discovered a large nodule of the slimy, runny substance—almost like a biological island or a storehouse.

She withdrew a sample of the unusual fluid and sealed it in an Extreme Hazard container. She would perform her own analysis of the specimen and send another sample to the Centers for Disease Control to supplement the samples already sent by the ME. Perhaps the pathogen specialists had seen something like this before. But she had a far more immediate concern.

"My primary conclusion, which is still pure speculation," Scully continued, "is that the biological research at DyMar Laboratory may have produced some sort of disease organism. We have not been able to track down full disclosure of David Kennessy's experiments or his techniques, and so I am at a disadvantage to go on the record with any more detailed conjectures."

She stared down at Ruckman's open body, unsettled. The tape recorder waited for her to speak again. If the situation was as bad as Scully feared, then they would certainly need much more help than either she or Mulder could give by themselves.

"The lumps and misshapen portions inside Vernon Ruckman's body look as if rapid outgrowths of cells engulfed his body with astonishing speed." Dr. Kennessy was working on cancer research. Could he have somehow produced a genetic or microbial basis for the disease? she wondered. Had he unleashed some terrible viral form of cancer?

She swallowed hard, frightened by her own idea. "All this is very far-fetched, but difficult to discount in light of the symptoms I have observed in this body—especially if this man was visibly healthy mere hours before his body was found."

The period from onset to death was at a maximum only part of an evening, perhaps much less. No time for treatment, no time even for him to realize his fate. . . .

Vernon Ruckman had had only minutes before a terminal disease struck him down.

Barely even time enough to pray.

9

Dr. Elliott Hughart was torn between intentionally putting the mangled black Labrador to sleep, or just letting it die. As a veterinarian, he had to make the same decision year after year after year. And it never got easier.

The dog lay on one of the stainless-steel surgical tables, still alive against all odds. The rest of the veterinary clinic was quiet and silent. A few other animals hunkered in their wire cages, quiet, but restive and suspicious.

Outside, it was dark, drizzling as it usually did this time of night, but the temperature was warm enough for the vet to prop open the back door. The damp breeze mitigated the smell of chemicals and frightened pets that thickened the air. Hughart had always believed in the curative properties of fresh air, and that went for animals as well as humans.

His living quarters were upstairs, and he had left the television on, the single set of dinner dishes unwashed—but he spent more time down here in the office, surgery, and lab anyway. *This* part was home for him—the other rooms upstairs were just the place where he slept and ate.

After all these years, Hughart kept his veterinary practice more as a matter of habit than out of any great hope of making it a huge success. He had scraped by over the years. The locals came to him regularly, though many of them expected free treatment as a favor to a friend or neighbor. Occasionally, tourists had accidents with their pets. Hughart had seen many cases like this black Lab: some guilt-ridden sightseer delivering the carcass or the still-living but grievously injured animal, expecting Hughart to work miracles. Sometimes the families stayed. Most of the time—as in this instance—they fled to continue their interrupted vacations.

The black Lab lay shivering, sniffing, whimpering. Blood smeared the steel table. At first, Hughart had done what he could to patch the injuries, stop the bleeding, bandage the worst gashes—but he didn't need a set of X-rays to tell that the dog had a shattered pelvis and a crushed spine, as well as major internal damage.

The black Lab wasn't tagged, was without any papers. It could never recover from these wounds, and even if it pulled through by some miracle, Hughart would have no choice but to relinquish it to the animal shelter, where it would sit in a cage for a few days and hope pathetically for freedom before the shelter destroyed it anyway.

Wasted. All wasted. Hughart drew a deep breath and sighed.

The dog shivered under his hands, but its body temperature burned higher than he had ever felt in an animal before. He inserted a thermometer, genuinely curious, then watched in astonishment as the digital readout climbed from 103 to 104. Normally a dog's temperature should have been 101.5, or 102 at most—and with the shock from his injuries, this dog's body temp should have dropped. The number on the readout climbed to 106 °F.

He drew a routine blood sample, then checked diligently for any other signs of sickness or disease, some cause for the fever that rose like a furnace from its body. What he found, though, surprised him even more.

The black Lab's massive injuries almost seemed to be healing rapidly, the wounds shrinking. He lifted one of the bandages he had pressed against a gash on the dog's rib cage, but though the gauze was soaked with blood, he saw no sign of the wound. Only matted fur. The veterinarian knew it must be his imagination, mere wishful thinking that somehow he might be able to save the dog.

But that would never happen. Hughart knew it in his mind, though his heart continued to hope.

The dog's body trembled, quietly whimpering. With his calloused thumb, Hughart lifted one of its squeezed-shut eyelids and saw a milky covering across its rolled-up eye, like a partially boiled egg. The dog was deep in a coma. Gone. It barely breathed.

The temperature reached 107°F. Even without the injuries, this fever was deadly.

A ribbon of blood trickled out of the wet black nostrils. Seeing that tiny injury, a little flaw of red blood across the black fur of the delicate muzzle, made Hughart decide not to put the dog through any more of this. Enough was enough.

He stared down at his canine patient for some time before he shuffled over to his medicine cabinet, unlocked the doors, and removed a large syringe and a bottle of Euthanol, concentrated sodium pentabarbitol. The dog weighed about sixty to eighty pounds, and the suggested dose was about 1 cc for each ten pounds, plus a little extra. He drew 10 ccs, which should be more than sufficient.

If the dog's owners ever came back, they would find the notation "PTS" in the records, which was a euphemism for "Put To Sleep"—which was itself a euphemism for killing the animal . . . or putting it out of its misery, as veterinarian school had always taught.

Once he had made the decision, Hughart didn't pause. He bent over the dog and inserted the needle into the skin behind the dog's neck and quietly but firmly injected the lethal dose. After its enormous injuries, the black Lab didn't flinch from the prick of the hypodermic.

A cool, clammy breeze eased through the cracked-open door, but the dog remained hot and feverish.

Dr. Hughart heaved a heavy sigh as he discarded the used syringe. "Sorry, boy," he said. "Go chase some rabbits in your dreams . . . in a place where you don't have to watch out for cars."

The chemical would take effect soon, suppressing the dog's respiration and eventually stopping his heart. Irrevocable, but peaceful.

First, though, Hughart took the blood sample back to the small lab area in the adjoining room. The animal's high body temperature puzzled him. He'd never seen a case like this before. Often animals went into shock if they survived the trauma of being struck by a motor vehicle, but they didn't usually have such a high fever.

The back room was perfectly organized according to a system he had developed over decades, though a casual observer might just see it as cluttered. He flicked on the overhead lights in the small Formica-topped lab area and placed a smear of the blood on a glass slide. First step would be to check the dog's white blood cell count to see if maybe he had some sort of infection, or parasites in the blood.

The dog could have been very sick, even dying, before he'd been hit by the car. In fact, that could explain why the animal had been so sluggish, so unaware of the large automobile bearing down on him. A fever that high would have been intolerable. If the dog suffered from some major illness, Hughart needed to keep a record of it.

Out in the adjoining operating and recovery area, two of the other dogs began to bark and whimper. A cat yowled, and the cages rattled.

Hughart paid little attention. Dogs and cats made a typical chaotic noise, to which he'd grown deaf after so many years. In fact, he'd been surprised at how quiet the animals were when thrown together in a strange situation, penned up in a cage for overnight care. They were already smarting from spaying or neutering or whatever ailments had brought them into the vet's office in the first place.

The only animal he was worried about was the dying black Labrador, and by now the Euthanol would be working.

Bothered by the distracting shadows, Hughart switched on a brighter fluorescent lamp tucked under the cabinets, then illuminated the slide under his microscope with a small lamp. Rubbing his eyes first, he gazed down at the smear of blood, fiddling with the focus knob.

The dog should even now be drifting off to perpetual dreams—but its blood was absolutely *alive*.

In addition to the usual red and white cells and platelets, Hughart saw tiny specks, little silvery components . . . like squarish glittering crystals that moved about on their own. If this was some sort of massive infection, it was not like any microorganism he had ever before laid eyes on. The odd shapes were as large as the cells and moved about with blurred speed.

"That's incredible," he said, and his voice sounded loud in the claustrophobic lab area. He often talked to the animals around him, or to himself, and it had never bothered him before.

Now, though, he wished he wasn't alone; he wished he had someone with him to share this amazing discovery.

What kind of disease or infection looked like this? After a long career in veterinary medicine, he would have thought he'd seen just about everything. But he had never before witnessed anything remotely like this.

And he hoped it wasn't contagious.

This revamped building had been Elliott Hughart's home, his place of work, for decades, but now it seemed strange and sinister to him. If this dog had some sort of unknown disease, he would have to contact the Centers for Disease Control.

He knew what to do in the case of a rabies outbreak or other diseases that normally afflicted household pets—but these tiny microscopic . . . slivers? They were utterly foreign to him.

In the back surgery room, the caged animals set up a louder racket, yowling and barking. The old man noticed it subconsciously, but the noise wasn't enough to tear him from his fascination with what he saw under the microscope.

Hughart rubbed his eyes and focused the microscope again, blurring the image past its prime point and then back to sharp focus again. The glittering specks were still there, buzzing about, moving cells. He swallowed hard; his throat was dry and cottony. What to do now?

Then he realized that the barking and meowing inside the operating room cages had become an outright din, as if a fox had charged into a henhouse.

Hughart spun around, bumped into his metal stool, knocked it over, and hopped about on one foot as pain shot through his hip. When he finally rushed into the operating room, he looked at the cages first to see the captive animals pressed back against the bars of their cages, trying to get away from the center of the room.

He didn't even look at the black Lab, because it should have been dead by now—but then he heard paws skittering across the slick surface of stainless steel.

The dog got to its feet, shook itself, and leaped down from the table, leaving a smear of blood on the clean surface. But the dog showed no more wounds, no damage. It trembled with energy, completely healed.

Hughart stood in total shock, unable to believe that the dog had not only regained consciousness—despite its grievous injuries and the euthanasia drug—but had jumped down from the table. This was as incredible as the swarming contamination in the blood sample.

He caught his breath, then eased forward. "Here, boy, let me take a look."

Quivering, the dog barked at him, then backed away.

10

Not long before sunset, a patch of bright blue sky made a rare appearance in the hills over Portland. Mulder squinted up, wishing he had brought along sunglasses as he maneuvered the rental car up the steep drive to the site of the DyMar Laboratory.

Much of the facility's structure remained intact, though entirely gutted by the fire. The walls were blackened, the wood support structure burned to charcoal, the office furniture slumped and twisted. Some overhead beams had toppled, while others balanced precariously against the concrete load-bearing walls and metal girders. Glass shards lay scattered among ashes and broken stone.

As they crested the hill and reached the sagging chain-link fence around the site, Mulder shifted the car into park and looked through the windshield. "A real fixer-upper," he said. "I'll have to talk to my real estate agent."

Scully got out of the car and looked over at him. "Too late to make an offer, Mulder—this place is scheduled to be demolished in a few days to make way for a new business park." She scanned the thick stands of dark pines and the sweeping view of Portland spread out below, with its sinuous river and necklace of bridges.

Mulder realized the construction crew was moving awfully fast, disturbingly so. He and Scully might not even be able to finish a decent investigation in the amount of time alloted to them.

He opened the chain-link gate; sections of the fence sagged and left wide gaps. Signs declaring "Danger" and "Warning" adorned the fence, marking the hazards of the half-collapsed building; he doubted those signs would discourage any but the meekest of vandals.

"Apparently Vernon Ruckman's death has proved a greater deterrent than any signs or guards," Scully said. She held on to the chain link for a moment, then followed Mulder into the burned area. "I contacted local law enforcement, trying to get a status on their arson investigation. But so far, all they would tell me is that it's 'pending—no progress.'"

Mulder raised his eyebrows. "A protest group large enough to turn into a destructive mob, and they can't find any members?"

The FBI crime lab was analyzing the note claiming responsibility. By late that evening they expected to have results on whoever was behind Liberation Now. From what Mulder had seen, the letter seemed to be a very amateurish job.

He stared at the blackened walls of the DyMar facility for a moment, then the two agents entered the shell of the building, stepping gingerly. The smell of soot, burned plastics, and other volatile chemicals bit into Mulder's nostrils.

As he stood inside the ruins, looking across the hilltop vista toward the forests and the city below, Mulder imagined that night two weeks earlier, when a mob of angry and uncontrolled protesters had marched up the gravel drive. He drew a deep breath of the ash-clogged air.

"Conjures up images of peasants carrying torches, doesn't it, Scully?" He looked up at the unstable ceiling, the splintered pillars, the collapsed walls. He gingerly took another step into what must have been a main lobby area. "A mob of angry people charging up the hill to burn down the evil laboratory, destroy the mad scientist."

Beside him, Scully appeared deeply disturbed. "But what were they so worried about?" she said. "What did they know? This was cancer research. Of all the different kinds of science, surely *cancer research* is something even the most vehement protesters will abide."

"I don't think it was the cancer part that concerned them," Mulder said.

"What then?" Scully asked, frowning. "The animal testing? I don't know what sort of experiments Dr. Kennessy was doing, but I've researched animal rights groups before—and while they sometimes break in and release a few dogs and rats from their cages, I'm unaware of any other situation that has exhibited this extreme level of violence."

"I think it was the type of research itself," Mulder said. "Something about it must have been very scary. Otherwise, why would all of his records be sealed away?"

"You already have an idea, Mulder. I can tell."

"David Kennessy and his brother had made some waves in the research community, trying unorthodox new approaches and treatments that had been abandoned by everyone else. According to Kennessy's resume, he was an expert in abnormal biochemistry, and his brother Darin had worked for years in Silicon Valley. Tell me, Scully, what sort of relationship could there be between electronics and cancer research?"

Scully didn't offer any of her thoughts as she poked around, looking for where the guard had been found. She saw the yellow-taped section and stood gazing at the rough outline of the body impressed into the loose ash, while Mulder ranged around the perimeter. He moved a fallen sheet of twisted metal out of the way and stumbled upon a fire safe, its door blackened but ajar. He called for Scully.

"Does it contain anything?" she asked.

Mulder raised his eyebrows and rummaged around in the sooty debris. "It's open, but empty. And the inside is dirty but not burned." He waited for that to sink in, then looked up at his partner. From her expression, it was clear she thought the same thing he did. The safe had been opened after the fire, not before. "Someone else was here that night, someone looking for the contents of this safe."

"That's why the guard came up here into the ruins. He saw someone."

Scully frowned. "That could explain why he was here. But it still doesn't tell us what killed him. He wasn't shot or strangled. We don't even know that he met up with the intruder."

"But it's possible, even likely," Mulder said.

Scully looked at him curiously. "So this other person took all the records we need?"

He shrugged. "Come on, Scully. Most of the other information on Kennessy's cancer research was locked away and classified. We can't get our hands on it. There may well have been some evidence here, too—but now that's gone as well, and a security guard is dead."

"Mulder, he was dead from a kind of disease."

"He was dead from some kind of toxic pathogen. We don't know where it came from."

"So whoever was here that night killed the guard, and stole the records from the safe?"

Mulder cocked his head to one side. "Unless someone else got to it first."

Scully remained tight-lipped as they eased around a burned wall, ducked under a fallen girder, and crunched slowly into the interior.

What remained of the lab areas sprawled like a dangerous maze, black and unstable. Part of the floor had collapsed, tumbling down into the basement clean rooms, holding areas, and storage vaults. The remaining section of floor creaked underfoot, demonstrably weakened after the fire.

Mulder picked up a shard of glass. The intense heat had bent and smoothed its sharp edges. "Even after his brother abandoned the research, I think Kennessy was very close to some sort of magnificent breakthrough, and he was willing to bend a few rules because of his son's condition. Someone found out about his work and tried to stop him from taking rash action. I suspect that this supposedly spontaneous protest movement, from a group nobody's ever heard of, was a violent effort to silence him and erase all the progress he had made."

Scully brushed her reddish hair back away from her face, leaving a little soot mark on her cheek. She sounded very tired. "Mulder, you see conspiracies everywhere."

He reached forward to brush the smudge from her face. "Yeah, Scully, but sometimes I'm right. And in this case it cost the lives of two people—maybe more."

11

Under Burnside Bridge
Portland, Oregon
Tuesday, 11:21 P.M.

X He tried to hide and he tried to sleep—but nothing came to him but a succession of vicious nightmares.

Jeremy Dorman did not know whether the dreams were caused by the swarms of microscopic invaders tinkering with his head, with his thought processes . . . or whether the nightmares came as a result of his guilty conscience.

Wet and clammy, clad in tattered clothes that didn't fit him right, he huddled under the shelter of Burnside Bridge, on the damp and trash-strewn shore of the Willamette River. The muddy green-blue water curled along in its stately course.

Years ago, downtown Portland had cleaned up River Park, making it an attractive, well-lit, and scenic area for the yuppies to jog, the tourists to sit on cold concrete benches and look out across the water. Young couples could listen to street musicians while they sipped on their gourmet coffee concoctions.

But not at this dark hour. Now most people sat in their

warm homes, not thinking about the cold and lonely night outside. Dorman listened to the soft gurgle of the slow-moving river against the tumbled rocks around the bridge pilings. The water smelled warm and rich and alive, but the cool mist had a frosty metallic tang to it. Dorman shivered.

Pigeons nested in the bridge superstructure above, cooing and rustling. Farther down the walk came the rattling sound of another vagrant rummaging through trash cans to find recyclable bottles or cans. A few brown bags containing empty malt liquor and cheap wine bottles lay piled against the green-painted wastebaskets.

Dorman huddled in the shadows, in bodily pain, in mental misery. Fighting a spasm of his rebellious body, he rolled into a mud puddle, smearing dirt all over his back . . . but he didn't even notice.

A heavy truck rumbled overhead across the bridge with a sound like a muffled explosion.

Like the DyMar explosion.

That night, the *last* night, came back to him too vividly—the darkness filled with fire and shouts and explosions. Murderous and destructive people: faceless, nameless, all brought together by someone pulling strings invisibly in the shadows. And they were malicious, destructive.

He must have fallen asleep . . . or somehow been transported back in time. His memory had been enhanced in a sort of cruel and unusual punishment, perhaps by the wild-card action of his affliction.

"A chain-link fence and a couple of rent-a-cops does not make me feel safe," Dorman had said to David Kennessy. This wasn't exactly a high-security installation they were working in—after all, David had smuggled his damned pet dog in there, and a handgun. "I'm starting to think your brother had the right idea to walk away from all this six months ago."

DyMar had called for backup security from the state police, and had been turned down. The ostensible reason was some buried statute that allowed the police to defer "internal company disputes" to private security forces. David paced around the basement laboratory rooms, fuming, demanding to know how the police could consider a mob of demonstrators to be an internal company dispute. It still hadn't occurred to him that somebody might want the lab unprotected.

For all his biochemical brilliance, David Kennessy was clueless. His brother Darin hadn't been quite so politically naive, and Darin had gotten the hell out of Dodge—in time. David had stayed—for his son's sake. Neither of them understood the stakes involved in their own research.

When the actual destruction started, Jeremy recalled seeing David scrambling to grab his records, his samples, like in all those old movies where the mad scientist strives to rescue a single notebook from the flames. David seemed more pissed off than frightened. He kicked a few stray pencils away from his feet, and spoke in his "let's be reasonable" voice. "Some boneheaded fanatic is always trying to stop progress—but it never works. Nobody can undiscover this new technology." He made a rude noise through his lips.

Indeed, biological manufacturing and submicroscopic engineering had been progressing at remarkable speed for years now. Genetic engineers used the DNA machinery of certain bacteria to produce artificial insulin. A corporation in Syracuse, New York, had patented techniques for storing and reading data in cubes made of bacteriorhodopsin, a genetically altered protein. Too many people were working on too many different aspects of the problem. David was right—nobody could undiscover the technology.

But Dorman himself knew that some people in the government were certainly intent on trying to do just that. And even with all the prior planning and the hushed agreements, they hadn't given Dorman himself time to escape, despite their promises.

While David was distracted, rushing to the phone to

warn his wife about the attack and her own danger, Dorman had not been able to find any of the pure original nanomachines, just the prototypes, the leftover and questionable samples that had been used—with mixed results—on the other lab animals, before their success with the dog. But still, the prototypes had worked . . . to a certain extent. They had saved him, technically at least.

Then Dorman heard windows smashing upstairs, the murderous shouts pouring closer—and he knew it was time.

Those prototypes had been his last resort, the only thing he could find. They had been viable enough in the lab rat tests, hadn't they? And the dog was just fine, perfectly healthy. What choice did he have but to take a chance? Still, the possibility froze Dorman with terror, uncertainty, for a moment—if he did this, it would be an irrevocable act. He couldn't just go to the drugstore and get the antidote.

But the thought of how those men had betrayed him, how they meant to kill him and tidy up all their problems, gave him the determination he needed.

After Dorman added the activation hormone and the self-perpetuating carrier fluid, the prototypes were supposed to adapt, reset their programming.

With a small *whumpp*, a Molotov cocktail exploded in the lobby, and then came running feet. He heard hushed voices in quiet discussion that sounded cool and professional—a contrast to the chanting and yelling that continued outside, the protests Dorman knew were staged.

Quickly, silently, Dorman injected himself, just before David Kennessy returned to his side. Now the lead researcher finally looked afraid, and with good reason.

Four of the gunshots struck Kennessy in the chest, driving him backward into the lab tables. Then the DyMar building erupted into flames—much faster than Jeremy Dorman could have imagined.

He tried to escape, but even as he fled, the flames swept along, closing in on him as the walls ignited. The shock wave of another large explosion pummeled him against one of the concrete basement walls. The stairwell became a chute of fire, searing his skin. He had watched his flesh bubble and blacken. Dorman shouted with outrage at the betrayal. . . .

Now he awoke screaming under the bridge. The echoes of his outcry vibrated against the river water, ricocheting across the river and up under the bridge.

Dorman hauled himself to his feet. His eyes adjusted to the dim illumination of streetlights and the moon filtering through clouds above. His body twisted and contorted. He could feel the growths squirming in him, seething, taking on a life of their own.

Dorman clenched his teeth, brought his elbows tight against his ribs, struggling to regain control. He breathed heavily through his nostrils. The air was cold and metallic, soured with the memory of burning blood.

As he swayed to his feet, Dorman looked down at the rock embankment where he had slept so fitfully. There he saw the bodies of five pigeons, wings splayed, feathers ruffled, their eyes glassy gray. Their beaks hung open with a trickle of blood curling down from their tongues.

Dorman stared at the dead birds, and his stomach clenched, turning a somersault with nausea. He didn't know what his body had done, how he had lost control during his nightmares. Only the pigeons knew.

A last gray feather drifted to the ground in silence.

Dorman staggered away, climbing up toward the road. He had to get out of Portland. He had to find his quarry, find the dog, before it was too late for any of them.

12

 Mulder didn't feel at all nondescript or unno-
ticeable as he and Scully stood in the lobby of
the main post office. They moved back and
forth, pretending to wait in line, then going
back to the counter and filling out unnecessary
Express Mail forms. The postal officials at the
counter watched them warily.

All the while, Scully and Mulder kept their eyes on the
wall of covered cubbyholes, numbered post office boxes, especially number 3733. Each box looked like a tiny prison cubicle.

Every time a new customer walked in and marched
toward the appropriate section of boxes, he and Scully
exchanged a glance. They tensed, then relaxed, as person
after person failed to fit the description, went to the wrong
cubbyhole, or simply conducted routine post office business,
oblivious to the FBI surveillance.

Finally, after about an hour and twenty minutes of stake-
out, a gaunt man pushed open the heavy glass door and
moved directly to the wall of P.O. boxes. His face was lean,
his head completely shaven and glistening as if he used

furniture polish every morning. His chin, though, held an explosion of black bristly beard. His eyes were sunken, his cheekbones high and protruding.

"Scully, that's him," he said. Mulder had seen various photos of Alphonse Gurik in his criminal file—but previously he had had long hair and no beard. Still, the effect was the same.

Scully gave a brief nod, then flicked her eyes away so as not to draw the man's suspicions. Mulder nonchalantly picked up a colorful brochure describing the Postal Service's selection of stamps featuring famous sports figures, raising his eyebrows in feigned interest.

The National Crime Information Center had rapidly and easily completed their analysis of the letter claiming responsibility for the destruction of the DyMar Lab. Liberation Now had mailed their note on a piece of easily traceable stationery, written by hand in block letters and sporting two smudged fingerprints. *Sloppy*. The whole thing had been sloppy and amateurish.

NCIC and the FBI crime lab had studied the note, using handwriting analysis and fingerprint identification. This man, Alphonse Gurik—who had no permanent address—had been involved in many causes for many outspoken protest groups. His rap sheet had listed name after name of organizations that sounded so outrageous they couldn't possibly exist. Gurik had written the letter claiming responsibility for the destruction and arson at DyMar.

But already Mulder had expressed his doubts. After visiting the burned DyMar site, it was clear to both of them that this had been a professional job, eerily precise and coldly destructive. Alphonse Gurik seemed to be a rank amateur, perhaps deluded, certainly sincere. Mulder didn't think him capable of what had happened at DyMar.

As the man reached for P.O. Box 3733, spun his combination, and opened the little window to withdraw his mail,

Scully nodded at Mulder. They both moved forward, reaching into their overcoats to withdraw their ID wallets.

"Mr. Alphonse Gurik," she said in a firm, uncompromising voice, "we're federal agents, and we are placing you under arrest."

The bald man whirled, dropped his mail in a scattershot on the floor, and then slammed his back against the wall of boxes.

"I didn't do anything!" he said, his face stricken with terror. He raised his hands in total surrender. "You've got no right to arrest me."

The other customers in the post office backed away, fascinated and afraid. Two workers at the counter leaned forward and craned their necks so they could see better.

Scully withdrew the folded piece of paper from her inner pocket. "This is an arrest warrant with your name on it. We have identified you as the author of a letter claiming responsibility for the fire and explosion at DyMar Laboratory, which resulted in the deaths of two researchers."

"But, but—" Gurik's face paled. A thread of spittle connected his lips as he tried to find the appropriate words.

Mulder came forward and grabbed the bald man's arm after removing a set of handcuffs from his belt. Scully hung back, keeping herself in a bladed position, ready and prepared for any unexpected action from the prisoner. An FBI agent always had to be prepared no matter now submissive a detainee might appear.

"We're always happy to hear your side of this, Mr. Gurik," Mulder said. He took advantage of Gurik's shock to bring the man's arms down and cuff his wrists behind him. Scully read the memorized set of Miranda rights, which Alphonse Gurik seemed to know very well already.

According to his file, this man had been arrested seven times already on minor vandalism and protest charges— throwing rocks through windows or spray-painting misspelled threats on the headquarters buildings of companies he didn't like. Mulder gauged him to be a principled man, well-read in his field. Gurik had the courage to stand up for what he believed in, but he gave over his beliefs a little too easily.

As Mulder turned the prisoner around, escorting him toward the glass door, Scully bent down to retrieve Gurik's scattered mail. They ushered him outside.

It took thirty seconds, almost like clockwork, until Gurik began to babble, trying to make excuses. "Okay, I sent the letter! I admit it, I sent the letter—but I didn't burn anything. I didn't kill anybody. I didn't blow up that building."

Mulder thought he was probably telling the truth. Gurik's previous minor pranks had made him a nuisance, but could not be construed as a dry run for the destruction of an entire research facility.

"It's a little convenient to change your story now, isn't it?" Scully said. "Two people are dead, and you'll be up for murder charges. This isn't a few out-of-hand protest activities like the ones you've been arrested for in the past."

"I was just a protester. We picketed DyMar a few times in the past . . . but suddenly the whole place just exploded! Everybody was running and screaming, but I didn't do anything wrong!"

"So why did you write the letter?" Mulder asked.

"Somebody had to take responsibility," Gurik said. "I kept waiting, but nobody sent any letters, nobody took credit. It was a terrible tragedy, yeah! But the whole scene would have been pointless if nobody announced what we were protesting against. I thought we were trying to free all those lab animals, that's why I sent the letter . . .

"Some of us got together on this, a few different independent groups. There was this one guy who really railed against the stuff at DyMar—he even drafted the letter to the paper and made sure we all had a copy before the protest. He showed us videotapes, smuggled reports. You wouldn't believe what they were doing to the lab animals. You should have seen what they did to that poor dog."

Scully crossed her arms over her chest. "So what happened to this man?"

"We couldn't even find him again—he must have turned chicken after all. So I sent the letter myself. Somebody had to. The world has to know."

Outside the post office, Gurik looked desperately toward an old woody station wagon with peeling paint, touched up with spots of primer coat.

Boxes of leaflets, maps, newspaper clippings, and other literature crammed the worn seats of the station wagon. Bumper stickers and decals cluttered the car body and rear. One of the car's windshield wipers had broken off, Mulder saw, but at least it was on the passenger side.

"I didn't *burn* anything, though," Gurik insisted fervently. "I didn't even throw rocks. We just shouted and held our signs. I don't know who threw the firebombs. It wasn't me."

"Why don't you explain to us about Liberation Now?" Mulder asked, falling into the routine. "How do they fit into this?"

"It's just an organization I made up. Really! It's not an official group—there aren't even any members but me. I can make any group I want. I've done it before. Lots of activists were there that night, other groups, people I'd never seen before."

"So who set up the protest at DyMar?" Scully said.

"I don't know." Still pressed against the side of his car, Gurik twisted his head over his other shoulder to look at her. "We have connections, you know. All of us activist groups. We talk. We don't always agree, but when we can join forces it's stronger.

"I think the DyMar protest was pulled together by leaders of a few smaller groups that included animal rights activists, genetic engineering protesters, industrial labor organizations, and even some fundamentalist religious groups. Of course, with all my work in the past they wouldn't dare leave me out."

"No, of course not," Mulder said. He had hoped Gurik would be able to lead them toward other members of Liberation Now, but it appeared that he was the sole member of his own little splinter group.

The violent protesters had materialized promptly, with no known leaders and no prior history, conveniently turned into a mob that burned the facility down and destroyed all records and research . . . then evaporated without a trace. Whoever had engineered the bloody protest had so smoothly pulled together the various groups that even their respective members didn't know they were being herded to the same place at the same time.

Mulder thought it was very clear that the entire incident had been staged.

"What were you fighting against at DyMar?" Scully said.

Gurik raised his eyebrows, indignant. "What do you mean, what were we fighting against? The horrible animal research, of course! It's a *medical facility*. You've got to know what scientists do in places like that."

"No," Scully said, "I don't know. What I do know is that they were trying to find medical breakthroughs that would help people. People dying of cancer."

Gurik snorted and turned his head. "Yeah, as if animals have any less right to a peaceful existence than humans do! By what standard do we torture animals so that humans can live longer?"

Scully blinked at Mulder in disbelief. How could you argue with someone like this?

"Actually," Mulder said, "our investigation hasn't turned up evidence of any animal experimentation beyond the lab rat stage."

"What?" Gurik said. "You're lying."

Mulder turned to Scully, cutting the protester off. "I think he's been set up, Scully. This guy doesn't know anything. Someone wanted to destroy DyMar and David Kennessy, while transferring the blame elsewhere."

Scully raised her eyebrows. "Who would want to do that, and why?"

Mulder looked hard at her. "I think Patrice Kennessy knows the answer to that question, and that's why she's in trouble."

Scully looked pained at the mention of the missing woman. "We've got to find Patrice and Jody," she said. "I suggest we question the missing brother, Darin, as well. The boy himself can't be too hard to find. If he's weak from his cancer treatments, he'll need medical attention soon. We've got to get to him."

"Cancer treatments!" Gurik exploded. "Do you know how they develop those things? Do you know what they do?" He growled in his throat as if he wanted to spit. "You should see the surgeries, the drugs, the apparatuses they hook to those poor little animals. Dogs and cats, anything that got lost and picked up on the streets."

"I'm aware of how . . . difficult cancer treatments can be," Scully said coldly, thinking of what she herself had endured, how the treatment had been nearly as lethal as the cancer itself.

But she had no patience for this now. "Some research is necessary to help people in the future. I don't condone excessive pain or malicious treatment of animals, but the research helps humans, helps find other methods of curing terminal diseases. I'm sorry, but I cannot sympathize with your attitude or your priorities."

Gurik twisted around enough so that he could look directly at her. "Yeah, and you don't think they're experimenting on humans, too?" His eyes were not panicky now, but burning with rage. He nodded knowingly at her. The skin on his shaven head wrinkled like leather.

"They're sadistic bastards," he said. "You wouldn't say that if you knew how some of the research was conducted!" He drew a deep breath. "You haven't seen the things I have."

13

X In a nondescript office with few furnishings, Adam Lentz sat at his government-issue desk and pondered the videotape in front of him. The tape still smelled of smoke from the DyMar fire, and he was anxious to play it.

Lentz's name wasn't stenciled on the office door, nor did he have a plaque on the new desk, none of the trappings of importance or power. Useless trappings. Adam Lentz had many titles, many positions, which he could adopt and use at his convenience. He simply had to select whichever role would allow him best to complete his real job.

The office had plain white walls, an interior room with no windows, no blinds—no means for anyone else to spy on him. The federal building itself sported completely unremarkable architecture, just another generic government building full of beehive offices for the unfathomable business of a sprawling bureaucracy.

Each evening, after working hours, Crystal City became a ghost town as federal employees—clerks and paper pushers and filing assistants—rushed home to Gaithersburg,

Georgetown, Annapolis, Silver Spring . . . leaving much of the area uninhabited. Lentz often stayed late just to witness the patterns of human tribal behavior.

Part of his role in the unnamed government office had been to oversee David and Darin Kennessy's research at DyMar Laboratory. Other groups at the California Institute of Technology, NASA Ames, the Institute for Molecular Manufacturing—even Mitsubishi's Advanced Technology Research and Development Center in Japan—had forged ahead with their attempts. But the Kennessys had experienced a few crucial lucky breaks—or made shrewd decisions—and Lentz knew DyMar was the most likely site for a breakthrough.

He had followed the work, seen the brothers' remarkable progress, egged them on, and held them back. Some of the earlier experiments on rats and small lab animals had been amazing—and some had been horrific. Those initial samples and prototypes had all been confiscated and, he hoped, destroyed. But David Kennessy, who had kept working even after his brother left, had proved too successful for his own good. Things had gotten out of control, and Kennessy hadn't even seen it coming.

Lentz hoped the confiscated tape had not been damaged in the cleansing fire that had obliterated DyMar. His clean-up teams had scoured the wreckage for any evidence, any intact samples or notes, and they had found the hidden fire safe, removed its contents, and brought the tape to him.

He swiveled a small portable TV/VCR that he had set on his desk and plugged into a floor socket. He closed and locked his office door, but left the lights on, harsh and flickering fluorescent fixtures in the ceiling. He sat back in his standard-issue desk chair—he wasn't one for extravagant amenities—and popped the tape into the player. He had heard about an extraordinary tape, but he had never personally seen it. After adjusting the tracking and the volume, Lentz sat back to watch.

In the clean and brightly lit lab, the dog paced inside his

cage, an enclosure designed for larger animals. He whined twice with an uncertain twitch of his tail, as if hoping for a quick end to his confinement.

"Good boy, Vader," David Kennessy said, moving across the camera's field of view. "Just sit."

Kennessy paced the room, running a hand through his dark hair, brushing aside a film of perspiration on his forehead. Oh, he was nervous, all right—acting cocky, doing his best to look confident. Darin Kennessy—perhaps the smarter brother—had abandoned the research and gone to ground half a year before. But David hadn't been so wise. He had continued to push.

People were very interested in what this team had accomplished, and he obviously felt he had to prove it with a videotape. Kennessy didn't know, though, that the success would be his own downfall. He had proven too much, and he had frightened the people who had never really believed he could do it.

But Lentz knew the researcher's own son was dying, which might have tempted him into taking unacceptable risks. That was dangerous.

Kennessy adjusted the camera himself, shoving his hand in the field of view, jittering the image. Beside him, near the dog's cage, the big-shouldered technical assistant, Jeremy Dorman, stood like Igor next to his beloved Frankenstein.

"All right," Kennessy said into the camcorder's microphone. A lot of white noise buzzed in the background, diagnostic equipment, air filters, the rattle of small lab rodents in their own cages. "Tonight, you're in for a *rilly big shew!*"

As if anybody remembered Ed Sullivan, Lentz thought.

Kennessy postured in front of the camera. "I've already filed my data, sent my detailed documentation. My initial rodent tests showed the amazing potential. But those progress reports either went unread, or at least were not understood. I'm tired of having my memos disappear in your piles of paper. Considering that this breakthrough will change the universe as we know it, I'd think somebody might want to give up a coffee break to have a look."

Oh no, Dr. Kennessy, Lentz thought as he watched, *your reports didn't disappear. We paid a great deal of attention.*

"They're management boobs, David," Dorman muttered. "You can't expect them to understand what they're funding." Then he covered his mouth, as if appalled that he had made such a comment within range of the camcorder's microphone.

Kennessy glanced at his watch, then over at Dorman. "Are you prepared, Herr Dorman?"

The big lab assistant fidgeted, rested his hand on the wire cage. The black Lab poked his muzzle against Dorman's palm, snuffling. Dorman practically leaped out of his skin.

"Are you sure we should do this?" he asked.

Kennessy looked at his assistant with an expression of pure scorn. "No, Jeremy. I want to just give up, shelve the work, and let Jody die. Maybe I should retire and become a CPA."

Dorman raised both hands in embarrassed surrender. "All right, all right—just checking."

In the background, on one of the poured-concrete basement walls, a poster showed Albert Einstein handing a candle to someone few people would recognize by sight—K. Eric Drexler; Drexler, in turn, was extending a candle toward the viewer. *Come on, take it!* Drexler had been one of the first major visionaries behind genetic engineering some years before.

Too bad we couldn't have gotten to him soon enough, Lentz thought.

Vader looked expectantly at his master, then sat down in the middle of his cage. His tail thumped on the floor. "Good boy," Kennessy muttered.

Jeremy Dorman went out of range, then returned a few moments later holding a handgun, a clunky but powerful

Smith & Wesson. According to records Lentz had easily obtained, Dorman himself had gone into a Portland gun shop and purchased the weapon with cash. At least the handgun hadn't come out of their funding request.

Kennessy spoke again to the camera as his assistant sweated. Dorman looked down at the handgun, then over at the caged dog.

"What I am about to show you will be shocking in the extreme. I shouldn't need to add the disclaimer that this is real, with no special effects, no artificial preparations." He crossed his arms and stared firmly into the camera eye. "My intention is to jar you so thoroughly that you are ready to question all your preconceptions."

He turned to Dorman. "Gridley, you may fire when ready."

Dorman looked confused, as if wondering who Kennessy meant, then he raised the Smith & Wesson. His Adam's apple bobbed up and down, exhibiting his nervousness. He pointed the gun at the dog.

Vader sensed something was wrong. He backed up as far as he could in the cage, then growled loud and low. His dark eyes met Dorman's, and he bared his fangs.

Dorman's hand began to shake.

Kennessy's eyes flared. "Come on, Jeremy, dammit! Don't make this any worse than it is."

Dorman fired twice. The gunshots sounded thin and tinny on the videotape. Both bullets hit the big black dog, and the impact smashed him into the mesh of the cage. One shot struck Vader's rib cage; another shattered his spine. Blood flew out from the bullet holes, drenching his fur.

Vader yelped and then sat down from the impact. He panted.

Dorman looked stupidly down at the handgun. "My God!" he muttered. "The animal rights activists would crucify us, David."

But Kennessy didn't allow the silence to hang on the tape. He stepped forward, delivering his rehearsed speech.

He was running this show. Melodramatic though it might seem, he knew it would work.

"My medical breakthrough opens the doorway to numerous other applications. That's why so many people have been working on it for so long. The first researchers to make this breakthrough work are going to shake up society like you won't be able to imagine." Kennessy sounded as if he was giving a speech to a board of directors, while his pet dog lay shot and bleeding in his cage.

Lentz had to admire a man like that.

He nodded to himself and leaned forward, closer to the television. He rested his elbows on the desktop. *All the more reason to make sure the technology is tightly controlled, and released only when we deem it necessary.*

On the screen, Kennessy turned to the cage, looking down with clinical detachment. "After a major trauma like this, the first thing that happens is that the nanocritters shut down all of the dog's pain centers."

In his cage, Vader sat, confused. His tongue lolled out. He had clumsily managed to prop himself upright. The dog seemed not to notice the gaping holes in his back. After a moment, the black Lab lay down on the floor of the cage, squishing his fur in the blood still running along his sides. His eyes grew heavy, and he sank down in deep sleep, resting his head on his front paws. He took a huge breath and released it slowly.

Kennessy knelt down on the floor beside the cage, reached his hand in to pat Vader on the head. "His temperature is already rising from the waste heat. Look, the blood has stopped flowing. Jeremy, get the camera over here so we can have a close-up."

Dorman looked befuddled, then scurried over to grab the camera. The view on the videotape rocked and shook, then came into focus on the dog, zooming in on the injuries. Kennessy let the images speak for themselves for a moment, before he picked up the thread of his lecture.

"A large-scale physical trauma like this is actually easier to fix than a widespread disease, like cancer. A gunshot injury needs a bit of patchwork, cellular bandages, and some reconstruction.

"With a genetic disease, though, each cell must be repaired, every anomaly tweaked and adjusted. Purging a cancer patient might take weeks or months. These bullet wounds, though—" He gestured down at the motionless black Lab. "Well, Vader will be up chasing squirrels again tomorrow."

Dorman looked down in amazement and disbelief. "If this gets to the newspapers, David, we're all out of a job."

"I don't think so," Kennessy answered, and smiled. "I'll bet you a box of dog biscuits."

Within an hour, the dog woke up again, groggy but rapidly recovering. Vader stood up in the cage, shook himself, then barked. Healthy. Healed. As good as new. Kennessy released him from the cage, and the dog bounded out, starved for attention and praise. Kennessy laughed out loud and ruffled his fur.

Lentz watched in astonishment, understanding now that Kennessy's work was even more frightening, even more successful than he had feared. His people had been absolutely right to take the samples, lock them away, and then destroy all the remaining evidence.

If something like this became available to the general public, he couldn't conceive of the earth-shattering consequences. No, everything had to be destroyed.

Lentz popped out the videotape and locked it within a repository for classified documents. The fire safe at DyMar had protected this tape and the other documents with it, but unfortunately he knew with a grim certainty that they had not recovered every scrap, every sample.

Now, after all he had seen, Lentz finally understood the frantic phone call they had tapped, when David Kennessy had dialed his home number on the night of the explosive protest, on the night of the fire.

Kennessy's voice had been frantic, ragged. He didn't even let his wife speak. "Patrice, take Jody and Vader and get out of there—*now*! Everything I was afraid of is going down. You have to run. I'm already trapped at DyMar, but you can get away. Keep running. Don't let them . . . get you."

Then the phone recording was cut off before Kennessy or his wife could say anything else. Patrice Kennessy had listened to her husband, had acted quickly. By the time the clean-up teams got to their suburban house, she had packed up with the boy and the dog, and vanished.

After seeing the videotape, Lentz realized what a grave mistake he had made. Before, he had worried that Patrice might have a few notes, some research information that Lentz needed to retrieve. Now, though, the danger had increased by orders of magnitude.

How could he have missed it before? The dog wasn't just a family pet that the Kennessys couldn't bear to leave behind. That black Lab was *the dog*. It was the research animal, it carried the nanomachines inside its bloodstream, lurking there, just waiting to spread around the world.

Lentz swallowed hard and grabbed for the phone. After a moment, though, he froze and gently set the receiver back in the cradle. This was not a mistake he wanted to admit to the man in charge. He would take care of it himself.

Everything else had been destroyed in the DyMar fire—but now Adam Lentz had to call in all of his resources, get reinforcements, spend whatever time or money was necessary.

He had a woman, a boy, and, especially, their pet dog to track down.

14

The midday sunlight dappled the patches in the Oregon hills where the trees had been shaved in strips from clearcut logging. Patrice and Jody sat by the table in the living room with the curtains open and the lights switched off, working on a thousand-piece jigsaw puzzle they had found in one of the cedar window seats.

The two of them had finished a lunch of cold sandwiches and an old bag of potato chips that had gone stale in the damp air. Jody never complained. Patrice was just glad her son had an appetite again. His mysterious remission was remarkable, but she couldn't allow herself to hope. Soon, she dreaded, the blush of health would fade, and Jody would resume his negotiations with the Grim Reaper.

But still, she clung to every moment with him. Jody was all she had left.

Now the two of them hunched over the scattered puzzle pieces. When finished, the image would show the planet Earth rising over lunar crags, as photographed by one of the Apollo astronauts. The blue-green sphere covered most of the small wooden table, with jagged gaps from a few continents not yet filled in.

They weren't having much fun, barely even occupying their minds. They were just killing time.

Patrice and Jody talked little, in the shared silence of two people who'd had only their own company for many days. They could get by with partial sentences, cryptic comments, private jokes. Jody reached forward with a jagged piece of the Antarctic ice cap, turning it to see how the interlocking pieces fit in.

"Have you ever known somebody who went to Antarctica, Mom?" Jody asked.

Patrice forced a smile. "That's not exactly on the standard tour list, kid."

"Did Dad ever go there? For his research? Or Uncle Darin?"

She froze her face before a troubled frown could pass over her features. "You mean to test out a new medical treatment on, say, penguins? Or polar bears?" *Why not? He had tested it on Vader....*

"Polar bears live at the *North* Pole, Mom." Jody shook his head with mock scorn. "Get your data right."

Sometimes he sounded just like his father.

She had explained to her son why they had to hide from the outside world, why they had to wait until they learned some answers and discovered who had been behind the destruction of DyMar.

Darin had split from his brother after a huge fight about the dangers of their research, about the edge they were skirting. He had walked away from DyMar, sold his home, left this vacation cabin to rot, and joined an isolated group of survivalists in the Oregon wilds. From that point on, David had spoken of Darin with scorn, dismissing the usual misguided complaints by Luddite groups, like the one his brother had joined.

Darin had insisted they would be in danger as soon as

more people found out about their research, but somehow David could not believe anybody but the technically literate would understand how significant a breakthrough he had made. "It's always nice to see that some people understand more than you give them credit for," David answered. "But I wouldn't count on it."

But Patrice knew he was naive. True this wasn't the type of thing ordinary people got up in arms about—it was too complicated and required too much foresight to see how the world would change, to sort the dangers they feared from the miracles he offered. But some people were paying attention. Darin had had good reason to fear, good reason to run. Patrice's question now was who was orchestrating all this?

The demonstrators outside DyMar consisted of an odd mix of religious groups, labor union representatives, animal-rights activists, and who knew what else. Some were fruit-cakes, some were violent. Her husband had died there, with only a crisp warning for her. *Go. Get away! Don't let them catch you. They'll be after you.*

Hoping it was just a temporary emergency, a flareup of destructive demonstrators, she had thrown Jody and the dog into their car, driving aimlessly for hours. She had seen the DyMar fire blazing on the distant bluff, and she feared the worst. Still not grasping the magnitude of the conspiracy, she had rushed home, hoping to find David there, hoping he had at least left her a message.

Instead, their place had been ransacked. People searching for something, searching for *them*. Patrice had run, taking only a few items they needed, using her wits and her fear as they raced away from Tigard, away from the Portland metropolitan area, into the deep wilderness.

She had swapped license plates several times in darkened parking lots, waited until near midnight and then grabbed a day's maximum cash from an ATM in downtown Eugene, Oregon; she had driven across town to another ATM, after midnight this time and therefore a new date, and gotten a second day's maximum. Then she had fled for the coast, for Darin's old, abandoned cabin, where she and Jody could go to ground, for however long it took for them to feel safe again.

For years she had worked freelance as an architect, doing her designs from home, especially in the last few months when Jody became more and more ill from his cancer and—worse—from the conventional chemo and radiation treatments themselves.

Patrice had designed this little hideaway as a favor for her brother-in-law several years ago. With rented equipment, Darin had installed the electricity himself, graded the driveway, cut down a few trees, but never gotten around to making it much of a vacation home. He had been too swallowed up in his eight-days-a-week research efforts. Corrupted by David, no doubt.

No one else would know about this place, no one would think to look for them here, in an unused vacation home built years ago for a brother who had disappeared half a year previously. It should have been a perfect place for her and Jody to catch their breath, to plan their next step.

But now the dog had disappeared, too. Vader had been Jody's last remaining sparkle of joy, his anchor during the chaos. The black Lab had been so excited to be out of the suburbs, where he could run through the forest. He had been a city dog for so long, fenced in; suddenly he had been turned loose in the Oregon forests.

She wasn't surprised that Vader had run off, but she always expected him to come home. She should have kept him on a rope—but how could she bear to do that, when she and her son were already trapped here? Prisoners in hiding? Patrice had been so afraid, she had stripped away the dog's ID tag. Now if Vader were caught, or injured somehow, there would be no way to get them back together—and no way to track them down.

Jody had taken it hard, trying his best to keep his hopes

up. His every thought was a wish for his dog to return. Apart from his gloom, he looked increasingly healthy now; most of his hair had grown back after the leukemia therapies. His energy level was higher than it had been in a long time. He looked like a normal kid again.

But his sadness over Vader was like an open sore. After every piece he placed in the Earth-Moon jigsaw puzzle, he glanced through the dingy curtains over the main windows, searching the treeline.

Suddenly he jumped up. "Mom, he's back!" Jody shouted, pushing away from his chair.

For a moment, Patrice reacted with alarm, thinking of the hunters, wondering who could have found them, how she might have given them away. But then, through the open screen door, she could hear the dog barking. She stood up from the puzzle table, astonished to see the black Labrador bounding out of the trees.

Jody leaped away from the table and bolted out the door. He ran toward the black dog so hard she expected her son to sprawl on his face on the gravel driveway or trip on a stump or fallen branch in the yard.

"Jody, be careful!" she called. Just what she needed—if the boy broke his arm, that would ruin everything. So far, she had managed to avoid all contact with doctors and any people who kept names and records.

Jody remained oblivious to everything but his excitement over the dog.

The boy reached his dog safely, and each tried to outdo the other's enthusiasm. Vader barked and danced around in circles, leaping into the air. Jody threw his arms around the dog's neck and wrestled him to the wet ground in a tumble of black fur, pale skin, and weeds.

Dripping and grass-stained, Jody raced Vader back to the cabin. Patrice wiped her hands on a kitchen towel and came out to the porch to greet him. "I told you he'd be okay," she said.

Idiotically happy, Jody nodded and then stroked the dog.

Patrice bent over and ran her fingers through the black fur. The wedding ring, still on her finger, stood out among the dark strands. The black Lab had a difficult time standing still for her, shifting on all four paws and letting his tongue loll out. His tail wagged like an out-of-control rudder, rocking his body off balance on his four paws.

Other than mud spatters and a few cockleburrs, she found nothing amiss. No injuries, no wounds. Not a mark on him.

She patted the dog's head, and Vader rolled his deep brown eyes up at her. With a shake of her head, she said, "I wish you could tell us stories."

15

As they approached the veterinary clinic in the sleepy coastal town of Lincoln City, Scully could hear the barking dogs.

The building was a large old house that had been converted into a business. The aluminum siding was white, smudged with mildew; the wooden shutters looked as if they needed a coat of paint. The two agents climbed the concrete steps to the main entrance and pushed open a storm door.

On their way to tracking down David Kennessy's survivalist brother, a report from this veterinarian's office had caught Mulder's attention. When Scully had requested a rush analysis of the strange fluid she had taken during the security guard's autopsy, the CDC had immediately recognized a distinct similarity to another sample—also submitted from rural Oregon.

Elliott Hughart had treated a dog, a black Labrador, who was also infected with the same substance. Mulder had been intrigued by the coincidence. Now at least they had someplace to start looking.

In the front lobby, the veterinarian's receptionist looked

harried. Other patrons sat in folding chairs around the lobby beside pet carriers. Kittens wrestled in a cage. Dogs whined on their leashes. Posters warned of the hazards of heartworm, feline leukemia, and fleas, next to a magazine rack filled with months-old issues of *Time*, *CatFancy*, and *People*.

Mulder flashed his ID as he strode up to the receptionist. "I'm Agent Fox Mulder, Federal Bureau of Investigation. We'd like to see Dr. Hughart, please."

"Do you have an appointment?" The information didn't sink in for a few seconds, then the harried woman blinked at him. "Uh, the *FBI*?"

"We're here to see him about a dog he treated two days ago," Scully said. "He submitted a sample to the Centers for Disease Control."

"I'll get the doctor for you as soon as possible," she said. "I believe he's performing a neutering operation at the moment. Would you like to go into the surgery room and wait?"

Mulder shuffled his feet. "We'll stay out here, thanks."

Three-quarters of an hour later, when Scully had a roaring headache from the noise and chaos of the distressed animals, the old doctor came out. He blinked under bushy gray eyebrows, looking distracted but curious. The FBI agents were easy to spot in the waiting room.

"Please come back to my office," the veterinarian said with a gesture to a small examining room. He closed the door.

A stainless-steel table filled the center of the room, and the smell of wet fur and disinfectants hung in the air. Cabinets containing thermometers and hypodermic needles for treatment of tapeworms, rabies, and distemper sat behind glass doors.

"Now, then," Hughart said in a quiet, gentle voice, but obviously flustered. "I've never had to deal with the FBI before. How can I help you?"

"You submitted a sample to the CDC yesterday from a

black Labrador dog you treated," Scully said. "We'd like to ask you a few questions."

Mulder held out a snapshot of Vader that they had taken from the family possessions at the ransacked Tigard home. "Can you identify the dog for us, sir? Is this the one you treated?"

Surprised, the veterinarian raised his eyebrows. "That's almost impossible to tell, just from a photograph like this. But the size and age look about right. Could be the same animal." The old veterinarian blinked. "Is this a criminal matter? Why is the FBI involved?"

Scully withdrew the photos of Patrice and Jody Kennessey. "We're trying to find these two people, and we have reason to believe they are the dog's owners."

The doctor shook his head and shrugged. "They weren't the ones who brought him in. The dog was hit by a car, brought in by a tourist. The man was real anxious to get out of here. Kids were crying in the back of the station wagon. It was late at night. But I treated the dog anyway, though there wasn't much cause for hope." He shook his head. "You can tell when they're about to die. They know it. You can see it in their eyes. But this dog . . . very strange."

"Strange in what way?" Scully asked.

"The dog was severely injured," the old man said. "Massive damage, broken ribs, shattered pelvis, crushed spine, ruptured internal organs. I didn't expect him to live, and the dog was in a great deal of pain." He distractedly wiped his fingers across the recently cleaned steel table, leaving fingerprint smears.

"I patched him up, but clearly there was no hope. He was hot, his body temperature higher than any fever I've seen in an animal before. That's why I took the blood sample. Never expected what I actually found, though."

Mulder's eyebrows perked up. Scully looked at her partner, then back at the veterinarian. "With severe trauma from a car accident, I wouldn't expect the temperature to rise," she said. "Not if the dog was in shock and entering a coma state."

The doctor nodded his head patiently. "Yes, that's why I was so curious. I believe the animal had some sort of infection before the accident. Perhaps that's why he was so disoriented and got struck by the car." Hughart looked deeply disturbed, almost embarrassed. "When I saw there was no hope, I gave the dog an injection of Euthanol—sodium pentabarbitol—to put him to sleep. Ten ccs, way more than enough for the body mass of a black Lab. It's the only thing to do in cases like that, to put the animal out of its misery . . . and this dog was in a world of misery."

"Could we see the body of the dog?" Scully asked.

"No." The veterinarian turned away. "I'm afraid that's impossible."

"Why?" Mulder asked.

Hughart looked at them from beneath his bushy gray eyebrows before glancing back down at his scrubbed-clean fingers. "I was working in the lab, studying the fresh blood sample, when I heard a noise. I came in and found that the dog had jumped off the table. I swear its forelegs were broken, its rib cage crushed."

Scully drew back, unable to believe what she was hearing. "And did you examine the dog?"

"I couldn't." Hughart shook his head. "When I tried to get to the dog, it barked at me, turned, then pushed its way through the door. I ran, but that black Lab bounded out into the night, as frisky as if he were just a puppy."

Scully looked at Mulder with eyebrows raised. The veterinarian seemed distracted by his own recollection. He scratched his hair in puzzlement. "I thought I saw a shadow disappearing toward the trees, but I couldn't be sure. I called for it to come back, but that dog knew exactly where he wanted to go."

Scully was astonished. "Are you suggesting that a dog struck by a car, as well as given an injection of concentrated sodium pentabarbitol . . . was somehow able to leap down from your operating table and run out the door?"

"Quite a lot of stamina," Mulder said.

"Look," the veterinarian said, "I don't have an explanation, but it happened. I guess somehow the dog . . . wasn't as injured after all. But I can't believe I made a mistake like that. I spent hours searching the woods around here, the streets, the yards. I expected to find the body out in the parking lot or not far from here . . . but I saw nothing. There've been no reports either. People around here talk about unusual things like that."

Scully changed the subject. "Do you still have the original blood sample from the dog? Could I take a look at it?"

"Sure," the veterinarian said, as if glad for the opportunity to be vindicated. He led the two agents to a small laboratory area where he performed simple tests for worms or blood counts. On one countertop underneath low fluorescent lights stood a bulky stereomicroscope.

Hughart pulled out a slide from a case where a dried smear of blood had turned brown under the cover slip. He inserted the slide under the lens, flicked on the lamp beneath it, and turned the knobs to adjust the lens. The old man stepped back and motioned for Scully to take a look.

"When I first glanced at it," the veterinarian said, "the blood was swarming with those tiny specks. I've never seen anything like it, and in my practice I've encountered plenty of blood-borne parasites in animals. Nematodes, amoebas, other kinds of pests. But these . . . these were so unusual. That's why I sent the sample to the CDC."

"And they called us." Scully looked down and saw the dog's blood cells, as well as numerous little glints that seemed too angular, too geometrical, unlike any other microorganism she had ever seen.

"When they were moving and alive, those things looked almost . . . I can't describe it," the old vet said. "They've all stopped now, hibernating somehow. Or dead."

Scully studied the specks and could not understand them either. Mulder waited patiently at her side, and she finally let him take a look. He looked at her knowingly.

Scully turned to the veterinarian. "Thank you for your time, Dr. Hughart. We may be back in touch. If you find any information on the location of the dog or its owners, please contact us."

"But what is this?" the doctor asked, following as Scully led Mulder toward the door. "And what prompted an FBI follow-up?"

"It's a missing persons case," Mulder said, "and there's some urgency."

The two agents made their way out through the reception area, where they encountered a different assortment of cats and dogs and cages. Several of the examining room doors were closed, and strange sounds came from behind them.

The veterinarian seemed reluctant to get back to his routine chaos of yowling animals, lingering in the door to watch them go down the steps.

Mulder held his comments until they had climbed back in the car, ready to drive off again. "Scully, I think the Kennessys were doing some very unorthodox research at DyMar Lab."

"I admit, it's some kind of strange infection, Mulder, but that doesn't mean—"

"Think about it, Scully." His eyes gleamed. "If DyMar developed some sort of amazing regenerative treatment, David might well have tested it on the pet dog." Scully bit her lip. "With his son's condition, he would have been desperate enough for just about anything."

She slumped into the seat and buckled her seatbelt. "But, Mulder, what kind of treatment could heal a dog from disastrous injuries after a car accident, then neutralize the effects of sodium pentabarbitol designed to put the dog to sleep?"

"Maybe something in the combined expertise of Darin and David Kennessy," Mulder said, and started the car.

She unfolded the state highway map, looking for the next stopping point on their search: the vicinity where Darin Kennessy had gone into hiding. "But, Mulder, if they really developed such a . . . miracle cure, why would Darin have abandoned the research? Why would someone want to blow up the lab and destroy all the records?"

Mulder eased out of the parking lot and waited as a string of RVs drove along the Coast Highway, before he turned right and followed the road through the small picturesque town. He thought of the dead security guard, the rampant and unexplained growths, the slime. "Maybe all of DyMar's samples weren't so successful. Maybe something much worse got loose."

Scully looked at the road ahead. "We've got to find that dog, Mulder."

Without answering, he accelerated the car.

16

Some people might have thought being alone in a morgue late at night would be frightening—or at least cause for some uneasiness. But Edmund found the silent and dimly lit hospital the best place to study. He had hours of quiet solitude, and he had his medical books, as well as popularized versions of true crime and coroner's work.

Someday he hoped to get into medical school himself and study forensic medicine. The subject fascinated him. Eventually, if he worked hard, he might become at least a first or second assistant to the county medical examiner, Frank Quinton. That was the highest goal Edmund thought he could reach.

Studying was somewhat hard for him, and he knew that medical school would be an enormous challenge. That was why he hoped to learn as much as he could on his own, looking at the pictures and diagrams, boning up on the details before he got a chance to enter college.

After all, Abraham Lincoln had been a self-educated man, hadn't he? Nothing wrong with it, no way, no how.

And Edmund had the time and the concentration and the ambition to learn as much as he could.

Fluorescent lights shone in white pools around him on the clean tile floor, the white walls. The steel and chrome gleamed. The air vents made a sound like the soft breath of a peacefully sleeping man. The hospital corridors were silent. No intercom, no elevator bell, no footsteps from crepe-soled shoes walking down the halls.

He was all alone down here in the morgue on the night shift—and he liked it that way.

Edmund flipped pages in one of his medical texts, refreshing his memory as to the difference between a *perforating* and a *penetrating* wound. In a penetrating wound, the bullet simply passed into the body and remained there, while in a perforating wound, the bullet plowed through the other side, usually tearing out a larger chunk of flesh in the exit wound, as opposed to the neat round entry hole.

Edmund scratched the bald top of his head as he read the distinction over and over again, trying to keep the terms straight. On another page, he analyzed gunshot diagrams, saw dotted lines indicating the passage of bullets through the body cavity, how one course could be instantly fatal while another could be easily healed.

At least it was quiet here so he could concentrate, and when Edmund finally got all of the explanations clear in his mind, they usually stayed in place. The back of his head throbbed with a tension headache, but Edmund didn't want to get more coffee or take aspirin. He would think his way through it.

Just when he thought he was on the verge of a revelation, ready to grin with exhilarated triumph, he heard something moving . . . stirring.

Edmund perked up, squaring his shoulders and looking around the room. Only a week before, another morgue attendant had told him a whopper about a cadaver—a man decapitated in an auto accident—that had supposedly gotten up and walked out of the Allegheny Catholic Medical Center. One of the lights flickered in the left corner, but Edmund saw no shambling, headless corpses . . . or any other manifestations of ridiculous urban legends.

He stared at the dying bulb, realizing that its strobe-light pattern was distracting him. He sighed and jotted a little note for the maintenance crew. Maintenance had already double-checked the temperature in the refrigerator drawers, had added more freon, and claimed that everything in the small vaults—including 4E—was exactly the way it should be.

Hearing no further sound, Edmund turned the page and flipped to another chapter about the various types of trauma that could be inflicted by blunt weapons.

Then he noticed the sound of movement again—a brushing, stirring . . . and then a loud *thump*.

Edmund sat bolt upright, blinking repeatedly. He knew this wasn't his imagination, no way, no how. He had worked here in the morgue long enough that he didn't get easily spooked by sounds of settling buildings or whirring support machinery.

Another thump. Something striking metal.

He stood up, trying to determine the source of the noise. He wondered if someone was hurt, or if some sinister lurker had slipped into the quiet morgue . . . but why? Edmund had been at his station for the previous three hours and he had heard nothing, seen nothing. He could remember everyone who had entered the place.

Again, he heard a pounding, and a thump, and a scraping. There was no pretense of quiet at all anymore. Someone hammered inside a chamber, growing more frantic.

Edmund scuttled to the rear of the room with growing dread—in his heart, he knew where he would find the source of the noise. One of the refrigerator drawers—one of the drawers that contained a cadaver.

He had read horror stories in school, especially Edgar

Allan Poe, about premature burials, people not actually dead. He had heard spooky stories about comatose victims slammed into morgue refrigerators until they died from the cold rather than their own injuries—patients who had been misdiagnosed, in a diabetic shock or epileptic seizures that gave all the appearance of death.

From his limited medical expertise, Edmund had dismissed each of these anecdotal examples as urban legends, old wives' tales . . . but right now there could be no mistaking it.

Someone was pounding from the *inside* of one of the refrigerator doors.

He went over, listening. "Hello!" he shouted. "I'll get you out." It was the least he could do.

A RESTRICTED sign marked the drawer making the sounds, yellow tape, and a BIOHAZARD symbol. Drawer 4E. This one contained the body of the dead security guard, and Edmund knew the blotched, lumpy, slime-covered corpse had been inside the drawer for days. *Days!* Agent Scully had even performed an autopsy on the man.

This guy could not still be alive.

The restless noises fell quiet after his shout, then he heard a stirring, almost like . . . rats crawling within the walls.

Edmund swallowed hard. Was this a prank, someone trying to spook him? People picked on him often, called him a geek.

If this was a joke, he would get even with them. But if someone needed help, Edmund had to take the chance.

"Are you in there?" he said, leaning closer to the sealed refrigerator door. "I'll let you out." He pressed his white lips together to squeeze just a little more bravery into his system, and tugged on the handle of 4E.

The door popped open, and something inside tried to push its way free. Something horrible.

Edmund screamed and fought against the door. He saw

a strange twisted shape inside the unlit chamber thrashing about, denting the stainless-steel walls. The sliding drawer rocked and rattled.

A fleshy appendage protruded, bending around in ways no jointed limb would ever move . . . more like a stubby *tentacle*.

Edmund wailed again and used his back to push against the door, squirming out of the way so the groping thing would not be able to touch him. His weight was more than enough to force back the attack. Other protrusions from the body core, twisted lumps that seemed to have been arms or hands at one point, scraped and scrabbled for a hold against the slippery metal door, trying to get in.

A sticky coating of slime, like saliva, drooled from the inside ceiling of the drawer.

Edmund pushed hard enough that the door almost closed. Two of the tentacles and one many-jointed finger were caught in the edge. Other limbs—far too many for the normal complement of arms and legs—flailed and pounded, struggling to get out.

But he heard no sound from vocal chords. No words. No scream of pain. Just frantic movement.

Edmund pushed harder, crushing the pseudo-fingers. Finally they jerked and broke away, yanking themselves back into the relative safety of the refrigerator drawer.

Biting back an outcry, Edmund slammed himself against the steel door, shoving until he heard the latch click and lock into place.

Trembling with a huge sigh of relief, he fiddled with the latch to make sure it was solid. Then he stood in shock, staring at the silent refrigerator drawer.

He had a moment of blessed peace—but then he heard the trapped thing inside pounding about in a frenzy. Edmund shouted at it in panic, "Be quiet in there!"

The best thing he could think of was to rush to the temperature controls, where he dialed the setting as low as it could possibly go—to hard freeze. That would knock the thing down, keep it still. The refrigerators had just been charged, and the freezers would do their work quickly. They were designed to preserve evidence and tissue without any chance of further decay or handling damage.

Inside the coffin-sized drawer, the cold recirculating air would even now be intense, stunning that *thing* that had somehow gotten inside where the guard's body was stored.

In a few moments he heard the frantic thrashing begin to subside—but it might have been just a ruse. Edmund wanted to run, but he didn't dare leave. He didn't know what to do. He couldn't think of any other way to deal with the problem. Cold . . . *cold*. That would freeze the thing.

The thumping and scrabbling slowed, and finally Edmund got up the nerve to hurry to the telephone. He punched a button and called Security.

When two hospital guards eventually came down—already skeptical and taking their sweet time, since they received more false alarms from night-shift morgue attendants than in any other place or any other time in the hospital—the creature inside the drawer had fallen entirely silent. Probably frozen by now.

They laughed at Edmund, thinking it was just his imagination. But he endured their joking for now.

He stood back, unwilling to be anywhere close by when they opened up drawer 4E. He warned them again, but they slid open the drawer anyway.

Their laughter stopped instantly as they stared down at the hideous remains.

17

The bridge spread out into the early morning fog. Its vaulted and lacy metal girders disappeared into the mist like an infinite tunnel.

To Jeremy Dorman it was just a route across the Willamette River on his long and stumbling trek out of the city, toward the wilderness . . . toward where he might find Patrice and Jody Kennessy.

He took another step, then another, weaving. He couldn't feel his feet; they were just lumps of distant flesh at the ends of his legs, which themselves felt rubbery, as if his body were changing, altering, growing joints in odd places.

At the peak of the bridge, he felt suspended in air, though the dawn murk prevented him from seeing the river far below. The city lights of skyscrapers and streetlamps were mere fairy glows.

Dorman staggered along, focusing his mind on the vanishing point, where the bridge disappeared into the fog. His goal was just to get to the other side of the bridge. One step at a time. And after he succeeded in that task, he would set another for himself, and another, until he finally made his way out of Portland.

The wooded coastal mountains—the precious dog—seemed an impossibly long distance away.

The morning air was clammy and cold, but he couldn't feel it, didn't notice his sticky clothes. His skin crawled with gooseflesh, but it had nothing to do with the temperature, just the rampant disaster happening within all of his cells. As a scientist, he should have found it interesting—but as the victim of the change, he found it only horrifying.

Dorman swallowed hard. His throat felt slick, as if clogged with slime, a mucus that oozed from his pores. When he clenched his teeth, they rattled loosely in their gums. His vision carried a black fringe of static around the edges.

He walked onward. He had no other alternative.

A pickup truck roared by on the deck plates of the bridge. The echoes of the engine and the tires throbbed in his ears. He watched the red taillights disappear.

Suddenly Dorman's stomach clenched, his spine whipped about like an angry serpent. He feared he would disintegrate here, slough off into a pool of dissociated flesh and twitching muscles, a gelatinous mass that would drip down beneath the grated walkway of the bridge.

"Noooo!" he cried, a howling inhuman voice in the stillness.

Dorman reached out with one of his slick, waxy hands and grabbed the bridge railing to support himself, *willing* his body to cease its convulsions. He was losing control again.

It was getting harder and harder to stop his body. All of his biological systems were refusing commands from his mind, taking on a life of their own. He gripped the bridge rail with both hands and squeezed until he thought the steel would bend.

He must have looked like a potential suicide waiting to leap over the edge into the infinite murk of whispering water below—but Dorman had no intention of killing himself. In fact, everything he was doing was a desperate effort to keep himself alive, no matter what. No matter the cost.

He couldn't go to a hospital or seek other medical attention—no doctor in the world would know how to treat his affliction. And any time he reported his name, he might draw the attention of . . . unwanted eyes. He couldn't risk that. He would have to endure the pain for now.

Finally, when the spasm passed and he felt only weak and trembly, Dorman set off again. His body wouldn't fall apart on him yet. Not yet. But he needed to focus, needed to reestablish the goal in his mind.

He had to find the damned dog.

He reached into his tattered shirt pocket and pawed out the wrinkled, soot-smudged photo he had taken from the broken frame in David Kennessy's desk. Lovely young Patrice with her fine features and strawberry blond hair, and wiry, tousle-haired Jody grinning for the camera. Their expressions reflected the peaceful times before Jody's leukemia, before David's desperate drive for research.

Dorman narrowed his eyes and burned the picture into his brain.

He had been a close friend of the Kennessys. He had been Jody's surrogate uncle, practically a member of the family—far more than the skittish and rude brother Darin, that's for sure. And because he knew her so well, Dorman had a good idea where Patrice would think to hide. She would imagine she was safe there, since Darin had loved his secrets so much.

In the deep pocket of his tattered jacket, the revolver he had taken from the security guard hung like a heavy club.

When he finally reached the far end of the Ross Island Bridge, Dorman stared westward. The forested, fog-shrouded mountains of the coast were a long distance away.

Once he found them, Dorman hoped he could get away with the dog without Patrice or Jody seeing him. He didn't want to have to kill them—hell, the kid was already a skeleton, nearly dead from his leukemia—but he would shoot them, and the dog, too, if it became necessary. In the big picture, it didn't really matter how much he cared for them.

He already had plenty of blood on his hands.

Once again, he cursed David and his naiveté. Darin had understood, and he had run to hide under a rock. But David, hot-headed and desperate to help Jody, had blindly ignored the true sources of funding for their work. Did he really think they were giving DyMar all those millions just so *David Kennessy* could turn around and decide the morally responsible approach to its use?

David had stumbled into a political minefield, and he had set in motion all the events that had caused so much damage—including Jeremy Dorman's own desperate gambit for survival.

A gambit that was failing. Though the prototype samples had kept him alive at first, now his entire body was falling into a biological meltdown, and he could do nothing about it.

At least, not until he found the dog.

18

 Mulder pulled up to the Mini Serve pump in the small, rundown gas station. As he got out of the car, he looked toward the glassed-in office and the tall, unlit Conoco sign. He half expected to see old men sitting in rocking chairs on the porch, or at least someone coming out to offer Andy Griffith–like hospitality.

Scully got out of the car to stretch. They had been driving for hours up Highway 101, seeing the rugged coastline, small villages, and secluded houses tucked away into the forested hills.

Somewhere out here David Kennessy's brother had joined his isolated group of survivalists, and it was the same general area where the black Lab had been hit by the car. That made too great a coincidence for Mulder's mind. He wanted to find Darin and get some straight answers about the DyMar research. If Darin knew why DyMar had been destroyed, he might also know why Patrice had gone missing.

But further information on the survivalists was vague. The group, by its very nature, kept its exact location secret, without phones or electricity. Finding the camp might be as hard as finding Patrice and Jody.

Mulder popped the gas tank and lifted the nozzle from the pump. Then the office door banged open, but instead of a "service with a smile" attendant, a short potbellied man with a fringe of gray-white hair scuttled out.

"Hey, don't touch that!" the potbellied man snapped, wearing a stormy expression. "This ain't no self-serve."

Mulder looked at the gas nozzle in his hand, then at the Mini Serve sign. The potbellied man came over and grabbed the nozzle out of Mulder's grasp as if it were a dangerous toy in the hands of a child. The man slid the nozzle into the gas tank, squeezed and locked on the handle, then stepped back proudly, as if only a professional could be trusted with such a delicate operation.

"What is the problem, sir?" Scully asked.

The potbellied man glowered at her, then at Mulder, as if they were incredibly stupid. "Damn Californians." He shook his head after glancing at the license plate of their rental car. "This is Oregon. We don't allow amateurs to pump their own gas."

Mulder and Scully looked at each other from across the roof of the car. "Actually, we're not Californians," Mulder said, reaching inside his overcoat. "We're federal agents. We work for the FBI—and I can assure you that pumping gas is one of the rigorous training courses we're required to undergo at Quantico." He flashed his ID and gestured over at Scully. "In fact, Agent Scully here is nearly as qualified as I am to fill up a tank."

The potbellied man looked at Mulder skeptically. His flannel shirt was oil-stained and tattered. His jowls had been shaved intermittently, giving him a rugged, patchy appearance. He didn't seem the type ever to have dirtied his hands with knotting a necktie.

Scully drew out the photo of Patrice and Jody Kennessy. "We're searching for these people," she said. "A woman, mid-thirties, her son, twelve years old."

"Never seen 'em," the man said, then devoted his entire attention to the gas nozzle. On the pump, numbers clicked around and around in circles.

"They're also with a dog," Mulder said, "a black Labrador."

"Never seen 'em," the man repeated.

"You didn't even look at the picture, sir." Scully pushed it closer to his face across the top of the car.

The man looked at it carefully, then turned away again. "Never seen 'em. I got better things to do than to keep my eye on every stranger that comes through here."

Mulder raised his eyebrows. In his mind this man was *exactly* the type who would keep a careful eye on every stranger or customer who came through—and he had no doubt that before the afternoon was over, everyone within ten miles would hear the gossip that federal agents were searching for someone on the isolated stretches of the Oregon coast.

"You wouldn't happen to have any idea where we might locate a survivalist compound in this area?" Mulder added. "We believe they may have been taken there, to be with a family member."

The potbellied man raised his eyebrows. "I know some of those places exist in the hills and the thick forest—nobody in their right mind goes looking too close for them."

Scully took out her business card. "If you do see anything, sir, we'd appreciate it if you give us a call. We're not trying to arrest these two for anything. They need help."

"Sure, always happy to do my duty," the man said, and tucked the card into his shirt pocket without even glancing at it. He topped off the gas tank to an even dollar amount and then, maliciously, it seemed, squirted a few cents more into the tank.

Mulder paid him, got a receipt, and then he and Scully climbed back in the car. "People around here sure value their privacy," Mulder said. "Especially outside of the cities,

Oregon has a reputation for harboring survivalists, isolationists, and anybody else who doesn't want to be bothered."

Scully glanced down at the photo in her hands, at Jody Kennessy's smiling face, and Mulder knew what must be occupying her mind. "I wonder why David Kennessy's brother wanted so badly to drop out of sight," she said.

After four more hours of knocking on doors, stopping at cafes, souvenir shops, and art galleries scattered along the back roads, Mulder wasn't sure they would get any benefit out of continuing their methodical search unless they found a better lead to the location of Darin Kennessy.

But they could either sit and cool their heels in their Lincoln City motel room, or they could do something. Mulder preferred to do something. Usually.

He picked up his cell phone to see if he could call Frank Quinton, the medical examiner, to check on any results of the analysis of the strange mucus, but he saw that the phone was out of range. He sighed. They could have missed a dozen phone calls by now. The wooded mountains were sparsely inhabited, often even without electrical utilities. Cellular phone substations were too widely separated to get reception. He collapsed the antenna and tucked the phone back into his pocket.

"Looks like we're on our own, Scully," he said.

The brooding pines stood dense and dominant on either side of the road, like a cathedral tunnel. Wet leaves, spruce needles, and slick moisture coated the pavement. Someone had bothered to put up an unbroken barbed-wire fence from which "No Trespassing" signs dangled at frequent intervals.

Mulder drove slowly, glancing from side to side. "Not too friendly, are they?"

"Seems like they're overdoing it a bit," Scully agreed. "Anybody who needs that much privacy must be hiding something. Do you think we're close to the survivalist compound?"

Out of the corner of his eye, Mulder saw a black shape moving, an animal loping along. He squinted at it intently, then hit the brakes.

"Look, Scully!" He pointed, sure of what he saw in the trees behind the barbed-wire fence: a black dog about the right size to be the missing pet, looking at them curiously, then loping back off into the trees. "Let's go check it out. Maybe it's Vader."

He swung the car onto the narrow gravel shoulder, then hopped out. Scully exited into the ditch, trying to maintain her footing.

Mulder sprinted to the barbed wire, pushing down on the rusted strands and ducking through. He turned to hold one of the wires up for Scully. Off in the trees, the dog looked at them before trotting nervously away.

"Here, boy!" Mulder called, then tried whistling. He ran crashing after it through the underbrush. The dog barked and turned and bolted.

Scully chased after him. "That's not the way to get a skittish dog to come back to you," she said.

Mulder paused to listen, and the dog barked again. "Come on, Scully."

Along the trees even this deep in the woods he saw frequent "No Trespassing" signs, along with "Private Property, Warning—Violators Will Be Prosecuted." Several of the signs were peppered with buckshot dents.

Scully hurried, but kept herself intensely alert, aware of the very real danger of excessive traps and the illegal countermeasures some of these survivalist groups were known to use. At any moment they could step into a hunting snare, snap a trip wire, or find themselves dropped into a trap pit.

Finally, as Mulder continued up the slope after the black dog, ducking between trees and wheezing from lack of breath, he reached the crest of the hill. A line of DANGER signs marked the area.

As Scully came close to him, flushed from the pursuit, they topped the rise. "Uh-oh, Mulder."

Suddenly dozens of dogs began barking and baying. She saw a chain-link fence topped with razor wire, surrounding an entire compound of half-buried houses, bunkers, prefabricated cabins, and guard shacks.

The black dog raced toward the compound.

Mulder and Scully skidded to a stop in the soft forest dirt as armed men rushed from the guard shacks at the corners of the compound. Other people stepped out of the cabins. Women peered through the windows, grabbing their children and protecting them from what they thought must be an unexpected government raid. The men shouted and raised their rifles, firing warning shots into the air.

Mulder instantly held up his hands. Other dogs came bounding out of the compound, German shepherds, rottweilers, and Doberman pinschers.

"Mulder, I think we found the survivalists we've been looking for," Scully said.

19

"We're federal agents," Mulder announced. "I'm going to reach for my identification." With agonizing slowness, he groped inside his topcoat.

Unfortunately, all the weapons remained leveled at him, if possible with even greater ire. He realized that radical survivalists probably wanted nothing to do with any government agency.

One middle-aged man with a long beard stepped forward to the fence and glowered at them. "And do federal agents not know how to read?" he said in a firm, intelligent voice. "You've passed dozens NO TRESPASSING signs to get here. Do you have a duly authorized search warrant?"

"I'm sorry, sir," Scully said. "We were trying to stop your dog, the black one. We're searching for a man named Darin Kennessy. We have reason to believe he may have information on these people." She reached inside her jacket and withdrew the photos. "A woman and her boy."

"If you come one step closer, you'll be into a minefield," the bearded man said. The other survivalists continued

113

watching Mulder and Scully with increased suspicion. "Just stay where you are."

Mulder couldn't imagine that the survivalists would let their dogs run loose if there were really a minefield around the compound . . . but, then again, it wasn't completely inconceivable either. He didn't feel like arguing with this man.

"Who are they?" one of the women asked, also holding a high-powered rifle. "Those two people you're looking for?" She looked at least as deadly as the men. "And why do you need to talk to Darin?"

Mulder kept his face impassive, not showing his excitement at learning they had finally tracked down the brother of David Kennessy.

"The boy is the nephew of Darin Kennessy. He desperately needs medical attention," Scully said, raising her voice. "They have a black Labrador dog. We saw your dog and thought it might be the one we were looking for."

The man with the beard laughed. "This is a spaniel, not a black Lab," he said.

"What happened to the boy's dad?" the woman asked.

"He was recently killed," Mulder said. "The laboratory where he worked—the same place Darin worked—was destroyed in a fire. The woman and the boy disappeared. We hoped they might have come here, to be with you."

"Why should we trust you?" the man with the beard asked. "You're probably the people Darin warned us about."

"Go get Darin," the woman yelled over her shoulder; then she looked at the bearded man. "He's the one who's got to decide this. Besides, we have plenty of firepower to take care of these two, if there's trouble."

"There won't be any trouble," Scully assured them. "We just need some information."

A lean man with bushy cinnamon-red hair climbed up the underground stairs of one of the half-buried shacks. Uncertainly, he came closer, approaching the bearded man and the angry-looking woman.

"I'm Darin Kennessy, David's brother. What is it you want?"

Shouting across the fence, Mulder and Scully briefly explained the situation, and Darin Kennessy looked deeply disturbed. "You suspected something beforehand, didn't you—before DyMar was destroyed and your brother was killed?" Mulder asked. "You left your research many months ago and came out here . . . to hide?"

Darin became indignant. "I left my research for philosophical reasons. I thought the technology was turning in a very alarming direction, and I did not like some of the funding . . . sources my brother was using. I wanted to separate myself from the work and the men associated with it. Cut loose entirely."

"We're trying to stay away from people like that," the man with the beard said. "We're trying to stay away from everything, build our own life here. We want to create a protected place to live with caring neighbors, with strong families. We're self-sufficient. We don't need any interference from people like you—people who wear suits and ties."

Mulder cocked his chin. "Did you folks by any chance read the *Unabomber Manifesto*?"

Darin Kennessy scowled. "I'm as repelled by the Unabomber's use of bomb technology as I am by the atrocities of modern technology. But not everything—just one facet in particular. Nanotechnology."

He waited for a beat. Mulder thought the rugged dress and homespun appearance of the man shifted subtly, so he could see the highly intelligent computer chip researcher hiding beneath the disguise. "Very tiny self-replicating machines small enough to work inside a human cell, versatile enough to assemble just about *anything* . . . and smart enough to know what they're doing."

Mulder looked at Scully. "Big things come in small packages."

Darin's eyes shone with fervor. "Because each nanomachine

is so small, it can move its parts very rapidly—think of a hummingbird's wings vibrating. A swarm of nanomachines could scour through a pile of rubble or a tank of seawater and separate out every single atom of gold, platinum, or silver and sort them into convenient bins, all in total silence, with no waste and no unsightly mess."

Scully's brow furrowed. "And this was your DyMar work?"

"I started long before that," Darin said. "But David and I took our ideas in even more exciting directions. Inside a human body, nano-scouts could do the same work as white corpuscles do in fighting diseases, bacteria, and viruses. But unlike white corpuscles, these nano-doctors can also inspect DNA strands, find any individual cell that turns cancerous, then reprogram the DNA, fixing any errors and mutations they find. What if we could succeed in creating infinitesimal devices that can be injected into a body to act as 'biological policemen'—submicroscopic robots that seek out and repair damage on a cellular level?"

"A cure for cancer," Mulder said.

"And everything else."

Scully flashed him a somewhat skeptical look. "Mr. Kennessy, I've read some speculative pieces in popular science magazines, but certainly nothing that would suggest we are within decades of having such a breakthrough in nanotechnology."

"Progress is often closer than you think," he said. "Researchers at the University of Wisconsin used lithographic techniques to produce a train of gears a tenth of a millimeter across. Engineers at AT&T Bell Laboratories created semiconductors out of clusters containing only six to twelve atoms at a time. Using scanning tunneling microscopy, scientists at the IBM Almaden Research Center drew a complete map of Earth's western hemisphere only a fiftieth the diameter of a human hair."

"But there must be a limit to how small we can physically manipulate tools and circuit paths," Mulder said.

The dogs set up a louder barking, and the man with the beard went over to shush them. Darin Kennessy frowned, distracted, as if torn by his need to hide and deny all his technological breakthroughs and his clear passion for the work he had abandoned.

"That's only tackling the problem from one direction. Between David and myself, we also started to build from the bottom up. Self-assembly, the way nature does it. Researchers at Harvard have made use of amino acids and proteins as templates for new structures smaller than the size of a cell, for instance.

"With our combined expertise in silicon microminiaturization techniques and biological self-assembly, we tried to match up those advances to yield a sudden breakthrough."

"And did you?"

"Maybe. It seemed to be working very well, up until the time I abandoned it. I suspect my fool brother continued pushing, playing with fire."

"So why did you leave your research, if it was so promising?"

"There's a dark side, Agent Mulder," Darin continued, glancing over at the other survivalists. "Mistakes happen. Researchers usually screw up half a dozen times before they achieve success—it's just part of the learning process. The question is, can we afford that learning process with nanotechnology?"

The woman with the shotgun grumbled, but kept her direct comments to herself.

"Just suppose one of our first nanomachines—a simple one, without fail-safe programming—happens to escape from the lab," Darin said. "If this one goes about copying itself, and each copy builds more copies, in about ten hours there would be sixty-eight billion nanomachines. In less than two days, the runaway nanomachines could take apart the entire Earth—*working one molecule at a time!* Two days, from beginning to end. Think of the last time you saw any government make a decision that fast, even in an emergency."

No wonder Kennessy's research was so threatening to people in well-established circles of power, Mulder realized. No wonder they might be trying to suppress it, at all costs.

"But you left DyMar before you reached a point where you could release your findings?" Scully asked.

"Nobody was ever going to release our findings," Darin said, his voice dripping with scorn. "I knew it would never be made available to society. David made noises about going public, releasing the results of our first tests with lab rats and small animals, but I always talked him out of it, and so did our assistant, Jeremy Dorman." He drew a deep breath. "I guess he must have come too close, if those people felt they finally had to burn down the lab facility and destroy all our records."

"Patrice and Jody aren't with you, are they?" Scully said, confirming her suspicions. "Do you know where they are?"

Darin snorted. "No, we went our separate ways. I haven't spoken to any of them since I came out here to join the camp." He gestured to the dogs, the guard shacks, the razor wire. "This wouldn't be scenic enough for them."

"But you are Jody's uncle," Mulder said.

"The only person that kid spent time with was Jeremy Dorman. He was the closest thing to a real uncle the boy had."

"He was also killed in the DyMar fire," Scully said.

"He was low man on the totem pole," Darin Kennessy said, "but he knew how to pull the business deals. He got us our initial funding and kept it coming. When I left to come out here, I think he was perfectly happy to step into my shoes, working with David."

Darin frowned. "But I had nothing more to do with them, not then and not now." He seemed deeply troubled, as if the news of his brother's death was just now breaking through his consciousness. "We used to be close, used to spend time out in the deep woods."

"Where?" Mulder asked.

"Patrice designed a little cabin for me, just to get away from it all."

Scully looked at Mulder, than at Darin. "Sir, could you tell us how we could locate the cabin?"

Darin frowned again, looking skittish and uneasy. "It's up near Colvain, off on some winding fire roads."

"Here's my card," Mulder said. "In case they do show up or you learn anything."

Darin frowned at him. "We don't have any phones here."

Scully grabbed Mulder's sleeve. "Thank you for your time."

"Be careful of the minefield," the man with the beard warned.

"We'll watch our step," Scully said.

Feeling tired and sweaty, Mulder was nonetheless excited by the information they had learned.

They made their way back through the thick woods past the dozens of warning signs to where they had parked their car at the edge of the road.

Scully couldn't believe how the survivalists lived. "Some people will do anything to survive," she muttered.

20

X On hearing Jody's cry, Patrice awoke from a restless sleep. She sat up in her narrow cot in the cabin's single back bedroom, throwing aside the musty-smelling blankets.

"Jody!"

The cabin was dark and too silent—until the dog woofed, once. She blinked the disorientation of sleep away and brushed mussed strawberry blond hair away from her eyes. She struggled free of the last tangles of blankets, as if they were a restraining net trying to keep her from the boy. He needed her.

On her way to the main room, she stumbled into an old wooden chair, hurt her foot as she kicked it away, then plunged blindly ahead into the darkness. "Jody!"

The moonlight gave just enough silvery light to guide her way once she got her bearings. On the sofa in the main room, she saw her boy lying in a sweat. The last embers of their fire in the hearth glowed red-orange, providing more wood smell than heat. After dark, no one should have been able to see the smoke.

121

For a moment the smoldering embers reminded her of the DyMar fire, where her husband had died in the raging flames. She shuddered at the thought, the reminder of the violence. David had been ambitious and impulsive and perhaps he had taken ill-advised risks. But David had believed passionately in his research, and he had tried to do his best.

Now he had died for his discoveries . . . and Jody had lost his father.

Vader sat erect close to Jody, a black guardian snuffling the boy's chest in concern. Seeing Patrice, Vader's tail thumped on the hardwood floor next to where one of the pillows had fallen. The black Lab pushed his muzzle into the blankets, whining.

Jody moaned and made another frightened sound.

Patrice stopped, looking down at her son. Vader stared back up with his liquid brown eyes, emitting another whine, as if asking why she didn't do anything. But she let Jody sleep.

Nightmares again.

Several times in the past week, Jody had awakened in the isolated and silent cabin, frightened and lost. Since the start of their desperate flight, he'd had good reason for nightmares. But was it his fear that brought on the dreams . . . or something else?

Patrice knelt down, and Vader squirmed with energy, pushing his nose against her side, anxious for her to reassure him. She patted him on the head, thumping hard, just the way he had always liked it. "It's okay, Vader," she said, attempting to soothe herself more than the dog.

With the flat of her palm, she touched Jody's forehead, feeling the heat. The boy stirred, and she wondered if she should wake him. His body was a war zone, a cellular battlefield. Though David had repeatedly denied what he had done, she knew full well what caused the fever.

Sometimes Patrice wondered if her son would be better off dead after all—and then she hated herself for even thinking such things. . . .

Vader padded across the floor toward the fireplace, nosed around the base of a faded overstuffed chair, and came back to Jody's bedside with a slobber-soggy tennis ball in his jaws. He wanted to play, as if convinced that would make everything all right.

Patrice frowned at Vader, turning away from the sofa. "You've got so damned much energy, you know that?"

Vader whined, then chewed on the tennis ball.

She remembered sitting at home in their living room, back in the old suburban house in Tigard—now trashed and ransacked—with David. Jody, in extreme pain from his cancer, had soaked in a hot, hot bath, taken his prescription painkillers, and gone to bed early, leaving his parents alone.

Vader didn't want to settle down, though, and if his boy wouldn't play, then he would pester the adults. David halfheartedly played tug-of-war with the black Lab, while Patrice watched with a mixture of uneasiness and fascination. The family dog was twelve years old already, the same age as Jody, and he shouldn't have been nearly so frisky.

"Vader's like a puppy again," Patrice said. Previously, the black Lab had settled into a middle-aged routine of sleeping most of the time, except for a lot of licking and tail-wagging to greet them every day when they came home. But lately the dog had been more energetic and playful than he had been in years. "I wonder what happened to him," she said.

David's grin, his short dark hair, and his heavy eyebrows made him look dashing. "Nothing."

Patrice sat up and pulled her hand away from him. "Did you take Vader into your lab again? What did you do to him?" She raised her voice, and the words came out with cold anger. "What did you do to him!"

Vader dropped the pull-toy in his jaws, staring at her as if she had gone insane. What business did she have yelling when they were trying to play?

David looked at her, hard. He raised his eyebrows in an expression of sincerity. "I didn't do anything. Honest."

With a woof, Vader lunged back with the pull-toy again, wagging his tail and growling as he dug his paws into the carpet. David fought back, leaning against the sofa to gain more leverage. "Just look at him! How can you think anything's wrong?"

But in their years of marriage, Patrice had learned one thing, and she had learned to hate it. She could always tell when David was lying. . . .

Her husband had been focused on his research, bulldozing ahead and ignoring regulations and restrictions. He didn't consult with her on many things, just barged along, doing what he insisted was right. That was just the way David Kennessy did things.

He had been too focused, too involved in his work to take note of the suspicious occurrences at DyMar until it was too late. She herself had noticed things, people watching their house at night, keeping an eye on her when she was out with David, odd clicks on the phone line . . . but David had brushed her worries aside. Such a brilliant man, yet so oblivious. At the last moment, at least, he had called her, warned her.

She had grabbed Jody and run, even as the protesters burned down the DyMar facility, trapping her husband in the inferno with Jeremy; she barely made it into hiding here with her son. Her *healthy* son.

On the sofa, Jody fell into a more restful sleep. His temperature remained high, but Patrice knew she could do nothing about that. She tucked the blankets around him again, brushed straight the sweat-sticky bangs across his forehead.

Vader let the tennis ball thump on the floor, giving up on the possibility of play. With a heavy sigh, the dog turned three times in a circle in front of the sofa, then slumped into a comfortable position, guarding his boy. He let out a long, heavy animal sigh.

Comforted by the dog's devotion, Patrice wandered back to her cot, glad she hadn't awakened her son after all. At least she hadn't switched on any lights . . . lights that could have been seen out in the darkness.

Leaving Jody to sleep, she lay awake in her own cot, alternately growing too hot, then shivering. Patrice longed for rest, but she knew she couldn't let her guard down. Not for an instant.

With her eyes closed, Patrice quietly cursed her husband and listened for sounds outside.

21

X Edmund was amazed at how fast the officials arrived, considering that they supposedly came all the way from Atlanta, Georgia. Their very demeanor unnerved him so much he didn't dare question their credentials.

He was just glad that somebody seemed to believe his story.

Edmund had sealed drawer 4E after the previous night's incident and lowered the temperature as far as it would go, though nobody showed much interest in looking for the monsters that had given him the willies. He was waiting to talk to his mentor Dr. Quinton, who was busy analyzing the mucus specimen taken during the autopsy. He expected the ME any minute now, and then he would feel vindicated.

But the officials showed up first, three of them, non-descript but professional, with a manner that made Edmund want to avert his eyes. They looked clean-cut, well-dressed, but grim.

"We're here from the Centers for Disease Control," one man said and ripped out a badge bearing a gold-plated shield and a blurry ID photo. He folded the identification back into his suit faster than Edmund could make out any of the words.

"The CDC?" he stammered. "Are you here for . . . ?"

"It's imperative that we confiscate the organic tissue you have stored in your morgue refrigerator," said the man on the left. "We understand you had an incident yesterday."

"We certainly did," Edmund said. "Have you seen this sort of thing before? I looked in all my medical books—"

"We have to destroy the specimen, just to be safe," said the man on the right. Edmund felt relieved to know that someone was in charge, someone else could take care of it from here.

"We need to inspect all records you have regarding the victim, the autopsy, and any specimens you might have kept," the man in the middle said. "We're also going to take extreme precautions to sterilize every inch of your morgue refrigerators."

"Do you think I'm infected?" Edmund said.

"That's highly unlikely, sir. You would have manifested symptoms immediately."

Edmund swallowed hard. But he knew his responsibilities.

"But—but I have to get approval," he said. "The medical examiner has explicit responsibility."

"Yes, I do," Frank Quinton said, walking into the morgue and scanning the situation. The medical examiner's grandfatherly face clouded over. "What's going on here?"

The man on the right spoke up. "I assure you, sir, we have the proper authority here. This is a potential matter of national security and public health. We are very concerned."

"And so am I," Quinton said. "Are you working with the other federal agents who were here?"

"This . . . phase of the operation is out of their jurisdiction, sir. This outbreak poses an extreme danger without proper containment procedures."

The central man's eyes were hard, and even the ME seemed intimidated.

"Sir," the first man said, "we need to get an entire team in here to remove the . . . biomaterial from the refrigerator. We'll inconvenience you as little as possible."

"Well, I suppose . . ." Quinton's voice trailed off, sounding flustered as the three CDC men quickly ushered them both out of the quiet and clean room.

"Edmund, let's go for a cup of coffee," Quinton finally said, glancing uneasily over his shoulder.

Happy for the coroner's invitation—he had never been so lucky before—Edmund took the elevator and went to the hospital cafeteria for a while, still trying to recover. He kept seeing the many-tentacled creature trying to escape from the morgue refrigerator drawer.

Normally he would have had a thousand questions for the ME, checking details, demonstrating all the trivia he had learned from his midnight studies in the morgue. But Quinton sat quiet and reticent, looking at his hands, deeply troubled. He took out the card the FBI agents had given him previously, turning it over and over in his hands.

When they returned to the basement level an hour later, they found that the morgue had been scoured and sterilized. Drawer 4E had been ripped out entirely, its contents taken away. The men had left no receipt, no paperwork.

"We don't have any way to contact them to find out their results," Edmund said.

But the medical examiner just shook his head. "Maybe that's for the best."

22

X The ocean crashed against the black cliffs with a hollow booming sound like boulders dropped from a great height. The breeze at the scenic overlook whipped cold and salty and wet against Scully's face.

"It's called the Devil's Churn," Mulder had said, though Scully could certainly read the Oregon State Scenic Marker sign.

Below, the water turned milky in a frothing maelstrom as the breakers slammed into a hollowed-out indentation in the cliff. Sea caves there had collapsed, creating a sort of chute; as the waves struck the narrow passage head-on, it funneled the force of the water and sprayed it into a dramatic tower, like a water cannon blasting as high as the clifftops above, drenching unwary sightseers.

According to the signs, dozens of people had died at this place: unsuspecting tourists picking their way down to the mouth of the Churn, caught standing in the wrong place when the unexpected geyser of water exploded upward.

Their bodies had been battered against the algae-slick rocks or simply sucked out to sea.

Station wagons, minivans, and rental cars were parked in the scenic area as families from out of state as well as locals came to stare down at the sea. Obnoxious seagulls screamed overhead.

A battered old vending coach stood open with aluminum awnings rattling in the breeze; a grinning man with a golf cap sold warmed-over hot dogs, sour coffee, bagged chips, and canned soft drinks. On the other side of the parking area, a woman with braids huddled in a down hunting vest, watching her handmade rugs flap vigorously on a clothesline.

Fighting back a headache and drawing a deep breath of the cool, salty breeze, Scully buttoned her coat to keep warm. Mulder went directly over to the cliff edge, eagerly peering down and waiting for the water to spray up. Scully withdrew her cell phone, glad to see that the signal here was strong enough, at last. She punched in the buttons for the Portland medical examiner.

"Ah, Agent Scully," Dr. Quinton said, "I've been trying to call you all morning."

"Any results?" she asked. After seeing the slide of the dog's contaminated blood at the veterinarian's, she had asked the medical examiner to look at his own sample of the slimy mucus she had taken during Vernon Ruckman's autopsy.

By the unsteady-looking guardrail, Mulder watched in fascination as a rooster tail of cold spray jetted into the air, curling up to the precipice, and then raining back down into the sea. She gestured for Mulder to come back to her as she pressed the phone tightly against her ear, concentrating on the ME's staticky words.

"Apparently something . . . unusual happened to the plague victim's body in the morgue refrigerator." Quinton seemed hesitant, at a loss for words. "Our attendant reported hearing noises, something moving inside the sealed drawer. And it's been sealed since you left it."

"That's impossible," Scully said. "The man couldn't still be alive. Even if the plague put him in some kind of extreme coma, I'd already performed an autopsy."

The ME said, "I know Edmund, and he's not the skittish sort. A little bit of a pest sometimes, but this isn't the kind of story he would make up. I was going to give him the benefit of the doubt, but . . ." Quinton hesitated again, and Scully pressed the phone closer to her ear, straining to hear the undertone in his voice. "Unfortunately, before I could check it out myself, some gentlemen from the Centers for Disease Control came in and sterilized everything. As a precaution, they took the entire refrigerator drawer."

"From the CDC?" Scully said in disbelief. She had worked many times with the CDC, and they were always consummate professionals, following official procedures rigorously. This sounded like something else entirely, some*one* else.

Now she was even more concerned about what she had learned earlier that morning when she called Atlanta to check on the status of the sample she had personally sent in. Apparently, their lab technician had lost the specimen.

Mulder came up to her, brushing his damp hair back, though the wind continued to blow it around. He looked at her, raising his eyebrows. She watched him as she spoke into the phone, keeping her voice carefully neutral. "Dr. Quinton, you kept a sample of the substance for your own analysis. Were you able to find anything?"

The ME pondered for a moment before answering. She heard static on the line, clicking, a warbling background tone. They still must be at the edge of reception for cellular transmissions. "I think it's an infestation of some kind," Quinton said finally. "Tiny flecks unlike anything I've seen before. The sample is utterly clotted with them. Under highest magnification they don't look like any microorganism I've ever seen. Squarish little boxes, cubes, geometrical shapes . . ."

Scully felt cold as she heard the ME's words, echoing what Darin Kennessy had told them at the survivalist camp.

133

"Have you ever seen anything like this, Agent Scully?" the ME persisted on the phone. "You're a doctor yourself."

Scully cleared her throat. "I'll have to get back to you on that, sir. Let me speak with my partner and compare notes. Thanks for your information." She ended the call and then looked at Mulder.

After she briefly recounted the conversation, Mulder nodded. "They sure were eager to get rid of the guard's body. Every trace."

Scully pondered as she listened to the roar of the ocean against the rocks below. "That doesn't sound like the way the Centers for Disease Control operates. No official receipt, no phone number in case Dr. Quinton has further information."

Mulder buttoned his coat against the chilly breeze. "Scully, I don't think that was the CDC. I think it could well be representatives from the same group that arranged for the destruction of DyMar Laboratory and pinned the blame on a scapegoat animal rights group."

"Mulder, why would anyone be willing to take such extreme action?"

"You heard Kennessy's brother. Nanotechnology research," he said. "It's gotten loose somehow, maybe from a research animal carrying something very dangerous. The mucus from the dead security guard sounds just like what we saw in the sample of the dog's blood—"

Scully put her hands on her hips as the sea wind whipped her red hair. "Mulder, I think we need to find that dog, and Patrice and Jody Kennessy."

Behind them the Devil's Churn erupted again with a loud booming sound. Spray shot high into the air. A group of children stood next to their parents at the guardrail and cheered and laughed at the spectacle. No one seemed to be paying any attention to the food vendor in his van or the braided woman with her handmade rugs.

"I agree, Scully—and after that report from the ME, I think maybe we aren't the only ones looking for them."

23

The cold rain sheeted down, drenching him and the roadside and everything all around—but Jeremy Dorman's other problems were far worse than a bit of lousy weather. The external world was all bad data to him now, irrelevant numbness. The forest of nerves inside him provided enough pain for a world all its own.

His shoes and clothes were soaked, his skin gray and clammy—but those discomforts were insignificant compared to the raging war within his own cells. Slick patches of the protectant carrier fluid coated his skin, swarming with the reproducing nanocritters.

His muscles trembled and vibrated, but he continued lifting his legs, taking steps, moving along. Dorman's brain seemed like a mere passenger in his body now. It took a conscious effort to keep the joints bending, the limbs moving, like a puppeteer working a complicated new marionette while wearing a blindfold and thick gloves.

A car roared past him, spraying water. Its tires struck a puddle in a depression in the road and jetted cold rainwater all over him. The taillights flickered red for an instant as the driver realized what he had done, and then, maliciously, the man honked a few times and continued weaving down the road.

Dorman trudged along the muddy shoulder, uncaring. He focused ahead. The long road curved into the wooded mountains. He had no idea how many miles he had gone from Portland, but he hoped he could find some way to hurry. He had no money and he didn't dare rent a car anyway, at the risk of someone spotting his identity. No one knew he was still alive, and he wanted to keep it that way. Not that he would trust his rebellious body or flickering depth perception if he was driving . . .

He shambled past a small county weigh station, a little shack with a gate and a red stoplight for trucks. Opaque miniblinds covered the windows, and a sign that looked as if it hadn't been changed in months said, "Weigh Station Closed."

As Dorman trudged past, he looked longingly at the shelter. It would be unheated, with no food or supplies, but it would be dry. He longed to get out of the rain for a while, to sleep . . . but he would likely never wake up again. His time was rapidly running out.

He continued past the weigh station. Waterlogged potato fields sprawled in one direction, with a marsh on the other side of the road. Dorman headed toward the gentle uphill slope leading into the mountains.

Strange and unfathomable shapes skirled across his vision like static. The nanocritters in his body were messing around with his optic nerves again, fixing them, making improvements . . . or just toying with them. He hadn't been able to see colors for days.

Dorman clenched his jaws together, feeling the ache in his bones. He almost enjoyed the ache—a real pain, not a phantom side effect of having his body invaded by self-programmed machines.

He picked up his pace, so focused on keeping himself moving forward that he didn't even hear the loud hum of the approaching truck.

The vehicle grew louder, a large log truck half-loaded with pine logs whose bark had been splintered off and most of their large protruding branches amputated. Dorman turned and looked at it, then stepped farther to the side of the road. The driver flashed his headlights.

Dorman heard the engine growl as the trucker shifted down through the gears. The air brakes sighed as the log truck came to a halt thirty feet in front of Dorman.

He just stood and stared, unable to believe what had happened, what a stroke of luck. This man was going to give him a ride. Dorman hurried forward, squelching water from his shoes. He huddled his arms around his chest.

The driver leaned over the seat and popped open the passenger door. The rain continued to slash down, pelting the wet logs, steaming off the truck's warm grille.

Dorman grabbed the door handle and swung it open. His leg jittered as he lifted it to step on the running board. Finally he gained his balance and hauled himself up. He was dripping, exhausted, cold.

"Boy, you look miserable," the truck driver said. He was short and portly, with dirty-blond hair and blue eyes.

"I *am* miserable," Dorman answered, surprised that his voice worked so well.

"Well, then, be miserable inside the truck cab here. You got a place to go—or just wandering?"

"I've got a place to go," Dorman said. "I'm just trying to get there."

"Well, you can ride with me until the Coast Highway turnoff. My name's Wayne—Wayne Hykaway."

Dorman looked at him, suspicious. He didn't want his identity known. "I'm . . . David," he said. He slammed the truck's door, shoving his hands into the waterlogged pockets of his tattered jacket, hunched over and huddling into himself. Hykaway had extended his hand but quickly drew it back when it became obvious Dorman had no intention of shaking it.

The interior of the cab was warm and humid. Heat blasted from the vents. The windshield wipers slapped back and forth in an effort to keep the view clear. News radio played across the speakers of a far-too-expensive sound system, crackling with static from poor reception out here in the wilderness.

The trucker wrestled with the stick shift and rammed the vehicle into gear again. With a groan and a labor of its engines, the log truck began to move forward along the wet road uphill toward the trees.

As the truck picked up speed, Dorman could only think that he was growing closer to his destination every minute, every mile. This man had no idea of the deadly risk he had just taken, but Dorman had to think of his ultimate goal of finding Patrice and Jody—and the dog. Whatever the cost.

Dorman sat back, pressed against the door of the truck, trying to ignore the guilt and fear. Water trickled down his face, and he blinked it away. He maintained his view through the windshield, watching the wipers tock back and forth. He tried to keep as far away from Wayne Hykaway as possible. He didn't dare let the man touch him. He couldn't risk the exposure another body would bring.

The cordial trucker switched off the talk radio and tried in vain to strike up a conversation, but when Dorman proved reticent, he just began to talk about himself instead. He chatted about the books he liked to read, his hobby of tai chi relaxation techniques, how he had once trained unemployed people.

Hykaway kept one hand on the steering wheel of the mammoth logging truck, and with the other he fiddled with the air vent controls, the heater. When he couldn't think of anything to say, he flicked on the radio again, tuning to a different station, then switched it off in disgust.

Dorman concentrated on his body, turning his thoughts inward. He could feel his skin crawling and squirming, his muscle growths moving of their own accord. He pressed his elbows against his ribs, feeling the clammy fabric of his jacket as well as the slick ooze of the nanomachine carrier mucus that seeped out of his pores.

After fifteen minutes of Dorman's trancelike silence, the trucker began to glance at him sidelong, as if wondering what kind of psychopath he had foolishly picked up.

Dorman avoided his gaze, staring out the side window—and then his gut spasmed. He hunched over and clenched his hands to his stomach. He hissed breath through his teeth. He felt something jerk beneath his skin, like a mole burrowing through his rib cage.

"Hey, are you all right?" the trucker said.

"Yes," Dorman answered, ripping the answer out of his voice box. He squeezed hard enough until he could finally regain control over his rebellious biological systems. He sucked in deep pounding breaths. Finally the convulsions settled down again.

Still, he felt his internal organs moving, exploring their freedom, twitching in places that should never have been able to move. It was like a roiling storm inside of him.

Wayne Hykaway glanced at him again, then turned back to concentrate on the wet road. He kept both hands gripped white on the steering wheel.

Dorman remained seated in silence, huddled against the hard comfort of the passenger-side door. A bit of slime began to pool on the seat around him.

He knew he could lose control again at any moment. Every hour it got harder and harder. . . .

24

Scully was already tired of driving and glad for the chance to stop and ask a few more people if they recognized Patrice and Jody Kennessy.

Mulder sat in the passenger seat, munching cheese curls from a bag in his lap and dropping a few crumbs on his overcoat. He plastered his face to the unfolded official road map of the state of Oregon. "I can't find this town on the map," Mulder said. "Colvain, Oregon."

Scully parked in front of a quaint old shake-shingle house with a hand-painted sign dangling on a chain on a post out front. *Max's General Store and Art Gallery.*

"Mulder, we're *in* the town and I can't find it."

The heavy wooden door of the general store advertised Morley cigarettes; a bell on the top jingled as they entered the creaking hardwood floor of Max's. "Of course they'd have a bell," Mulder said, looking up.

Old 1950s-style coolers and refrigerators—enameled white with chrome trim—held lunch meats, bottled soft drinks, and frozen dinners. Boxes around the cash register

141

displayed giant-size Slim Jims and seemingly infinite varieties of beef jerky.

T-shirts hung on a rack beside shelves full of knick-knacks, most made from sweet-smelling cedar and painted with witty folk sayings related to the soggy weather in Oregon. Shot glasses, placemats, playing cards, and key chains rounded out the assortment.

Scully saw a few simple watercolor paintings hanging aslant on the far wall above a beer cooler; price tags dangled from the gold-painted frames. "I wonder if there's some kind of county ordinance that requires each town to have a certain number of art galleries," she said.

Behind the cash register, an old woman sat barricaded by newspaper racks and wire trays that held gum, candy, and breath mints. Her hair was dyed an outrageous red, her glasses thick and smudged with fingerprints. She was reading a well-thumbed tabloid with headlines proclaiming *Bigfoot Found in New Jersey*, *Alien Embryos Frozen in Government Facility*, and even *Cannibal Cult in Arkansas*.

Mulder looked at the headlines and raised his eyebrows at Scully. The red-headed woman looked up over her glasses. "May I help you folks? Do you need maps or sodas?"

Mulder flashed his badge and ID. "We're federal agents, ma'am. We're wondering if you could give us directions to a cabin near here, some property owned by a Mr. Darin Kennessy?"

Scully withdrew the much-handled Kennessy photos and spread them on the counter. The woman hurriedly folded her tabloid and shoved it beside the cash register. Through her smudged glasses, she peered down at the photos.

"We're looking for these two people," Scully said, offering no further information.

Jody Kennessy smiled optimistically up from the photograph, but his face was gaunt and sunken, his hair mostly fallen out, his skin grayish and sickly from the rigorous chemo and radiation treatments.

The woman removed her glasses and wiped them off with a Kleenex, then put them on her face again. "Yes, I think I've seen these two before. The woman at least. Been out here a week or two."

Mulder perked up. "Yes, that's about the time frame we're talking about."

Scully leaned forward, unable to stop herself from telling too many details, so as to enlist the woman's aid. "This young man is very seriously ill. He's dying of leukemia. He needs immediate treatment. He may have gotten significantly worse since this photo was taken."

The woman looked down at Jody's photograph again. "Well, then, maybe I'm wrong," she said. "As I recall, the boy with this woman seemed pretty healthy to me. They could be staying out at the Kennessys' cabin. It's been empty a long time."

The woman rocked back on her chair, which let out a metal squeal. She pressed the thick glasses up against the bridge of her nose. "Nothing much moves around here without us knowing about it."

"Could you give us directions, ma'am?" Scully repeated.

The redheaded woman withdrew a pen, but didn't bother to write down directions. "About seven or eight miles back, you turn on a little road called Locust Springs Drive, go about a quarter of a mile, turn left on a logging road—it's the third driveway on your right." She toyed with her strand of fake pearls.

"This is the best lead we've got so far," Scully said softly, looking eagerly at her partner. The thought of rescuing Jody Kennessy, helping him out in his weakened state, gave her new energy.

As an FBI agent, Scully was supposed to maintain her objectivity and not get emotionally involved in a case lest her judgment be influenced. In this instance she couldn't help it. She and Jody Kennessy both shared the shadow of cancer, and the connection to this boy she'd never met was too strong. Her desire to help him was far more powerful than Scully had anticipated when she and Mulder had left Washington to investigate the DyMar fire.

The bell on the door jingled again, and a state policeman strode in, his boots heavy on the worn wooden floor of the general store. Scully looked over her shoulders as the trooper walked casually over to the soft drink cooler and grabbed a large bottle of orange soda.

"The usual, Jared?" the woman called from the cash register, already ringing him up.

"Would I ever change, Maxie?" he answered, and she tossed him a pack of artificially colored cheese crackers from the snack rack.

The policeman nodded politely to Mulder and Scully and noticed the photographs as well as Mulder's badge wallet. "Can I help you folks?"

"We're federal agents, sir," Scully said. She picked up the photographs to show him and asked for his assistance. Perhaps he could escort them out to the isolated cabin where Patrice or Jody might be held captive—but suddenly the radio at Jared's hip squelched.

A dispatcher's voice came over, sounding alarmed but brisk and professional. "Jared, come in, please. We've got an emergency situation here. A passing motorist found a dead body up the highway about three quarters of a mile past Doyle's property."

The trooper grabbed his radio. "Officer Penwick here," he said. "What do you mean by a dead body? What condition?"

"A trucker," the dispatcher answered. "His logging rig is half off the road. The guy's sprawled by the steering wheel, and . . . well, it's weird. Not like any accident injuries I've ever heard of."

Mulder quickly looked at Scully, intrigued. They both

understood that this sounded remarkably like their own case. "You go ahead, Scully. I can ride out to the location of the body with Officer, uh, Penwick here and take a look around. If it's nothing, I'll have him take me to the cabin and meet up with you."

Uneasy about being separated from him, but realizing that they had to investigate both possibilities without delay, she nodded. "Make sure you take appropriate precautions."

"I will, Scully." Mulder hurried for the door.

The bell jangled as the trooper left, clutching his cheese crackers and orange soda on one hand as he sent off an acknowledgment on his walkie-talkie. He glanced over his shoulder. "Put it on my tab, Maxie—I'll catch you later."

Scully hurried behind them, letting the jingling door swing shut. Mulder and the trooper raced for his police vehicle, parked aslant in front of the general store.

Mulder called back at her, "Just see if you can find them, Scully. Learn what you can. I'll contact you on the cell phone."

The two car doors slammed, and with a spray of wet gravel the highway patrolman spun around and raced up the road with his red lights flashing.

She returned to their rental car, grabbing her keys. When she glanced down at the unit on the car seat, she finally noticed to her dismay that her cellular phone wasn't working. They were out of range once more.

25

Outside the cabin, Vader barked. He stood up on the porch and paced, letting a low growl loose in his throat.

Patrice stiffened and hurried to the lace curtains. Her mouth went dry. She had owned Vader for a dozen years, and she knew that this time the dog was not making one of his puppy barks at a squirrel.

This was a bark of warning. She had been expecting something like this. Dreading it.

Outside, the trees girdling the hollow stood tall and dark, claustrophobic around the hills that sheltered them. The rough trunks seemed to have approached silently closer, like an implacable army . . . like the mob she had imagined surrounded DyMar.

The grassy, weed-filled clearing stirred in a faint breeze, laden with moisture from the recent downpour. She had once thought of the meadow as beautiful, a perfect set-piece to display the wilderness cabin to best effect—a wonderful spot, Darin had said, and she had shared his enthusiasm.

147

Now, though, the broad clearing made her feel exposed and vulnerable.

Vader barked again and stepped forward to the edge of the porch, his muzzle pointed toward the driveway that plunged into the forest. His black nostrils quivered.

"What is it, Mom?" Jody asked. From the drawn expression on his face, she could tell he felt the fear as much as she did. In the past two weeks she had trained him well enough.

"Someone's coming," she said.

Forcing bravery upon herself, she doused the lights inside the cabin, let the curtains dangle shut, then swung open the front door to stand guard on the porch. They had run here, gone to ground, without preparation. She had to count on their hiding place, since she had no gun, no other weapons. Patrice had ransacked the cabin, but Darin had not believed in handguns. She had only her bare hands and her ingenuity. Vader looked over his shoulder at her, then turned toward the driveway again.

Jody crowded next to her, trying to see, but she pushed him back inside. "Mom!" he said indignantly, but she pointed a scolding finger at him, her face hard. He backed away quickly.

The mother's protective instinct hung on her like a drug. She had been helpless in the face of his cancer, she had been helpless when his father was murdered by shadowy men pretending to be activists, the same people who had tapped their phones, followed them, and might even now be trying to track them down. But she had taken action to get her son to safety, and she had kept him alive so far. Patrice Kennessy had no intention of giving up now.

A figure appeared in the trees, approaching on foot down the long driveway bordered by dark pines, coming closer, intent on the cabin.

Patrice didn't have time to run.

She had taken Jody out to the coastal wilderness because of its abundance of survivalists, of religious cults and extremists—all of whom knew how to be left alone. David's own brother had joined one such group, abandoning even this cabin to find deeper isolation, but she hadn't dared to go to Darin and ask for protection. The people hunting them down would think to find David's brother. She had to do the unexpected.

Now her mind raced, and she tried to think of even the smallest misstep she might have made to tip off who she was and where she and Jody were staying. Suddenly she remembered that the last time she had gone into a grocery store, she had noticed the cover of a weekly Oregon newspaper depicting the fenced-off and burned ruins of DyMar Laboratory.

Surprised, she had flinched and tried to maintain her composure, cradling her groceries in front of the *TV Guides* and beef jerky strips and candy bars. The old woman with shockingly dyed red hair had looked up at her from behind smeared eyeglasses. No one, Patrice insisted to herself, would have put such a coincidence together, would have taken note of a woman traveling alone with her twelve-year-old son, would have connected all the details.

Still, the clerk had stared at her too intently. . . .

"Who is it, Mom?" Jody asked in a stage whisper from the cold fireplace. "Can you see?" Patrice was glad she hadn't built a fire that morning, because the telltale wisp of gray-white smoke would have attracted even more attention.

They had made a plan for such a situation, that they would both try to slip away unnoticed and vanish in the trees, hiding out in the wooded hills. Jody knew the surrounding forest well enough. But this intruder had taken them by surprise. He had come on foot, with no telltale engine noise. And now neither of them had time to run.

"Jody, you stay back there. Take Vader, go to the back door, and hide. Be ready to run into the trees if you have to, but right now it'll be a tipoff."

He blinked at her in alarm. "But I can't leave you behind, Mom."

"If I buy you some time, then you can get a head start. If they don't mean any harm, then you don't have anything to worry about." Her face turned to stone, and Jody flushed as he realized what she meant.

She turned back to the door, squinting her eyes. "Now keep yourself out of sight. Wait until the timing's right."

With a grim expression on her face, Patrice crossed her arms over her chest and waited on her front porch to meet the approaching stranger. The terror and urgency nearly paralyzed her. This was the moment of confrontation she had dreaded ever since receiving David's desperate phone call.

The figure was a broad-shouldered man walking with an odd injured gait. He looked as if he had passed on foot through a car wash with open cans of waste oil in his arms. He staggered toward the cabin, but stopped dead in his tracks when he noticed her on the porch.

Vader growled.

Even from a distance, Patrice could see his dark gaze turn toward her, his eyes lock with hers. He had changed, his facial features distorted somehow—but she recognized him. She felt a flood of relief, a sensation she had not experienced in some time. A friend at last!

"Jeremy," she said with a sigh. "Jeremy Dorman!"

26

X "Patrice!" Dorman called in a hoarse voice, then walked toward her at an accelerated, somehow ominous pace.

She had bought newspapers from unattended machines on shadowy street corners, and had read that her husband's lab partner had also perished in the DyMar fire, murdered by the men who wanted to keep David's nanotech research from becoming public knowledge.

"Jeremy, are those men after you, too? How did you get away?"

The fact that Jeremy Dorman had somehow escaped gave her a flash of hope that perhaps David might have survived as well. But she could not grasp the thought; it slipped through her mental fingers. She had a thousand questions for him, but most of all she was glad just to see a familiar face, another person facing the same predicament as she was . . .

But something was very wrong about Jeremy's presence here. He had known to look for her and Jody in this cabin.

151

She knew that David had always talked too much. Even his brother's secret hideaway would never have been a secret for long, after tedious hours of small talk in the laboratory, David and Jeremy together.

She was suddenly wary. "Were you followed? If they come after us here, we don't have any weapons—"

"Patrice," he interrupted her, "I'm desperate. Please help me." He swallowed hard . . . and his throat continued to move far longer than it should have. "I need to come inside."

As he stepped closer, the burly man looked very sick, barely able to move, as if suffering from a hundred ills. His skin had a strange, wet cast—and not just from the misty moisture in the air, but with a kind of slickness. Like slime.

"What happened to you, Jeremy?" She gestured toward the door, wondering why she felt so uneasy. Dorman had spent a great deal of time with her family, especially after Darin had abandoned the work and fled to his survivalist camp. "You look awful."

"I have a lot to explain, but not much time. Look at me, at the shape I'm in. This is very important—do you have the dog here as well?"

She remained frozen in place; then it was all she could do to step forward and grip the damp, mossy handrail. Why did he want to know about Vader, hidden inside with Jody? Even though this was *Jeremy*, Jeremy Dorman, she felt the need to be cautious.

"I *want* some answers first," she said, not moving from the porch. He stopped in his tracks, uncertain. "How did you survive the fire at DyMar? We thought you were dead."

"I was supposed to die there," Dorman said, his voice heavy.

"What do you mean, you were *supposed* to die there? On the phone, in his last message to me, David said the DyMar protest was some kind of setup, that it wasn't just animal rights people after all."

Dorman's dark, hooded eyes bored into her. "I was betrayed, just like David was." He took two steps closer.

"What are you saying?" After what she had been through, Patrice thought almost anything might sound believable by now.

Dorman nodded. "They had orders to make sure nothing would survive, no record of our nanotechnology research. Only ashes."

Patrice stood her ground, silently warning him not to approach closer. "David said the conspiracy went much deeper in the government than he had thought. I didn't believe him until I went back to our house—only to find it ransacked."

Dorman lurched to a halt ten feet from the porch, stopping in the weeds of the meadow. He walked away from the cleared driveway, on the trampled path toward the door of the cabin. "They're all after you now, too, Patrice. We can help each other. But I need Vader. He carries the stable prototypes in his bloodstream."

"Prototypes? What are you talking about?"

"The nanotechnology prototypes. I had to use some of the defective earlier generations, samples from the small lab animals, but many of those exhibited shocking . . . anomalies. I didn't have any choice, though. The lab was on fire, everything was burning. I was supposed to be able to get away, but this was the only way I could survive." He looked at her, pleading, then lowered his voice. "But they don't work the way they were supposed to. With Vader's blood, there is a chance I can reprogram them in myself."

Her mind reeled. She knew what David had been working on, had suspected something wrong with their black Lab.

"Where's Jody?" Dorman said, peering past her to see through the curtains or the half-closed door. "Hey, Jody! Come out here! It's all right."

Jody had always looked at Dorman as a friend of his father's, a surrogate uncle—especially after Darin had left. They played video games together; Jeremy was just about the only adult who knew as many Nintendo 64 tricks as Jody did. They exchanged tips and techniques for *Wave Race*, *Mortal Kombat Trilogy*, and *Shadows of the Empire*.

Before Patrice could collect her thoughts, understand exactly where the situation stood, Jody pulled open the cabin door, accompanied by his black dog. "Jeremy!"

Dorman looked down at Vader, delighted and relieved, but the dog curled back his dark lips to expose fangs. The low growl sounded like a chainsaw embedded in the dog's throat, as if Vader had some kind of grudge against Dorman.

But Dorman paid no attention. He was staring at Jody— healthy Jody—in amazement. The skin on Dorman's face blurred and shifted. He winced, somehow forcing it back into place. "Jody, you're . . . you're recovered from the cancer."

"It's a miracle," Patrice said stiffly. "Some kind of spontaneous remission."

The sudden predatory expression on Dorman's oddly glistening face made a knot in her stomach. "No, it's not a spontaneous remission. Is it, Jody? My God, you have it, too."

The boy paled, took a step backward.

"I know what your dad did to you." For some odd reason, Dorman kept his eyes fixed upon Jody and the dog.

Patrice looked at Jody in confusion, then an instant of dawning horror as she realized the magnitude of what David had done, the risk he had taken, the real reason why his brother had been so frightened of the research. Jody's recent good health was not the result of another remission. All of David's hard work and manic commitment had paid off after all. He had found his cure for cancer, without telling Patrice.

But in the space of an indrawn breath, her incredible joy and relief and lingering heartbreak tempered with fear of Jeremy Dorman. Fear of his predatory glances at Jody, of his unnaturally shifting features, his slipping control.

"This is even better than Vader." Dorman's dark eyes blazed, taking on a distorted look. "I just need a sample of your son's blood, Patrice. Some of his blood. Not much."

Shocked and confused, Patrice flinched, but stood defiantly on the porch, not moving. She wasn't going to let anyone touch her son. "His *blood*? What on earth—"

"I don't have time to explain to you, Patrice. I didn't know they meant to kill David! They were staging the protest, they meant to burn the place down, but they were going to move the research to a more isolated establishment." His face contorted with anger. "I was supposed to be their lead researcher in the new facility, but they tried to murder me, too!"

Patrice's mind reeled; her perception of reality was being assaulted from too many directions at once. "You knew all along they intended to burn the place down? You were part of the conspiracy."

"No, I didn't mean that! It was all supposed to be under control. They lied to me, too."

"You let David be killed, you bastard. You wanted the credit, wanted his research."

"Patrice . . . *Jody*, I'll die without your help. Right now." Dorman strode toward the porch with great speed, but Patrice moved to block his path.

"Jody, get back in the cabin—right now. We can't trust him! He betrayed your father!" Her voice was ice cold, and the boy was already frightened. He quickly moved to do as she asked.

Dorman stopped five feet away, glowering at her. "Don't do this. You don't understand."

"I know I've got to protect my son, after all he's been through. You're probably still working for those men, hunting us. I'm not letting you near him." She held her fists at her sides, ready to tear this man apart with her bare hands. "Jody, go out and hide in the forest! You know where to go, just like we planned before," she shouted into the gap of the half-open door. "Go!"

Something squirmed beneath Dorman's chest. He hunched over, covering his stomach and his ribs. Finally, he rose up with his eyes glassy and pain-stricken. "I can't . . . wait . . . any longer, Patrice." He swayed in his step, coming closer.

In the back of the cabin, the rear door banged shut. Jody had run outside, making a beeline for the forest. Inside, she thanked her son for not arguing. She had feared he would side with Jeremy and want to help the man.

Vader bounded around the side of the cabin after Jody, barking.

Dismissing Patrice, Dorman turned toward the back. "Jody! Come here to me, boy!" He trudged away from the porch over to the side of the cabin.

Patrice felt an animal scream build within her throat. "You leave my boy alone!"

Dorman spun about and withdrew a revolver from his pants pocket. He gripped it with unsteady hands, holding it in front of her disbelieving gaze. "You don't know what you're doing, Patrice," he said. "You don't know anything about what's going on. I can just shoot the dog—or Jody—and get the blood I need. Maybe that would be easiest after all."

His muscle control was sporadic, though, and he could not keep a steady bead on her. Patrice could not believe he would shoot her anyway. Not Jeremy Dorman.

With an outcry, she vaulted over the porch railing, throwing herself in a battering-ram tackle toward Dorman.

As he saw her charging him, he flinched backward with a look of horror on his face. "No! Don't touch me!"

Then she plowed into him, knocking his gun away and driving the man to the ground. "Jody, run! Keep running!" she screamed.

Dorman thrashed and writhed, trying to kick her away. "No, Patrice! Stay away. Stay away from me!" But she fought with him, clawing, pummeling. His skin was slick and slimy . . .

Without a word, Jody and the dog raced into the forest.

27

X The dense trees clawed at him. Their branches scratched his face, tugged his hair, grabbed his shirt—but Jody kept sprinting anyway. The last words he heard were his mother's desperate shout. "Jody, run! Keep running!"

Over the past two weeks Patrice had drilled into him her fear and paranoia. They had made contingency plans. Jody knew full well that people were after them, powerful and deadly people. Someone had betrayed his father, burned down the whole laboratory facility.

He and his mother had driven away into the night, sleeping in their car parked off the road, going from place to place before finally arriving at the cabin. Again and again his mother had pounded into him that they must trust no one—and now it appeared that she might even have meant Jeremy Dorman himself. Jeremy, who had been like an uncle to him, who had played with him whenever he and his father could tear themselves away from work.

Now Jody didn't think; he just responded. He ran out the back door, across the meadow to the trees. Vader bounded into the fringe of pines ahead of him, barking as if scouting a safe path.

The cabin quickly fell behind, and Jody turned abruptly left, heading uphill. He hopped over a fallen tree, crunching broken branches and plowing through thick, thorny shrubs. Vines grabbed at the toes of his shoes, but Jody kept stumbling along.

He had explored these back woods in the last few weeks. His mother had hovered over him, making sure he didn't get into trouble or stray too far away, but still Jody had found time to poke around in the trees. He understood where he was supposed to go, how best to elude pursuit. He knew his way. He knew a few of the secret spots in the forest, but he didn't remember a hiding place that would be good enough or safe enough. His mother had told him to keep running, and he couldn't let her down.

If I buy you some time, then you can get a head start, she had said.

"Jody, wait!" It was Jeremy Dorman's voice, but it carried a strange and strangled undertone. "Hey, Jody—it's okay. I'm not going to hurt you."

Jody hesitated, then kept pushing ahead. Vader barked loudly and dashed under another fallen tree, then bounded up a rocky slope. Jody scrambled after him.

"Come here, boy. I need to talk to you," Dorman called from far back, near the cabin. Jody knew the man had just ducked into the trees, following him.

He paused for a moment, panting. His joints still ached sometimes with the strange tingly feeling, as if parts of his body had gone to sleep—but this discomfort was nothing like what he had experienced before, when the leukemia was at its worst, when he had honestly felt like dying just to stop the bone-deep ache. Now Jody felt healthy enough to go through with this effort—but he didn't want to keep it up for long. His skin crawled, and sweat prickled on his back, on his neck.

He heard Dorman lumbering through the trees, crashing branches aside, alarmingly close. How could the man have moved so fast? "Your mother wants to see you. She's waiting back at the cabin."

Jody hurried down a slope into a small gully where a stream trickled over rocks and fallen branches. Two days ago, as a game, he had skipped and hopped from stone to tree trunk to outcropping, crossing the stream and daring himself not to fall. Now the boy ran as fast as he could. Halfway across he slipped on a moss-covered boulder, and his right foot plunged into the icy water that chuckled along the banks.

He hissed in surprise, yanked his dripping foot back out of the stream, and continued across the stream. His mom had always warned him against getting his shoes wet . . . but right now Jody knew simple escape was much more important, was worth any sort of risk.

Dorman shouted again, "Jody, come here." He seemed a little more angry, his words sharper. "Come on, please. Only you can help me. Hey, Jody, I'm begging you!"

With his shoe soggy, Jody climbed back onto the bank. He heaved a deep breath to keep running. Grabbing a pine branch and getting sticky resin on his palm, he used it to haul himself up out of the gully to more level ground so he could run again.

He had a stitch in his side, which sent a sharp pain around his kidneys, his stomach, but he pressed his hand against the ache so he could keep fleeing. Jody didn't understand what was going on, but he trusted his fear, and he trusted his mother's warning. He vowed not to let Jeremy Dorman catch him.

He paused in his tracks, gasping beside a tree as he listened intently for further pursuit.

Down the slope on the other side of the stream, he saw the heavy form of Jeremy Dorman and his tattered shirt. Their eyes met from across the great distance in the shadowy forest.

Seeing a complete stranger behind Jeremy's eyes, Jody

ran with redoubled effort. His heart pounded, and his breath came in great gasps. He dove through clawing bushes that held him back. Behind him, Dorman had no difficulty charging through the underbrush.

Jody scrambled up a slope, slipping on loose wet leaves. He knew he couldn't keep up this incredible effort for long. Dorman didn't seem to be slowing at all.

He ran to a small gully, thick with deadfall and lichen-mottled sandstone outcroppings. The trees and shadows stood thick enough around him that he knew Dorman couldn't see him, and he had a chance to duck down in a damp animal hollow between a rotting tree stump and a cracked boulder. Twigs, vines, and underbrush crackled as he tried to huddle in the shelter.

He sat in silence, his lungs laboring, his pulse hammering. He listened for the man's approach. He had heard nothing at all from his mother, and he feared she might be hurt back at the cabin. What had Dorman done to her, what had she sacrificed so that he could get away?

Heavy footsteps crunched on the forest floor, but the man had stopped calling out now. Jody remembered playing chase games on his Nintendo system, how he and Jeremy Dorman would be opponents in death-defying races across the country or on alien landscapes.

But this was real, with a lot more at stake than a mere highest score.

Dorman came closer, pushing shrubs away, looking through the forest murk. Jody sat in tense silence, praying that his hiding place would remain secure.

In the distance Vader barked, and Dorman paused, then turned in a different direction. Jody saw his chance and attempted to slip away, but as he moved one of the fallen branches aside, a precariously balanced log crunched down into the brittle deadwood.

Dorman froze again, and then came charging toward Jody's hiding place.

The boy ducked down under the fallen trunk again, scuttled along next to the slick rock, and wormed his way out the other side of the gully. He stood up and raced off again, keeping his head low, pushing branches out of the way as Dorman yelled at him, fighting through the front of the thicket. Jody risked a glance over his should to see how close his pursuer had come.

Dorman reached up with a meaty hand, pointing toward him. Jody recognized a handgun at the same moment he saw a blaze of light flare from its muzzle.

A loud crack echoed through the forest. A chunk of splintered bark and wood exploded away from the pine tree only two feet above his head. Dorman had shot at him!

"Come here right now, dammit!" Dorman yelled.

Biting back an outcry, Jody scrambled away into the thick underbrush behind the tree that had protected him.

Through the forest murk, he heard Vader barking, whining as if in encouragement. Jody trusted his dog a lot more than he would ever trust Jeremy Dorman.

Jody ran off again, holding his side. His head pounded, his heart ran like a race car engine.

Back behind him, Dorman sloshed across the cold stream, not even trying to use the stepping stones. "Jody, come here!"

Jody fled desperately toward the sound of the barking dog—and, he hoped, safety.

28

The logging truck sat half off the road in a shallow ditch, its cab tilted at an odd angle like a metallic behemoth with a broken back.

As they drove up in the police cruiser, Mulder could tell instantly that something was wrong. This was more than a standard traffic accident. A red Ford pickup sat parked on the shoulder beside the logging truck, and a man with a plastic rain poncho climbed out of the driver's side as Officer Jared Penwick pulled to a halt.

Studying the scene, Mulder spotted sinuous tire marks in the wet grass. The logging truck had weaved back and forth out of control before grinding to a stop here. A few raindrops spattered the police cruiser's windshield, and Jared left the wipers streaking back and forth. He picked up his handset, clicked the transmit button, and reported in to the dispatcher that they had arrived at the scene.

The man in the pickup truck waited beside his vehicle, hunched over in the plastic slicker as the trooper crunched toward him. Mulder followed, pulling his topcoat closed to keep himself warm. The wind and the rain mussed his hair, but there was nothing he could do about it.

"You didn't touch anything in there did you, Dominic?" Jared said.

"I'm not going near that thing," the man in the pickup answered with a suspicious glance at Mulder. "That guy in there is gross."

"This is Agent Mulder of the FBI," Jared said.

"I was just driving down the road," Dominic said, still keeping his eyes on Mulder, until he flicked his gaze toward the tilted log truck. "When I saw that truck there, I thought the driver maybe lost control in the rain. Either that, or sometimes truckers just pull off the road and sleep—not too much traffic on this stretch, you know—but it was dangerous the way he had parked. Didn't have an orange triangle set up around the back of the truck bed, like he should. I was going to chew his ass."

Dominic flicked rainwater away from his face before shaking his head. He swallowed hard. "But then I got a look inside the cab. My God, never seen anything like that."

Mulder left Jared to stand with the pickup owner as he went over to the logging truck. He held the driver's-side door handle and cautiously raised himself up by stepping on the running board.

Inside the cab, the driver of the truck sprawled back with his arms akimbo, his legs jammed up, and his knees wedged behind the steering wheel like a cockroach that had been sprayed with an exterminator's poison.

The pudgy man's face was contorted and swollen with lumps, his jaw slack. The whites of his eyes were gray and smoky, laced with red lines of worse-than-bloodshot veins. Purplish-black blotches stood out like leopard spots all over his skin, as if a miniaturized bombing raid had taken place in his vascular system.

The truck window was tightly rolled up. The rain continued to trickle off the slanted roof of the cab and down the passenger-side window. From inside, the windshield was fogged in some places. Mulder thought he saw faint steam rising from the body.

Still balanced on the running board, he turned back to the state trooper, who stood looking at him curiously. "Can you run the plates and registration?" Mulder asked. "See if you can find out who this guy was and where he might have been going."

It made Mulder very uneasy to see another hideous death so close to the possible location of Patrice and Jody Kennessy—so close to where Scully had gone to look for them.

The trooper came forward and took his turn peering through the driver's-side window, as if it were a circus peep show. "That's disgusting," he said. "What happened to the guy?"

"No one should touch the body until we can get some more help out here," Mulder said briskly. "The medical examiner in Portland has dealt with this before. He should probably be called in, since he'll know how to handle this."

The trooper hesitated, as if he wanted to ask a dozen more questions, but instead he trotted back to talk on his radio.

Mulder walked around the front of the truck, saw how the cab had shifted to the right, nearly jackknifing the vehicle. The splintered logs were still securely fastened by chains to the long truck bed.

If the driver had gone into convulsions and swerved the heavy vehicle off the road, luckily his foot had slipped from the accelerator. The log truck had come to a stop on this rise without careening into a tree or crashing over a steeper embankment.

Mulder stared at the grille of the truck as the rain picked up again. Trickles of water slithered down his back, and he shrugged his shoulders, pulling up the collar of his topcoat in an effort to keep himself a little drier.

Mulder continued walking around the truck, descending into the ditch. His shoes splashed in the water, and the weeds danced along his pant cuffs. Once he got completely drenched, he supposed, it wouldn't matter if the rain got any heavier.

Then he saw that the log truck's passenger door hung ajar.

He froze, suddenly considering possibilities. What if someone else had been in the truck, a passenger—someone with the driver, maybe even a hitchhiker? The carrier of this lethal biological agent?

Mulder walked carefully over to the open door, glancing behind him into the close trees, the tall weeds, wondering if he would see another corpse, the body of a passenger who had undergone similar convulsions but managed to stagger away and collapse outside.

But he saw nothing. The rain began to sheet down harder.

"What did you find, Agent Mulder?" the trooper called.

"Still checking," he said. "Stay where you are."

The trooper called out again. "I've got the Portland ME and some other local law enforcement on their way. We'll have a real party scene here in a little while." Then, happy to let Mulder continue his business, Officer Penwick turned back to chat with the pickup driver.

Mulder carefully opened the heavy passenger-side door, and the metal swung out with a groan of hinges. He stepped back to peer inside.

The dead trucker looked even more bent and twisted from this perspective. Condensed steam had formed a halo across the windshield and the driver's-side door. The air smelled humid, but without the sour sharpness of death. The body hadn't been here for long, despite its horrible condition.

The passenger seat interested Mulder the most, though. He saw threads and tatters of cloth from a shirt that had been split or torn. Runnels of a strange translucent sticky substance clung to the fabric of the seat. A kind of congealed . . . slime, similar to what Mulder had seen on the dead security guard.

He swallowed hard, not wanting to get any closer, careful not to touch anything. This was indeed the same thing they had encountered before at the morgue. Mulder was sure this strange toxin, this lethal agent, was the result of Kennessy's renegade work.

Perhaps the unfortunate trucker had picked up someone and had become infected in close quarters. After the truck had crashed and the driver had died, the mysterious passenger had slipped away and escaped.

But where would he go?

Mulder saw a square of something like paper lying in the footwell beneath the passenger seat. At first he thought it was a candy wrapper or some kind of label, but then he realized it was a photograph, bent and half-hidden in the shadow of the seat.

Mulder withdrew a pen from his pocket and leaned forward, still careful not to touch any of the slimy residue. It was risky, but he felt a growing sense of urgency. Extending the pen, he reached in and drew the bent photo toward him. The edges were surrounded by other threads, as if the photo had fallen out of a shirt pocket during some sort of violent struggle.

He used the pen to flip over the photograph. It was a picture Mulder had not seen before, but he certainly recognized the faces of the woman and the young boy. He had seen them often enough in the past few days, had shown other photos to hundreds of people in their search for Patrice and Jody.

That meant whoever had been a passenger here in the truck, whoever had carried the nanotech plague, was also on his way, also connected to the woman and her son.

Headed to the same place Scully had gone.

Mulder tossed the pen into the truck, not daring to put it back in his pocket. As he hurried back around to the road, the trooper called to him from his patrol car, waving him over. "Agent Mulder!"

Mulder stepped away from the truck, wet and cold, feeling a deeper tension now. Distracted, Mulder went to see what Officer Penwick wanted.

"There's a truck weigh station a few miles back on this road. It's rarely open, but they have Highway Patrol surveillance cameras that operate automatically. I had somebody run them back a few hours to see if we could grab an image of this truck passing." Penwick smiled, and Mulder nodded at the man's good thinking. "That way we can at least establish a solid time frame."

"Did you find anything?" Mulder asked.

The trooper smiled. "Two images. One, we got the log truck barreling past—10:52 A.M. And a few minutes before that, we caught a man walking past. Very little traffic on the road."

"Can we get a video grab?" Mulder said eagerly, sliding into the front seat of the patrol car, looking down at the small screen mounted below the dash for their crime computer linkups.

"I thought you might want that," Penwick said, fiddling with the keypad. "I just had it up here . . . ah, there we go."

The first image showed the log truck heading down the road, obviously the same vehicle now stalled in the ditch. The digital time code on the bottom of the picture verified what the trooper had said.

But Mulder was more interested in something else. "Let me see the hitchhiker, the other man." His brows knitted as he tried to think of other possibilities. If the nanotechnology pathogen was as lethal as he suspected, the trucker wouldn't have lasted long in close quarters with it.

The new image was somewhat blurry, but showed a man

walking on the muddy shoulder, seemingly impervious to the rain. He looked directly at the camera, at the weigh station, as if longing to stop there and take shelter, but then he walked on.

Mulder had seen enough, though. He had looked at the file pictures, the DyMar background dossiers, the photos of the two researchers supposedly killed in the devastating fire.

It was Jeremy Dorman—David Kennessy's assistant. He was still alive.

And if Dorman had been exposed to something at DyMar, he was even now carrying a substance that had already killed at least two people.

He slid out of the front of the patrol car, looking urgently at the trooper. "Officer Penwick, you have to stay here and protect the scene. This is a highly hazardous place. Do not let anyone go near the body or even inside the cab of the truck without proper decontamination equipment."

"Sure, Agent Mulder," the trooper said. "But where will you be?"

Mulder turned toward Dominic. "Sir, I'm a federal agent. I need the use of your vehicle."

"My truck?" Dominic said.

"I need to reach my partner. I'm afraid she may be in grave danger." Before Dominic could argue with him, Mulder opened the door of the Ford pickup and extended his left hand. "The keys, please."

Dominic looked questioningly over at the state trooper, but Officer Penwick simply shrugged. "I've seen his ID. He is who he says." Then the trooper tucked his hat down against the rain. "Don't worry, Dominic. I'll give you a ride home."

The pickup driver frowned, as if this hadn't been the part that concerned him at all. Mulder slammed the door, and the old engine started with a comforting roar. He wrestled with the stick shift, trying to remember how to apply the clutch and nudge the gas pedal.

"You take good care of my truck!" Dominic yelled. "I don't want to waste time messing with insurance companies."

Mulder pushed down hard on the accelerator, hoping he would reach Scully in time.

29

X Scully became disoriented on the winding dirt logging roads, but after making a cautious Y-turn on the narrow track, she finally found the driveway as described by Maxie at the general store and art gallery. She saw no mailbox, only a metal reflector post that bore a cryptic number designating a specific plot for fire control or trash pickup.

It was just a nondescript private road chewed through the dense underbrush, climbing over a rise and vanishing somewhere back into a secluded hollow. This was it, though—the place where Patrice and Jody Kennessy had supposedly been taken, or gone into hiding.

Scully drove down the driveway as quickly as she dared through mud puddles and over bumps. Up the rise on either side of her, the forest seemed too close. Branches ticked and scraped along the sideview mirrors.

She accelerated over a large bump, some long-buried log, and reached the top of the rise. The bottom of the car scraped on the gravel as she headed down the slope. Ahead of her, in a cleared meadow surrounded on all sides by dense trees, sat a single isolated cabin. A perfect place for hiding.

This modest, rugged home seemed even more out of the way and invisible than the survivalist outpost she and Mulder had visited the day before.

She drove forward cautiously, noticing a muddy car parked to one side of the cabin, where a corrugated metal overhang protected it from the rain. The car was a Volvo, the type a yuppie medical researcher would have driven—not the old pickup or sport utility vehicle a regular inhabitant of these mountains would have purchased.

Her heart raced. This place felt right: isolated, quiet, ominous. She had come miles from the nearest assistance, miles from reliable phone reception. Anyone could hide out here, and anything could happen.

She eased the car to a stop in front of the cabin and waited for a few moments. This was a dangerous situation. She was approaching alone with no backup. She had no way of knowing whether Patrice and Jody were hiding voluntarily, or if someone held them hostage here, someone with weapons.

As Scully stepped out of the car, her head pounded. She paused for a moment as colors flashed before her eyes, but then with a deep breath she calmed herself and slammed the car door. "Hello?"

She wasn't approaching in secret. Anyone who lived in this cabin would have heard her approach, perhaps even before her car topped the rise. She couldn't be stealthy. She had to be apparent.

Scully stood beside the car for a few seconds, waiting. She withdrew her ID wallet with her left hand and kept her right hand on the Sig Sauer handgun on her hip. She was ready for anything.

Most of all, though, she just wanted to see Jody and make sure he got the medical attention he needed.

"Hello? Anybody there?" Scully called, speaking loudly enough to be heard by anyone inside the house. She took two steps away from the car.

The cabin seemed like a haunted house. Its windows were dark, some covered with drapes. Nothing stirred inside. She heard no sounds from within . . . but the door was ajar.

Beside the door she saw a fresh gouge in the wood siding, pale splinters . . . the mark from a small-caliber bullet

Scully stepped up onto the slick wooden porch. "Anybody home?" she said again. "I'm a federal agent."

As she hesitated in front of the door, though, Scully looked to her left and spotted a figure in the tall grass beside the cabin. A human figure, lying still.

Scully froze, all senses alert, then approached to the edge of the porch, peering over the railing. It was a woman, sprawled on her chest in the tall grass.

Scully rushed back down the steps, then pulled herself to a halt as she looked down at a woman she recognized as Patrice Kennessy, with strawberry blond hair and narrow features—but the resemblance ended there.

Scully recalled the smiling woman whose photo she had looked at so many times—her husband a well-known and talented researcher, her son laughing and happy before the leukemia had struck him.

But Patrice Kennessy was no longer vivacious, no longer even on the run to protect her son. Now she lay twisted in the meadow, her head turned toward Scully and her expression grim and desperate even in death. Her skin was blotched with numerous hemorrhages from subcutaneous damage, distorted with wild growths in all shapes and sizes. Her eyes were squeezed shut, and Scully saw tiny maps of blood on the lids. Her hands were outstretched like claws, as if she had died while fighting tooth and nail against something horrible.

Scully stood stricken. She had arrived too late.

She moved back, knowing not to approach or touch the possibly contagious body. Patrice was already dead. Now the only thing that remained was to find Jody and keep him safe—unless something had already happened to him.

She listened to the wind whispering through the tall pines, a shushing sound as needles scraped against each other. The clouds overhead were thick with the constant threat of rain. She heard a few birds and other forest sounds, but the silence and abandonment of the place seemed oppressive, surrounding her.

Then she heard a dog bark off in the forest, a sharp excited sound—and a moment later came the distinctive crack of a gunshot.

"Come here right now, dammit!" She heard the words, a voice flattened by distance, made gruff with a threat. "Jody, come here!"

Scully drew her handgun and advanced toward the forest, following the sound of voices. Jody was still out here, running for his life—and a man who must have carried the plague, the man who had exposed Patrice Kennessy, was now after the boy.

Scully had to catch him first. She ran toward the forest.

30

 No matter how far Jody ran, Dorman followed. The only shelter he could think of was the cabin, endlessly far back through the trees. The small building was not much of an island of safety, but he could think of no better place to go. At least there he could find some crude weapons, something with which to fight back.

His mother was resourceful, and Jody could be, too. He had learned a lot from her in the past weeks.

Jody circled through the trees in a long arc, looping around the meadow and approaching from the rear. Vader continued to bark in the trees, sometimes running close to Jody and then bounding off, as if ready to hunt or play. Jody wondered if the black Lab thought it was all some kind of game.

He continued stumbling along, his legs aching as if sharp metal pins had been inserted into his knees. His side was aflame with pain. His face had been scratched by sharp branches and whipping pine needles, but he paid no attention to the minor injuries; they would fade quickly. His throat was dry, and he couldn't draw in enough breath.

As quietly as he could move, he stumbled along without trails, without guidance, but after weeks of nothing to do but play in the woods, he knew how to find the cabin. Vader would follow him. Together they could get out of this, and his mother . . . if she was still safe.

From above, Jody could see the small building and the meadow ahead. He'd come farther than he had thought, but now he could see another car in the driveway. A strange vehicle.

He felt a rush of cold fear. Someone else had tracked him down! One of those others his mother had warned him about. Even if he succeeded in outsmarting Jeremy Dorman and escaping back to the cabin, would others be waiting there for him? Or did they mean to help? He had no way of knowing.

But right now his greatest fear was much closer at hand.

Dorman continued to charge after him like a truck, plowing through the trees and underbrush, closing the gap. Jody couldn't believe how fast the broad-shouldered man was moving, especially because the big lab assistant did not look at all healthy.

"Jody, please! I won't hurt you if you just let me talk to you for a second."

Jody didn't waste his breath answering. He ran back, arrowing toward the cabin, but abruptly came to a steep slope where a mudslide had sheared off the gentle hillside. Two enormous trees had uprooted, tumbling down and leaving a gash in the dirt like an open wound.

Jody didn't have time to go around. Dorman was approaching too fast, rushing along the hillside, holding onto trees and pulling himself along.

The slope looked too steep. He couldn't possibly get down it.

He heard the dog bark again. Halfway to the bottom, off to the left of the mudslide, Vader stood with his paws spread, his fur tangled with cockleburrs and weeds. He barked up at his boy.

With no other choice, Jody decided to follow. He eased himself over the lip of the mudslide and started to descend, using his hands, digging his fingers into the cold ground, stepping on loose rocks, and looking for support. He heard twigs snapping, branches crashing aside, as Dorman came closer.

Jody tried to move faster. He looked up and glimpsed the burly figure at the upper edge of the hillside. He gasped—and his hand slipped.

Jody's foot stepped on an unstable rock, which popped out of the raw dirt like a rotten tooth coming loose from a gum. He bit back an outcry as he began to fall.

He scrabbled with his fingers, digging into the mud, but his body slid down, tumbling, rolling, covering his clothes in dirt and mud. Rocks pattered around him.

As he bounced and slid, Jody saw Dorman standing at the lip of the mudslide, his hands outstretched like claws, ready to bend down and grab him—but the boy was too far away, still falling, still picking up speed.

Jody rolled, struck his side, and then his head—but he remained conscious, terrified that he would break his leg so that he couldn't keep running away from Dorman.

Dirt and rocks showered around him, but he didn't scream, didn't even cry out—and he finally came to rest at the bottom of the slide, up against one of the toppled trees. Its matted root system stuck out like a dirt-encrusted scrubbing pad. He slammed hard against the bark and lay gasping, struggling, trying to move. His back hurt.

Then, to his horror, he saw Jeremy Dorman bounding down the sharp slope up above, somehow keeping his balance. Dirt and gravel flew up from his feet as he stomped heavy indentations in the soft hillside. He waved the revolver in his hand in a threat to keep Jody where he was—not that Jody could have gotten up and moved fast enough anyway.

Dorman skidded to a halt just above the boy. His face

was flushed . . . and his skin looked as if it were *crawling*, writhing, seething like a pot of candle wax slowly coming to a boil. Rage and exertion contorted the man's face.

He held the handgun up, gripping it with both hands and pointing the barrel directly at Jody. It looked like a cyclopean eye, a deadly open-mouthed viper.

Then Dorman's shoulders sagged, and he just stared at the boy for a few moments. "Jody, why do you have to make this so hard? Haven't I been through enough—haven't *you* been through enough?"

"Where's my mom?" Jody demanded, drawing deep breaths. His heart thumped like a jackhammer and his breath felt cold and frosty, like knives in his lungs. He struggled to get to his knees.

Dorman gestured with the revolver again. "All I need is some of your blood, Jody, that's all. Just some blood. Fresh blood."

"I said, where's my mom?" Jody shouted.

Dorman looked as if a thunderstorm passed across his face. Both the boy and the man were so intent on each other, neither heard the other person approach.

"Freeze! Federal agent!"

Dana Scully stood in the trees fifteen feet away, her feet braced, her arms extended and gripping her handgun in a precise firing position.

"Don't move," she said.

Scully had breathlessly followed the sounds of pursuit, the barking dog, the angry shouted words. When she came upon the hulking man who loomed too close over Jody Kennessy, she knew she had to prevent this man—this carrier of something like a deadly viral cancer—from so much as touching the boy.

Both the intimidating man and the twelve-year-old Jody snapped their glances aside to look at her, astonished. Jody's expression flooded with relief, then rapidly turned to suspicion.

"You're one of *them*!" the boy whispered.

Scully wondered how much Patrice Kennessy had told him, how much Jody knew about the death of his father and the possible conspiracy involving DyMar.

But what astonished her the most was the appearance of the boy. He seemed healthy, not gaunt and haggard, not at all pale and sickly. He should have been in the final stages of terminal lymphoblastic leukemia. Granted, Jody looked exhausted, battered . . . haunted perhaps by constant fear and lack of sleep. But certainly not like a terminal cancer patient.

Nearly a month earlier, Jody had been bedridden, at death's doorway. But now the boy had run vigorously through the forest and been caught by this man only because he had stumbled and fallen down a steep hillside.

The large man scowled at Scully, dismissed her, and tried to ease closer to the boy.

"I said don't move, sir," Scully said. Seeing the revolver hanging loosely in his hand, she feared he might take Jody in a hostage situation. "Put your gun down," she said, "and identify yourself."

The man looked at her with such pure disgust and impatience that she felt cold. "You don't know what's going on here," he said. "Stop interfering." He looked hungrily back down at the trapped Jody, then snapped his glance toward Scully once more. "Or are you one of *them*? Just like the boy says? Out to annihilate both of us?"

Before she could answer or question him further, a black shape like a rocket-propelled battering ram bounded from the underbrush and launched itself toward the man threatening Jody.

In a flash Scully recognized the dog, the black Lab that had somehow survived being struck by a car, that had escaped from the veterinarian's office and gone on the run with Patrice and Jody.

"Vader!" Jody cried.

The dog lunged. Black Labradors were not normally used as attack dogs, but Vader must have been able to sense the fear and tension in the air. He knew who the enemy was, and he fought back.

The burly man whirled, raising his gun and gripping the trigger with the sudden unexpected threat—but the dog crashed into him, growling and snarling, spoiling his aim. The man cried out, threw up his free hand to ward off the attack—and his finger squeezed the trigger.

The explosion roared through the quiet isolation far from the main road.

Instead of taking off Jody's head, the .38-caliber shell slammed into the boy's chest before he could hurl himself out of the way. The impact sprayed blood behind him, knocking the boy's lean frame back against the fallen tree, as if someone with an invisible piano wire had just jerked him backward. Jody cried out, and slid down the rain-slick bole of the tree.

Vader bore the gunman to the ground. The man tried to fight the dog off, but the suddenly vicious black Lab bit at his face, his throat.

Scully raced over to the wounded boy, dropped to her knees, and cradled Jody's head. "Oh my God!"

The boy blinked his eyes, wide with astonishment and seemingly far away. Blood bubbled out of his mouth, and he spat it aside. "So tired." She stroked his hair, unable to leave him to rescue the big man who had shot him.

The dog continued growling, snapping his jaws, digging his muzzle into the man's throat, ripping at the tendons. Blood sprayed onto the forest floor. The man dropped his smoking revolver and pounded on the black Lab's rib cage, trying to knock him away, but growing weaker and weaker.

Scully stared at where foamy scarlet blood blossomed from the center of Jody's chest. A hole with neat round edges stood out against a welling, pulsing lake of blood. She could tell from the placement of the wound that no simple first aid would do Jody any good.

"Oh, no," she said and bent down, tearing Jody's shirt wider and looking at the gunshot wound that had penetrated his left lung and perhaps struck the heart. A serious wound—a deadly wound.

He would never survive.

Jody's skin turned gray and pale. His eyes were closed in unconsciousness. Blood continued to pour from the bullet hole.

Leaning forward, Scully pushed aside her empathy for Jody, mentally clicking into her emergency medical mindset, slapping the heel of her hand on the wound and pressing down, pushing hard against the cloth of his shirt to stop the flow of blood. At her side, she could hear the dog continuing his attack on the fallen man—a vicious attack, a personal vendetta, as if this man had once hurt the dog very badly. Scully concentrated, though, on helping the boy. She had to slow the terrible bleeding from the bullet wound.

31

X The sudden carnage astonished Scully, and time seemed to stop as the forest pressed around her, the smell of blood and black powder from the gunshots. The birdsong and the breeze fell silent.

She hesitated for only a moment before snapping back into her mindset as a federal agent. After pressing down her makeshift bandage, she stood up jerkily from the mortally wounded boy and ran over to the dog, who was still growling and snapping at the fallen man. She grabbed Vader by the skin of his neck, grappling with his strong shoulders and front forepaws to pull him away. His bloodied victim lay twitching in the mud, leaves, and twigs.

She tugged at the dog, dragging him away.

The dog continued to growl, and Scully realized the danger of throwing herself upon a vicious animal that had just ripped out the throat of a man. A killer. But the black Lab acquiesced and staggered away, sitting down obediently in the forest debris. Frothy blood covered his muzzle, and his sepia eyes were bright and angry, still fixed on the fallen form. Scully saw his red teeth and shivered.

She glanced down at the man who had held Jody at bay, who had shot the boy. His throat was mangled. His shirt hung in tatters, shredded as if it had burst from the inside.

Though he was obviously dead, the man's hand jittered and jerked like a frog on a dissection table, and his skin squirmed as if alive from the inside, the home of a colony of swarming cockroaches. Patches of his exposed skin glistened, wet and gelatinous . . . like the mucus Scully had found during her autopsy of Vernon Ruckman.

His skin also had an uneven darkish cast . . . but the blotches shifted and faded, mobile hemorrhages that healed and passed across his complexion. This man must be the carrier of the instantly disruptive disease that had killed Patrice Kennessy and Vernon Ruckman, and probably the trucker Mulder had gone to investigate. She had no idea who this was, but he looked oddly familiar to her. He must have some connection with DyMar Laboratory, with David Kennessy's research, and the radical cancer treatment he had meant to develop for his son.

As time seemed to stand still, Scully looked over at the black Lab to see if Vader might be suffering from the effects of the plague as well—but apparently the cellular destruction did not transfer readily across species boundaries. Vader sat patiently, not wagging his tail but focused intently on her reaction. He whined, as if daring her to challenge what he had done to protect his boy.

She whirled back toward Jody, who still lay gasping and bleeding from the bullet wound in his chest. She tore off more of his shirtsleeve and pressed the wadded cloth hard upon the open bubbling wound.

This was a penetrating wound—the bullet had not passed through the other side of Jody's back, but remained lodged somewhere in his lung, in his heart . . .

Scully couldn't imagine how the boy might survive—but

she kept on treating him, doing what she knew best. She had lost fellow agents before, other people injured on cases—but she felt a unique affinity with Jody.

The twelve-year-old also suffered from a form of terminal cancer; both he and Scully were victims of the vagaries of fate, the mutations of one cell too many. Jody had already been given a death sentence by his own biology, but Scully didn't intend to let a tragic accident rob him of his last month or so of life. This was one thing she could control.

She fumbled in her pocket and pulled out the cellular phone. With shaking, blood-tipped fingers, she punched in the programmed number for Mulder's phone—but all she received was a burst of static. She was out of range in the isolated wooded hills. She tried three times, hoping for at least a faint signal, some stray opening of the electromagnetic window in the ionosphere . . . but she had no such luck. It was almost as if someone was jamming her phone. Scully was alone.

She thought about running back to the car, driving it across the rugged meadows as close as she could get to the slide area, then rushing to Jody and carrying him to the car. It would be easier that way, if the car could travel over the wet and uneven meadow.

But that would also mean she'd have to leave Jody's side. She looked at the blood on her hands from pressing down on his gunshot wound, saw his pale complexion, and noted his faint fluttery breathing. No, she would not leave him. Jody might well die before she made it back here with the car, and she vowed not to let the boy die alone.

"Looks like I'll have to take you myself, then," she said grimly, and bent over to gather up the young man. "Above and beyond the call of duty."

Jody's frame was slight and frail. Though he appeared to have fought back the worst ravages of his wasting disease, he still had not put on much weight, and she could lift him. It was lucky they were close to the cabin.

Vader whined next to her, wanting to come close.

Jody moaned when she moved him. She tried not to hurt him further, though she had no choice but to get him back to her car, where she could drive at breakneck speed to the nearest hospital . . . wherever that might be.

She left the mangled and bloody form of the attacker lying on the trampled forest floor. The burly man was dead, killed before her eyes.

Later on, evidence technicians would come here and study the body of this man, as well as Patrice's. But that was in the future. There would be plenty of time to pick up the loose threads, to explain the pieces.

For now, the only thing that mattered to Scully was to get this boy to medical attention.

She felt so helpless. She was sure that whatever first aid she could give him—even whatever emergency room surgery the doctors could perform whenever she arrived at a medical center—would be too little, too late.

But she refused to give up.

In her arms, Jody felt warm and feverish. Incredibly hot, in fact. But Scully couldn't waste time thinking of explanations. She trudged ahead at her best speed, lugging him out of the forest, taking him to help. The black Lab followed close at her heels, silent and worried.

Jody continued to bleed, spilling crimson droplets along the forest floor, the grass, finally out to the clearing around the cabin. Scully focused her attention straight ahead and kept moving toward her rental car. She had to get out of here, had to hurry.

She looked off to one side as she bypassed the plague-ridden body of Patrice Kennessy. She was glad Jody didn't have to see his mother like this. Perhaps he didn't even know what had happened to her.

Scully reached the car and gently set the boy down on

the ground, leaning his back against the back fender as she opened the rear door. Vader barked and jumped in, then barked again, as if urging her to hurry.

Scully picked up Jody's limp form and gently positioned him inside the car. Her makeshift bandage had fallen off, soaked with blood. But the bleeding from his huge wound had slowed remarkably, congealing. Scully worried that meant Jody's heartbeat was weak, at the edge of death. She pressed more cloth against the bullet hole, and then jumped into the driver's seat and started the car.

She drove off at a reckless speed up the bumpy dirt driveway, over the rise. She scraped the bottom of her car again as she headed back toward the logging road, but she accelerated this time, ignoring all caution.

The isolated cabin with all of its murder and death fell behind them.

In the back seat, Vader looked through the rear window and continued barking.

32

Federal Office Building
Crystal City, Virginia
Friday, 12:08 P.M.

 The phone rang in Adam Lentz's plain government office, and he grabbed for it immediately. Very few people knew his direct number, so the call had to be important, though it startled him from his quiet and intense study of maps and detailed local survey charts of the Oregon wilderness.

"Hello," he said, keeping his voice neutral.

Lentz listened to the voice on the other end of the phone, feeling a sudden chill. "Yes, sir," he answered. "I was about to have a progress report for you."

Indeed, he had put together a careful map of his ongoing search, a listing of all the attempts he had made, the professional hunters and investigators combing the wooded, mountainous area of western Oregon.

"In fact," Lentz said, "I have my briefcase packed and a ticket voucher. My plane leaves for Portland within the hour. I'm going to head up the mobile tactical command center there. I want to be on site so I can take care of things personally."

He listened to the voice, detecting no displeasure, no scorn, only the faintest background lilt of sarcasm.

The man didn't want a formal report. Not at this time. In fact, he tended to avoid anything on paper whatsoever, so Lentz verbally gave him a summary of what he had done to track down Patrice and Jody Kennessy and their pet dog.

Lentz looked at his topographical maps. With a flat voice he listed where the six teams had concentrated their searches, rattling off one after another. He did not need to make his efforts sound extravagant or impressive—just competent.

Finally, though, a hint of criticism came from the other end of the phone conversation. "We had thought all of the uncontrolled samples of Kennessy's nanomachines were destroyed. Your previous reports stated as much. This was a very important goal of ours, and I'm quite disappointed to learn that this isn't so. And the dog—that's a rather large mistake."

Lentz swallowed. "We believed those efforts had been successful after the fire at DyMar. We had sent sterilization crews in to retrieve any unburned records. We found the fire safe and the videotape, but nothing else."

"Yes," the man said on the phone, "but from the condition of the dead security guard—as well as several other bodies—we must assume that some of the nanomachines have now escaped."

"We'll get them, sir," Lentz said. "We're doing our best to track down the fugitives. Finding the dog should be no problem. When we complete our mission, I assure you, there won't be any samples remaining."

"That isn't a suggestion," the voice said. "That's the way it must be."

"I understand, sir," Lentz replied. "I've narrowed down my search, concentrating on a particular area in rural Oregon."

He rolled up the maps as he talked, folded other documents, and slid them into his briefcase. He glanced at his watch. His plane would be departing soon. He had only unmarked carry-on luggage, and he had papers that allowed him to bypass normal ticketing requirements. Lentz could take advantage of one of those empty seats the airlines were required to keep on all flights for important military or government personnel. His passes allowed him to move about at will with no written record of his travel plans or his movements. Such things were required in his line of work.

"And one last thing," said the man on the phone. "I've suggested this before, but I will reiterate it. You would do well to keep your eye on Agent Mulder. Make sure part of your team is specifically assigned to shadowing his movements, following everything he does. Eavesdrop on every conversation he has.

"You already have the manpower that you need, but Agent Mulder has a certain . . . talent for the unexpected. If you stay close to him, he may well lead you exactly where you need to be."

"Thank you, sir," Lentz said, then glanced at his watch again. "I need to get to National Airport. I'll remain in touch, but for now I've got a plane to catch."

"And a mission to accomplish," the man said without the slightest hint of emotion.

33

The red pickup truck Mulder had commandeered handled surprisingly well. With its big
tires and high clearance, it ran like a steam-
roller over the potholes, puddles, and broken
branches on the old logging road and the over-
grown half-graded driveway that led back to
the isolated cabin.

After seeing the dead trucker's body and the image of
supposedly dead Jeremy Dorman on the surveillance videotape, he felt an urgency to find Scully, to warn her. But the
cabin was quiet, empty, abandoned.

Leaving the truck and walking around, he saw fresh tire
marks embedded in the soft mud and gravel. Someone had
driven here recently and then departed again. Could Scully
have gone already? Where would she go?

When he discovered the woman's body lying in the
grass, he knew it was Patrice Kennessy, without a doubt.

Mulder frowned and stepped back away from her.
Patrice's skin had been ravaged by the same disease he had
just seen on the dead truck driver. He swallowed hard.

"Scully!" He moved with greater urgency. The scarlet blood spatters on the ground were obvious, bright red coins splashed in an uneven pattern.

With a sheen of sweat on his forehead, Mulder broke into a trot, looking ahead, then back down to the ground as he followed the blood trail back into the forest.

Now he saw footprints. Scully's shoes. Paw prints from a dog. His heart beat faster.

Mulder found his way to the base of a steep slope where a mudslide had gouged the hillside. Near one of the horizontal tree trunks Mulder saw the blood-smeared man with broad shoulders, tattered clothes, and a mangled throat ripped all the way down to the neck bone.

He recognized the burly man from the DyMar personnel photos, from the surveillance video at the truck weigh station. Jeremy Dorman—certainly dead now.

Mulder also smelled gunpowder beyond the blood. The dead man's hand clutched a service revolver. From the smell, Mulder could tell it had been recently fired—but Dorman didn't look as if he'd be firing it again anytime soon.

Mulder bent over to inspect the gaping wound in the man's throat. Had the black Lab attacked him?

But even as he watched, Dorman's mangled larynx and the muscle tissue and skin around it looked melted, smoothing itself over, as if someone had sealed it with wax. His throat injury was filled with translucent mucus, slime oozing over the mangled skin.

Around him, Mulder saw signs of a struggle where rocks and mud had slid down the slope. It looked as if someone had fallen over the edge, and then been pursued. He saw more of the dog's footprints, Scully's shoe prints.

And smaller prints—the boy's?

"Scully!" he called out again, but he heard no answer, only the rustle of pine trees and a few birds. The forest remained hushed, fearful or angry. Mulder listened, but he heard no answer.

Then the dead man on the ground lurched up as if spring-loaded.

His claw-like left hand grabbed the edge of Mulder's overcoat. Mulder cried out and struggled backward, but the desperate man clung to his coat.

Without changing his cadaverous expression, Jeremy Dorman brought up the revolver he held in his hand, pointing it threateningly at Mulder. Mulder looked down and saw the clutching hand, its covering of skin squirming, moving—infested with nanomachines?—slicked with a coating of slime. A contagious mucus . . . the carrier of the deadly nanotech plague.

34

X Fifty miles at least to the nearest hospital, along tangled roads through wooded mountains— and Scully didn't know exactly where she was going. She raced away as the lowering sun glittered through the trees, and then the clouds closed over again.

She kept driving, pushing her foot to the floor and wrestling with the curves of the county road, heading north. Dark pine trees flashed by like tunnel walls on either side of her.

In the backseat, Vader whimpered, very upset. Clumps of blood and foam bristled from his muzzle. She hadn't taken time to clean him up. He snuffled at the motionless boy on the seat beside him.

Scully remembered the brutal way the dog had attacked the hulking man who had carried the plague that killed Patrice Kennessy, who had threatened Jody. Now, despite the spattered evidence of dried blood on his fur, he seemed utterly loyal and devoted to guarding his master.

Before driving away from the cabin, she had checked Jody's pulse. It was faint, his breathing shallow—but the boy still lived, clinging tenaciously. He seemed to be in a coma. In the past twenty minutes Jody hadn't made a sound, not even a groan. She glanced up in the rearview mirror, just to reassure herself.

From the trees on her right, a dog stepped into the road in front of her, and she spotted it out of the corner of her eye. Scully slammed the brakes and yanked the steering wheel.

The dog bounded back out of sight, into the underbrush. She swerved, nearly lost control of the car on the slick road, then at the latest minute regained it. Behind her, in the rearview mirror, she saw the dark shape of the dog trot back across the road, undaunted by its close call.

In the backseat Jody gasped, and his spine arched with some kind of convulsion. Scully jerked the car to a stop in the middle of the road and unbuckled her seatbelt to reach back, dreading to find that the boy had finally succumbed to death, that he had reached the limits of endurance.

She touched him. Jody's skin was hot and feverish, damp with sweat. His skin burned. Sweat trickled along his forehead. His eyes were squeezed shut. Despite all her medical training, Scully still didn't know what to do.

In a moment the convulsion faded, and Jody breathed a little more easily. Vader nudged the boy in the shoulder and then licked Jody's cheek, whimpering.

Seeing him stabilized for the moment, Scully didn't dare waste any more time. She shifted back into gear and roared off, her tires spinning on the leaf-covered asphalt. Trees swallowed the curves ahead, and she was forced to concentrate on the road rather than her patient.

Beside her the cell phone still displayed "No Service" on its little screen. She felt incredibly isolated, like the survivalists in the group where Jody's uncle had gone to hide. Those people wanted it that way, but right now Scully would have much preferred a large, brightly lit hospital with lots of doctors and other specialists to help.

She wished Mulder were here. She wished she could at least call him.

When Jody coughed and sat up in the back seat, looking groggy but otherwise perfectly healthy, Scully nearly drove off the road.

Vader barked and nuzzled the young man, crawling all over him, slobbering on him, utterly happy to see Jody restored.

Scully slammed on the brakes. The car slewed onto the soft shoulder, and she came to a stop near an unmarked dirt road.

"Jody!" she cried. "You're all right."

"I'm hungry," he said, rubbing his eyes. He looked around in the backseat. His shirt still hung open, and though dried blood was caked on his skin, she could see that the wound itself had closed over.

She popped open her door and raced to the back of the car, leaving the driver's side open. The helpful chiming bell scolded her for leaving the keys in the ignition. In the back she bent over, grasping Jody by the shoulders.

"Sit back. Are you all right?" She touched him, checking his skin. His fever had dropped, but he still felt warm. "How do you feel?"

She saw that skin had folded over the gunshot wound in his chest, clean and smooth, with a plastic appearance. "I don't believe this," Scully said.

"Is there anything to eat?" Jody asked.

Scully remembered the bag of cheese curls Mulder had left in the front seat, and she moved around to the other side of the car to get it. The boy grabbed the bag of snack food and ate greedily, chomping handfuls as powdery orange flavoring covered his lips and fingers.

The black Lab wiggled and squirmed in the backseat, demanding as much attention as his boy could give him, though Jody was more interested in just eating. Offhandedly, he patted Vader on the shoulders.

Finished with the cheese curls, Jody leaned forward to scrounge around. Scully saw something glint. With a quiet sound, a piece of metal dropped away from his back.

Scully reached behind him, and Jody distractedly shifted aside to give her room. She picked up a slug—the bullet that had been lodged inside him. She lifted the back of his shirt, saw a red mark, a puckered scar that faded even as she watched. She held the flattened bullet between her fingertips, amazed.

"Jody, do you know what's happened to you?" she said.

The boy looked up at her, his face smeared with cheese powder. Vader sat next to him and laid his chin on Jody's shoulder, blinking his big brown eyes and looking absolutely at peace, enthralled to have the boy back and ready to pay attention to him.

Jody shrugged. "Something my dad did." He yawned. "Nanotech . . . no, he called them nanocritters. Biological policemen to make me better from the leukemia, fix me up. He made me promise not to tell anybody—not even my mom."

Before she could think of another thing to ask, Jody yawned again and his eyes dulled. Now that he had eaten, an overpowering weariness came over him. "I need to rest," he said, and though Scully tried to ask him more questions, Jody was unable to answer.

He blinked his heavy eyelids several times and then drew a deep breath, fading backward into the seat, where he dropped into a deep and restful sleep, not the shock-induced coma she had seen before. This sleep was healing and important for his body.

Scully stood back up and stepped away from the car, her mind reeling with what she had seen. The dull bell tone continued to remind her that she had her door open and the keys dangling in the ignition.

The implications astounded her, and she stood completely at a loss. Mulder had suspected as much. She would have been skeptical herself, unable to believe the cellular technology had advanced so far—but she'd witnessed Jody Kennessy's healing powers with her own eyes, not to mention the fact that he had visibly recovered from the terrible wasting cancer that had left him an invalid, weak and skeletal, according to the photos and records she had seen.

Scully moved slowly, in a daze, as she climbed back behind the steering wheel. Her head pounded. Her joints ached, and she tried to tell herself that it was just from the stressful several days of sleeping in hotel rooms, traveling across country, and not an additional set of symptoms from her own cancer, the affliction that had resulted perhaps from her abduction, the unfathomable tests that had been done on her . . . the experiments.

Scully buckled her seatbelt and pulled the door closed, if only to halt the idiotic bell. In the backseat, Vader heaved a heavy sigh and rested his head on Jody's lap. His tail bumped against the padded armrest of the rear door.

She drove off, slower this time, aimless.

David Kennessy had developed something wonderful, something astonishing—she realized the power he had tapped into at DyMar Laboratory. It had been a federally funded cancer research facility, and this work had a profound meaning for the millions of cancer patients each year—people like herself.

It was appalling and unethical for Dr. Kennessy to have given his own son such an unproven and risky course of treatment. As a medical doctor, she was indignant at the very idea that he had bypassed all the checks and balances, the control groups, the FDA analysis, other independent studies.

But then again, she understood the heartache, the desperate need to do *something*, anything, taking unorthodox measures when none of the normal ones would suffice. Was it so different from laetrile therapy, prayer healers, crystal meditation, or any number of other last-ditch schemes that terminal patients tried? She had found that as hope diminished, the gullibility factor increased. With nothing to lose, why not try everything? And Jody Kennessy had indeed been dying. He'd had no other chance.

However, prayer healers and crystal meditation offered no threat to the population at large, and Scully realized with a sick tenseness in her stomach that the risk was far greater with Kennessy's nanotechnology experiments. If he had made the slightest mistake in tailoring or adapting his "biological policemen" to human DNA, they could become profoundly destructive on a cellular level. The "nanocritters" could reproduce and transmit themselves from person to person. They could cause a radical outrage of growths inside other people, healthy people, scrambling the genetic pattern.

That would have been a concern only if the nanomachines didn't work properly . . . and Kennessy had brashly gambled that he had made no mistakes.

Scully set her jaw and drove along, tugging down the sun visor in an effort to counteract the flickering tree shadows that danced in an interlocking pattern across her windshield.

After the plague victims she and Mulder had seen, it appeared that something must have gone wrong—very wrong.

35

X The wounds in Jeremy Dorman's throat had sealed, and a tangible heat emanated from him, a pulsing warmth that radiated from his skin and body.

The supposedly dead man opened his mouth and formed words, but only a whispery gurgle came from his ruined voice box. He jabbed with the revolver and hissed words using only modulated breath. "Your weapon—drop it!"

Mulder slowly reached to the other side of his overcoat, found the handgun in its pancake holster. He dropped his handgun on the forest floor with a thump. It struck the mud, slid to one side, and rested against a clump of dried pine needles.

"Nanotechnology," Mulder said, trying to quell the wonder in his voice. "You're healing yourself."

"You're one of *them*," Dorman said, his voice harsh, his breath still grievously wounded. "One of those men."

Then he released his grip on Mulder's overcoat, leaving

a handprint of slime that seeped into the fabric, spreading, moving of its own accord like an amoeba.

"Can I take off my coat?" Mulder asked, trying to keep the alarm out of his voice.

"Go ahead." Dorman heaved himself to his feet, still holding the revolver. Mulder shed his outer jacket, keeping only his dark sportcoat.

"How did you find me?" Dorman said. "Who are you?"

"I'm with the FBI. My name is Mulder. I've been looking for Patrice and Jody Kennessy. I'm after them, not you . . . though I would certainly like to know how you survived the DyMar fire, Mr. Dorman."

The man snorted. "FBI. I knew you were involved in the conspiracy. You're trying to suppress information, destroy our discoveries. You thought I was dead. You thought you had killed me."

Mulder would have laughed under any other circumstances. "No one's ever accused me of being involved in a conspiracy. I assure you, I had never heard of you, or David Kennessy, or DyMar Laboratory before the destruction of the facility." He paused. "You're contaminated with something from Kennessy's research, aren't you?"

"I *am* the research!" Dorman said, raising his voice, which was still rough and rocky.

Something in his chest squirmed beneath the tattered covering of his shirt. Dorman winced, nearly doubled over. Mulder saw writhing lumps like serpents, growths of a strange oily color that flickered into motion beneath his skin, and then calmed, seeping back into his muscle mass.

"It looks to me like the research still needs a little work," Mulder said.

Dorman gestured with the revolver for Mulder to turn around. "You have a vehicle here?"

Mulder nodded, thinking of the battered pickup. "So to speak."

"We're going to get out of here. You have to help me find Jody, or at least the dog. They're with the other one . . . the woman. She left me for dead."

"Considering the condition of your throat, that would have been a reasonable assumption," Mulder said, covering his relief at hearing confirmation that Scully had been here, that she was still alive.

"You're going to help me, Agent Mulder." Now Dorman's voice had an edge. "You are my key to tracking them down."

"So you can kill them both like you murdered Patrice Kennessy and the truck driver and the security guard?" Mulder said.

Dorman winced again as an inner turmoil convulsed through his body. "I didn't mean to. I had to." Then he snapped his gaze back toward Mulder. "But if you don't help me, I'll do the same to you. Don't try to touch me."

"Believe me, Mr. Dorman"—he glanced down at the slime-encrusted wounds on the man's exposed skin—"touching you is absolutely the last thing on my mind."

"I don't want to hurt anybody," Dorman said, his face twisted with anguish. "I don't. I never meant for any of this to happen . . . but it's rapidly becoming impossible not to hurt anyone else. If I can just get a few drops of fresh blood—preferably the boy's blood, but the dog might do—no one else needs to get hurt, and I can be well again. It's all so simple. Everybody wins."

For once Mulder let his skepticism show. He knew the dog had been used as some sort of research animal—but what did the boy have to do with it? "What will that accomplish? I don't understand."

Dorman flashed him a look of pure scorn. "Of course you don't understand, Agent Mulder."

"Then explain it to me," Mulder said. "You've got those nanotechnology machines inside your body, don't you?"

"David called them 'nanocritters'—very cute."

"The dog has them inside his bloodstream," Mulder

guessed. "Developed by David and Darin Kennessy for Jody's cancer."

"And apparently Jody's nanocritters work just fine." Dorman's dark eyes flashed. "He's already cured of leukemia."

Mulder froze under the tangled, shadowy forest branches as he tried to digest the information. "But if . . . if the dog and the boy are infected, if the dog recovers from his injuries and Jody's healthy now—why are you falling apart? Why do you bring death to anyone you touch?"

Dorman practically shouted, "Because their nanocritters function perfectly! Unlike mine." He gestured for Mulder to march out of the forest, back toward the isolated cabin where he had parked the pickup truck. "I didn't have time. The lab was burning, and I was supposed to die, just like David. They betrayed me! I took . . . whatever was available."

Mulder's eyes widened, turning to look over his shoulder. "You used early generation nanocritters, the ones not fully tested. You injected yourself so your body could heal, so you could escape while everyone else thought you were dead."

Dorman scowled. "That dog was our first real success. I realize now that David must have immediately taken a fresh batch of virgin nanocritters and secretly injected them in his son. Jody was almost dead already from his leukemia, so what difference did it make? I doubt Patrice even knew. But after seeing Jody today—he's cured. He's healthy. The nanocritters worked perfectly inside him." Dorman's skin shuddered and rippled in the dim forest light.

"Unlike yours," Mulder pointed out.

"David was too paranoid to leave anything valuable within easy reach. He'd learned that much at least from his brother. I only had access to what remained in our cryostorage. Some of our prototypes had produced . . . alarming results. I should have been more careful, but the facility was burning around me. When the machines got into my system, they reproduced and adjusted to my genetics, my cell structure. I thought it would work."

As he trudged into the meadow, Mulder's mind raced ahead, sifting the possibilities. "So DyMar was bombed because someone else was funding your research, and they didn't want the nanotechnology to get loose. They didn't want David Kennessy testing it out on his pet dog or his son."

Dorman's voice carried a strange tone. "The cure to disease, the possibility of immortality—why wouldn't they want it all to themselves? They intended to take the samples to an isolation laboratory where they could continue the work in secret." He continued under his breath. "I was supposed to be in charge of that work, but those people decided to obliterate me as well as David and everyone else."

He gestured again with the revolver, and Mulder stepped carefully, swallowing hard as understanding crystallized around him.

The prototype nanocritters had adapted themselves to the DNA of the initial lab animals, but when Dorman had brashly injected them into himself, the cellular scouts were forced to adapt to completely different genetics: biological policemen with conflicting sets of instructions. The drastic shift must have knocked the already unstable machines out of whack.

Mulder continued to speculate. "So your prototype nanocritters are confused with conflicting programming. When they hit a third person, a new genetic structure, they grow even more rampant. That's what causes this viral form of cancer whenever you touch someone, a shutdown in the nervous system that grows like wildfire throughout the human body."

"If that's what you believe," Dorman said with a low mutter. "I haven't exactly had time to run a lot of tests."

Mulder frowned. "Is that mucus"—he carefully pointed

at Dorman's throat, which was glistening with slime—"a carrier substance for the nanocritters?"

Dorman nodded. "It's infested with them. If someone gets the carrier fluid on them, the nanomachines quickly penetrate their body . . ."

The battered red pickup stood parked in the muddy driveway right in front of them now. As he walked, Dorman made every effort to avoid the fallen body of Patrice Kennessy.

"And now the same thing is happening to you as happened to your victims," Mulder said, "but much more slowly. Your body is falling apart, and you think Jody's blood will save you somehow."

Dorman sighed, at the end of his patience. "The nanocritters in his system are completely stable. That's what I need. They're working the way they should, not flawed with contradictory errors like mine. The dog's nanocritters are good, too, but Jody's are already conformed to human DNA."

Dorman drew a deep breath, and Mulder realized that the man had no reason to believe his own theory; he merely hoped against hope that his speculation was true. "If I can get an infusion of stable nanocritters, they'll be stronger than my warped ones. They will supersede the infestation in my own body and give them a new blueprint." He looked intensely at Mulder, as if he wanted to grab the FBI agent and shake his shoulders. "Is that so wrong?"

When the two men reached the old pickup parked in front of the cabin, Dorman told Mulder to take out his car keys.

"I've left them in the ignition," Mulder said.

"Very trusting of you."

"It's not my truck," Mulder said, making excuses, hesitating, trying to figure out what to do next.

Dorman yanked open his creaking door. "Okay, let's go."

He slid onto the seat, but remained as far toward the passenger door as possible, avoiding contact. "We've got to find them."

Mulder drove off, trapped in the same vehicle with the man whose touch caused instant death.

36

 To Adam Lentz and his crew of professionals, the fugitives were leaving a trail of clues like muddy footprints on a snow-white carpet.

He didn't know the members of his team by name, but he knew their skills, that they had been hand-picked for this and other similar assignments. This group could handle everything themselves, but Lentz wanted to be on the scene in person to watch over them, to intimidate them . . . and to be sure he could claim the proper credit when this was all over.

In his line of work, he didn't get official promotions, awards, or trophies. In fact, his successes didn't even amount to tangible pay raises, though income was never a factor for him. He had many sources of cash.

He had flown into Portland, discreet and professional. He had been met at the airport and whisked off to the rendezvous point. Other team members converged at the site of a local police call, their first stop.

Their high-tech mobile sanitation van arrived, escorted by a black sedan. Men in black suits and ties boiled out of the open doors next to where a logging truck had swerved off the road. The report had come in over the airwaves, and Lentz's response team had scrambled.

A state trooper, Officer Jared Penwick, had remained at the scene. Next to him, huddled in the patrol car passenger seat—obviously not a prisoner—was an old man wearing a red wide-billed cap and a rain slicker. The man looked miserable and worried.

The men in suits flashed their badges and announced themselves as operatives from the federal government. They all wore sidearms. They moved quickly as a unit.

The doors to the cleanup van popped open and men in spacesuit-like anti-contamination gear clambered out, armed with plastic bags and foam guns. The team member in the rear carried a flamethrower.

"What's going on here?" Officer Penwick said, stepping toward them.

"We're the official cleanup team," Lentz answered. He hadn't even bothered to take out his badge. "We would appreciate your full cooperation."

He stood stoically out of range beyond the risk of contamination as the crew opened the truck driver's door and descended upon the victim with plastic wrapping. They sprayed thick foam and acid, using extreme decontamination efforts. They quickly had the dead trucker bundled, his arms and legs bent so he could be wrapped up like a dying caterpillar in a cocoon.

The trooper watched everything, wide-eyed. "Hey, you can't just take—"

"We're doing this to eliminate all risk of contamination, sir. Did you or this gentleman here"—he nodded toward the man in the rain slicker—"actually open up the truck cab or go inside?"

"No," Officer Penwick said, "but there was an FBI agent with us. Agent Mulder. One of your people, I suppose?"

Lentz didn't answer.

The trooper continued, "He commandeered this man's pickup truck and headed off. He said he had to meet his partner, which had something to do with this situation. I've been waiting here for"—he glanced at his watch—"close to an hour."

"We'll take care of everything from this point on, sir. Don't concern yourself." Lentz stepped back, shielding his eyes as the suited man with the flamethrower sprayed jellied gasoline inside the cab of the logging truck and then ignited it with a *whump* and a roar.

"Holy shit!" said the man in the rain slicker. He slammed the door of the patrol car as a wave of heat ruffled over them, sending clouds of steam from the wet weeds and asphalt.

"You'd best step back," Lentz said to the trooper. "The gas tank will blow at any minute."

They hustled away, ducking low. The rest of the team had gotten the trucker's body wrapped up and tucked inside a sterile isolation chamber within the cleanup vehicle. They would shuck their suits and incinerate them as soon as they got inside.

The log truck burned, an incandescent torch in the gray rainy afternoon. The gas tank exploded with a deafening roar, and all the men ducked just long enough to avoid the flying debris before they turned back to their work.

"You mentioned Agent Mulder," Lentz said, returning to the trooper. "Can you tell us where he's gone?"

"Sure, I know where he's headed," Officer Penwick said, still astounded at the fireball, how the men had so efficiently obliterated all the evidence. The sound of the fire crackled and roared, while the black smoke stank of gasoline, chemicals, and wet wood.

The trooper gave Lentz directions on how to find Darin Kennessy's cabin. Lentz wrote nothing down, but memorized every word. He had to restrain himself from shaking his head.

A trail like muddy footprints on a snow-white carpet . . .

The men climbed back into the black sedan, while the rest of the crew sealed the cleanup van and its driver started the engine.

"Hey!" The old man in the rain slicker opened the passenger door of the trooper's car and stood up. He shouted at Lentz, "When do I get my pickup back?"

If the image of Agent Fox Mulder driving around in a battered redneck pickup truck amused Lentz, his face betrayed no expression.

"We'll do everything we can, sir. There's no need to worry."

Lentz then climbed into the sedan, and the team raced off to Kennessy's isolated cabin.

37

With a brief sigh from the backseat, Jody woke up again at dusk, refreshed, fully healed—and ready to talk.

"Who are you, lady?" Jody asked, startling her again. He woke up so quickly and fully.

Vader sat up next to him, panting and happy, as if all was right with the world again.

"My name is Dana Scully," she said, intent on the darkening road. "Dana—just call me Dana. I was here looking for you. I wanted to make sure you got to the hospital before your cancer got any worse."

"I don't need the hospital," Jody said with a lilt in his voice that made it clear he thought the answer to that was plain. "Not anymore."

Scully drove on into the dusk. She hadn't been able to reach Mulder.

"And why is it that you don't need a hospital?" Scully asked. "I've seen your medical records, Jody."

"I was sick. Cancer." Then he closed his eyes, trying to remember. "Acute lymphoblastic leukemia, that's what it's called—or 'ALL.' My dad said there were lots of names for it, cancer in the blood."

"It means your blood cells are being made wrong," Scully said. "They're not working properly and killing the ones that are."

"But I'm fixed now—or most of the way," Jody said confidently. He patted Vader on the head, then hugged his dog. The black Lab absolutely loved it.

Though Scully suspected the answers, she still had a hard time wrestling with the actual facts.

Jody suddenly looked forward at her with suspicion. "Are you one of those people chasing after us? Are you the one my mom was so afraid of?"

"No," Scully said, "I was trying to *save* you from those people. You were very hard to find, Jody. Your mom did a good job of hiding you." She bit her lip, knowing what he was going to ask next . . . and he did, looking around the backseat, suddenly realizing where he was.

"Hey, what happened to my mom? Where is she? Jeremy was chasing her, and she told me to run."

"Jeremy?" Scully asked, hating herself for so blatantly avoiding his question.

"Jeremy Dorman," Jody said, as if she should already know this information. "My dad's assistant. We thought he was killed in the fire, too, but he wasn't. I think there's something wrong with him, though. He said he needed my blood." Jody hung his head, absently patting the dog. He swallowed hard. "Jeremy did something to my mom, didn't he?"

Scully drew a deep breath and slowed the car. She didn't want to be distracted by any sharp curves or road hazards as she told Jody Kennessy that his mother was dead.

"She tried to protect you, I think," Scully said, "but that man, Mr. Dorman, who came after you . . ." She paused as her mind raced through possible choices of words. "Well, he is very sick. He's got some kind of disease. You were smart not to let him touch you."

216

"And did my mom catch the disease?" Jody asked.

Scully nodded, looking straight ahead and hoping he would still see her answer. "Yes."

"I don't think it was a disease," Jody said. He spoke bravely, his voice strong. "I think Jeremy has nanocritters inside him, too. He stole them from the lab . . . but they're not working right in him. His nanocritters kill people. I saw what he looked like."

"Is that why he was after you?" Scully asked. She was impressed by his intelligence and composure after such an awful ordeal—but his story seemed so fantastic. Yet, after what she had seen, how could he be making it up?

Jody sighed and his shoulders slumped. "I think those people are probably after him, too. We're carrying the only samples left, carrying them inside us. Somebody doesn't want them to get loose."

He blinked up, and Scully glanced in the rearview mirror, seeing his bright eyes in the fading light. He seemed terrified and innocent. She thought of the cancer ravaging him, how he faced a similar fate but a much greater risk than she herself did.

"Do you think I'm a threat, Dana? Are other people going to die because of me?"

"No." Scully said. "I've touched you, and I'm fine. I'm going to make sure you're okay."

The boy said nothing—it was hard to tell whether her words had the reassuring effect she intended.

"These 'nanocritters'," Jody. What did your dad say to you about them?"

"He told me they were biological policemen that went through my body looking for the bad cells and fixing them one at a time," Jody said. "The nanocritters can also protect me when I get hurt."

"Like from a gunshot," she said.

Scully realized that if the nanomachines were able to repair well-entrenched leukemia, a gunshot would have been simple patchwork. They could easily stop the bleeding, plug up holes, seal the skin.

Altering acute leukemia, though, was a monumentally more difficult task. The biological policemen would have to comb through billions of cells in Jody's body, a massive restructuring. It was the difference between a Band-Aid and a vaccine.

"You're not going to take me to a hospital, are you?" Jody asked. "I'm not supposed to be out in public. I'm not supposed to let my name get around anywhere."

Scully thought about what he had said. She wished she could talk this over with Mulder. If Kennessy's nanotechnology actually worked—as was apparent from the evidence of her own eyes—Jody and his dog were all that remained of the DyMar research. Everything else had been systematically destroyed, and these two in her backseat were living carriers of the functional nanocritters . . . and somebody wanted to destroy them.

It could be a grave mistake for her to take the boy to a hospital and entrust him into the care of other unsuspecting people. Scully had no doubt that before long Jody and Vader would fall into the hands of those men who had caused the destruction of DyMar.

As she drove on, Scully knew she couldn't let this boy be captured and whisked away, his identity erased. Jody Kennessy would not be swept under the rug. She felt too close to him.

"No, Jody," Scully said, "you don't have to worry. I'll keep you safe."

38

Oregon Back Roads
Friday, 6:24 P.M.

As the pickup truck droned on and the darkness deepened, at least Mulder didn't have to look at Jeremy Dorman, didn't have to see the sickening squirming and unexplained motion of his body.

After a long period of uneasiness, restlessness, and barely suppressed pain, Dorman seemed to be dropping into unconsciousness. Mulder could see that the former researcher, the man who had faced—and been seemingly killed by—the other conspirators, was in anguish. He clearly didn't have long to live. His body could no longer function with such severe ravages.

If Dorman didn't get his help soon, there would be no point.

But Mulder didn't know how much to believe the man's story. How much had he himself been responsible for the DyMar disaster?

Dorman lifted his heavy-lidded eyes, and when he noticed the antenna of Mulder's cellular phone poking from the pocket of his suit jacket, he sat up at once. "Your phone, Agent Mulder. You have a cell phone!"

Mulder blinked. "What about my phone?"

"Use it. Pull it out and dial your partner. We can find them that way."

So far Mulder had avoided bringing this monstrously distorted man anywhere close to Scully or the innocent boy in her possession—but now he didn't see any way he could talk himself out of it.

"Take out your phone, Agent Mulder," Dorman growled, the threat clear in his voice. "Now."

Mulder gripped the steering wheel with his left hand, compensating from side to side to maintain a steady course on the uneven road. He yanked out the phone and extended the antenna with his teeth. With some relief, he saw that the light still blinked NO SERVICE.

"I can't," Mulder said and turned the phone so that Dorman could see. "You know how far out we are. There aren't any substations nearby or booster antennas." He drew a deep breath. "Believe me, Mr. Dorman, I've wanted to call her many times."

The big man slumped against the passenger-side door until the armrest creaked. Dorman used his fingertip to rub at an imaginary mark on the pickup window; his finger left a tracing of sticky, translucent slime on the glass.

Mulder kept his eyes on the road. The headlights stabbed into the mist.

When Dorman looked at Mulder, in the shadows his eyes seemed very bright. "Jody will help me. I know he will." Dark trees flickered past them in the twilight. "He and I were pals. I was his foster uncle. We played games, we talked about things. Jody's dad was always busy, and his uncle—that jerk—told them all to go to hell when he had his fight with David and ran off to stick his head in the sand. But Jody knows I would never hurt him. He has to know that, no matter what else has happened."

He gestured to the phone lying between them on the seat. "Try it, Agent Mulder. Call your partner. Please."

The sincerity and desperation in Dorman's voice sent tingles down Mulder's spine. Reluctantly, without any faith that it would work, he picked up the phone and punched in Scully's speed-dial number.

This time, to his surprise, the phone rang.

39

 As the two vehicles toiled down the muddy rutted drive, Lentz couldn't believe they had missed the obvious connection all this time.

Earlier, they had quietly checked out the survivalist enclave where David Kennessy's brother Darin had gone to ground, thinking himself invisible and protected. But Patrice had not gone there. There was no sign of the dog or the twelve-year-old boy.

She had come instead to this land and this cabin, which had belonged to Kennessy's brother, purchased long ago and seemingly ignored. Focused on the red herring of the survivalist enclave, Lentz had not spotted this hiding place on any of their computer searches of where Patrice might have gone.

This cabin would have been a perfect place for Patrice to shelter her son and the dog.

But now it appeared that someone had found them first.

The team again sprang out of their vehicles, this time fully armed, their automatic rifles and grenade launchers pointed toward the small, silent building.

They waited. No one moved—nobody inside, nobody on the team. They were like a set of plastic army men forever frozen in attack positions.

"Move closer," Lentz said without raising his voice. In the still-misty air, his words carried clearly. The team members shuffled about, exchanging positions, moving closer, tightening a noose around the cabin. Others sprinted around the back to secure the site.

Lentz flicked his glance around, confident that every member of the group had noticed the twin sets of fresh tire tracks on the driveway. Agent Mulder had already been here, as had his partner Scully.

One of the men shouted, gesturing toward a thick patch of tall grass and weeds near the front porch. Lentz and the others hurried over to find a woman's body sprawled on the ground, blotched from the ravages of rampant nanotech infestation. She had been tainted. The disease had gotten her, too.

The viral infestation was spreading, and with each victim the prospect for containment grew worse and worse. The team members had just barely thwarted an outbreak in the Mercy Hospital morgue, where the nanomachines had continued their work on the first victim, crudely reanimating some of the cadaver's bodily systems.

It was Lentz's job to ensure that such a close call never happened again.

"They've gone," Lentz said, "but we've got more tidying up to do here."

He directed the teams in the cleanup van to put on fresh protective gear and prepare for another sterilization routine.

Lentz stood back and drew a deep breath, inhaling the resiny scent of the nearby forest, the damp perfume of the clean fresh meadow. He turned to one of the men. "Burn the cabin to the ground," he said. "Make sure nothing remains."

He turned to see the crew already swaddling Patrice

Kennessy's body with the plastic and the foam. Another man took out pumping equipment and began to spray jellied gasoline around the exterior cabin walls, then made a special effort to douse the meadow where Patrice had lain.

Lentz didn't bother to stay and watch the fire. He went back to the car, where the radio systems connected to other satellite uplinks and receiving dishes, to cellular phone tapping or jamming devices and security descramblers.

Other members of the extended tactical squadron had been keeping tabs on Agent Mulder, and now Lentz required whatever information they could give him.

Mulder could be the one to lead them right where they needed to be.

40

Scully's cellular phone rang in the quiet darkness of the car's front seat, like an electronic chipmunk chittering. She snatched it up, knowing who it must be, relieved to be back in touch with her partner at last.

In the rear of the car Jody remained quiet, curious. The dog whimpered, but fell silent. She yanked out the antenna while driving with one hand.

"Scully, it's me." Mulder's voice was surrounded by a nimbus of static, but still understandable.

"Mulder, I've been trying to reach you for hours," she said quickly, before he could say anything. "Listen, this is important. I've got Jody Kennessy with me. He's healed from his leukemia, and he's got amazing regenerative abilities—but he's in danger. We're both in danger." Her breath caught in her throat. "Mulder, he doesn't have the plague— he has the *cure*."

"I know, Scully. It's Kennessy's nanotechnology. The actual plague carrier is Jeremy Dorman—and he's sitting right here next to me . . . a little too close, but I don't have much choice at the moment."

Dorman was alive! She couldn't believe it. She had looked at the blood-soaked body, his hand still twitching. No human being could have survived an injury such as that.

"Mulder, I saw the dog attack him, tear his throat out—"

But then, Scully realized, she never would have believed young Jody could live after the gunshot wound he had received.

"Dorman's got the nanomachines in him as well," Mulder said, "but his are malfunctioning. Rather spectacularly, I'd say."

Jody leaned forward, concerned. "What is it, Dana? Is Jeremy after us?"

"He's got my partner," Scully muttered quietly to the boy.

Mulder's voice continued at the same time. "Those nano-critters are amazing things with remarkable healing abilities, as we've both seen. No wonder somebody wants to keep them under wraps."

"Mulder, we saw what happened at the DyMar Lab. We know people came in and confiscated all evidence of the dead security guard in the hospital morgue. I'm not going to let Jody Kennessy or the dog be captured, taken in, and somehow erased."

"I don't think that's what Mr. Dorman wants, either," Mulder said. "He wants to meet." She heard a mumbled discussion on the phone, Dorman saying something in a threatening tone. She remembered his gruff, dismissive voice from her confrontation with him in the forest, just before he had accidentally shot Jody. "In fact, he insists on it."

She pulled into a clearing at the side of the road. The trees were thinning, becoming scrubbier, and she looked down a shallow grade to a small city ahead. She hadn't noticed the town's name as she drove along, but from the direction she had been heading, Scully knew she must be nearing the suburbs around Portland.

"Mulder, are you all right?" she said.

"Dorman needs something from Jody. Some of his blood."

Scully interrupted. "I stopped him before . . . or at least I tried. I won't let Jody get hurt."

Mulder's voice fell silent for a few seconds on the phone, then she heard a scuffle. "Mulder! Are you all right?" she called out, wondering what was happening and how far away she was from helping him.

He didn't answer her.

As Mulder tried to think of something to say, Dorman finally gave up in frustration and reached over to snatch the telephone from Mulder's hand.

"Hey!" he said, then flinched away to keep from touching the slime-slick man.

Dorman cradled the cellular phone and pushed it against his fluctuating face. The skin on his cheeks glistened and squirmed. The mucus on his hands left sticky patches on the black plastic.

"Agent Scully, tell Jody I'm sorry I shot him," Dorman said into the phone. "But I knew he would heal, just like the dog. I didn't mean to hurt him. I don't want to hurt anybody."

He reached up to flick on the dome light in the pickup's cab so that Mulder could see the intent look on his face and the revolver still held in his hand. "You need to tell the boy something for me, please. I need to explain to him."

Mulder knew his own conversation with Scully was now over. He couldn't touch the telephone again, or else the nano-critters would infiltrate his body too and leave him a splotched, convulsing wreck like Dorman's other victims.

Dorman swallowed, and from the anguished look on his face and the yellow shadows cast from the dim dome light, Mulder thought perhaps the distorted man really was sorry for all that had happened. "Tell him his mother is dead—and it's because of me. But it was an accident.

She was trying to protect him. She didn't know that just touching me would be deadly."

His lips pressed together. "The nanocritters in my body are going wrong, very wrong. They didn't heal her, like Jody's do—they destroyed his mother's systems, and she died. There was nothing I could do." He spoke faster and faster. "I warned her to stay away from me, but she"— he drew a deep breath—"she moved too fast. Jody knows how tough his mom was."

Dorman looked up, turning his gleaming, hooded eyes at Mulder.

Mulder kept driving. The red pickup rattled over a pothole, and a loose wrench in the rear bed clanged and bounced. He hoped one of the bumps would knock it free so he wouldn't have to hear the grating noise any more.

"Listen, Agent Scully." Dorman's voice was soothing; his mangled voice box must have healed quite nicely. "Jody's nanocritters work just fine—and that's what I need his blood for. I think the nanocritters his dad gave him might be able to fix the ones in me. It's my only chance."

Dorman winced as his body convulsed again, and he tried not to gasp into the phone. The hand holding the revolver twitched and jerked. Mulder hoped his fingers wouldn't clench around the trigger and shoot a hole through the roof of the pickup.

"You saw how I look," he said. "Jody remembers what I was like, how everything was between us. Me and him playing *Mario Kart* or *Cruisin' USA*. Remind him about the one time I let him beat me."

Then he sat back, curling his mouth in a little bit of a smile, perhaps nostalgic, perhaps predatory. "David Kennessy was right. There are government men after us. They want to destroy everything we created—but I got away, and so did Jody and Vader. But we're marked for eradication. I'm going to die in less than a day unless my nanocritters can be fixed. Unless I can see Jody."

Mulder looked over at him. The broad-shouldered, devastatingly sick man was very persuasive. On the phone he could hear faint voices, a discussion—presumably Jody talking to Scully. By the expression on Dorman's face, Jody seemed swayed by the big man's arguments. And why not? Dorman was the only connection remaining to the boy's past. The twelve year old would give him the benefit of the doubt. Dorman's shoulders sagged with relief.

Mulder felt sick in the pit of his stomach, still not sure whether to believe Dorman or not.

Finally Dorman growled into the phone again. "Yes, Agent Scully. Let's all go back to DyMar. The lab will be burnt and abandoned, but it's neutral ground. I know you can't trick me there."

He rested the revolver in his lap, calmer and confident now. "You have to understand how desperate I am—that's the only reason I'm doing this. But I won't hesitate. Unless you bring Jody to meet me, I *will* kill your partner."

He raised his eyebrows. "I don't even need a gun. All I need to do is touch him." As if in an effort to provoke Mulder, he dropped the revolver onto the worn seat between them.

"Just be at DyMar." He punched the END button.

He looked at the sticky residue on the black plastic of the phone, frowned in disappointment. He rolled down his window and tossed the phone away. It bounced on the gravel and shattered.

"I guess we won't be needing that anymore."

41

X Satellite dishes mounted atop the van tilted at different azimuths to tap into various relay satellites. Computer signal processors sifted through the complex medley of transmissions broadcast by hundreds of thousands of unsuspecting people.

The van sat parked at the terminus of a short dirt road that ended in a shallow dumping ground. Compost, deadwood, rotting garbage, and uprooted stumps stood in a massive pile like a revolutionary's barricade. Some farmer or logger had been tossing his debris here for years rather than pay a disposal fee at the county dump. "Private Property" and "Keep Out" signs offered impotent threats; Adam Lentz had far more serious methods of intimidation at his disposal.

No one had been out here for some time, though, especially not after dark. The men on the professional surveillance team had the area to themselves—and with the black-program technology rigged into the van, they had most of North America at their fingertips.

Tree branches bristling with pine needles offered a mesh

233

of camouflage overhead, and the thick clouds made the night dark and soupy, blocking the stars—but neither the trees nor the clouds hampered satellite transmissions.

The computers in the dashboard of the mobile tactical command center scanned thousands of frequencies, ran transmissions through voice-recognition algorithms, searched for key words, targeted on likely transmission points.

They had continued their invisible surveillance for hours with no success, but Adam Lentz was not a man to give up. Unless he broached the subject himself, the rest of his team members would not dare to comment on the matter either.

Lentz was also not one to lose patience. He had cultivated it over the years, when patience and a cool lack of emotion as well as an absence of remorse had allowed him to rise to this unrecognized yet still substantial position of power. Though few people understood what he was all about, Lentz was content with his place in the world, with the importance of his activities.

But he would have been much more content if he could just find Agent Fox Mulder.

"He can't know we're looking for him," Lentz muttered. The man at the command console looked over, his face stony, reflecting no surprise whatsoever. "We've been very discreet," the man said.

Lentz tapped his fingertips on the dashboard, pondering. He knew Mulder and Scully had split up. Agent Mulder had seen the dead trucker whose body Lentz's team had cleanly eliminated. Both Mulder and Scully had been to Dorman's isolated cabin out in the hollow, which—along with the body of Patrice Kennessy—was now a pile of smoldering ashes.

Then they had fled, and Lentz believed either Agent Mulder or Scully had the boy Jody and his nanotech-infected dog.

But something else was spreading the plague. Patrice Kennessy and the boy had feared something. Was the dog going rampant? Had the nanomachines within it—as Lentz had witnessed so clearly and so brutally in the videotaped demonstration—somehow gone haywire so that they now destroyed human beings?

The prospect frightened even him, and he knew that his superiors were absolutely right in insisting that all such dangerous research be contained. Only responsible, *authorized* people should know about it.

He had to restore order to the world.

Outside, the awakening night insects in the Oregon deep woods made a humming, buzzing sound. Grasshoppers, tree bugs . . . Lentz didn't know their scientific names. He had never been much interested in wildlife. The hive behavior of humanity in general had been enough to capture his interest.

He sat back and waited, clearing his mind, thinking of nothing.

A man with many pressures, burdens, and dark secrets, Lentz found it most restful when he could make his mind entirely blank. He had no plans to set in motion, no schemes to concoct. He proceeded with his missions one step at a time.

And in this instance, he couldn't proceed to the next step until they heard from Agent Mulder.

The man at the command deck sat up quickly. "Incoming," he said. He pushed down his earphones and fiddled with switches on his receiver.

"Transmission number confirmed, frequency confirmed." He almost allowed himself a smile, then turned to Lentz. "Voice pattern match confirmed. It's Agent Mulder. I'm recording."

He handed the earphones to Lentz, who quickly snugged them in place. The technician fiddled with the controls and the recorder.

Lentz listened to a staticky, warbled conversation between Mulder and Scully. In spite of his own tight control over his reactions, Lentz's eyes went wide, and his eyebrows lifted.

Yes, Scully had the boy and the dog in her custody—and the boy had healed himself from a grievous wound . . . but the most astonishing news of all was that the organization's patsy, Jeremy Dorman, had not been killed in the DyMar fire after all. He was still alive, still a threat . . . and now Dorman too was a carrier of the rogue nanotechnology.

And so was the boy! The infestation was already spreading.

After various threats and explanations, Dorman and Agent Scully worked to arrange a time and a place where they could meet. Mulder and Scully, Dorman, Jody, and the dog were all falling right into his lap—if Lentz's team could set up their trap sufficiently ahead of time.

As soon as the cellular transmission ended, Lentz launched his team into motion.

Every member of his group was well aware of how to reach the burned-out ruins of the laboratory. After all, each one of the mercenaries had been part of the supposed protest group that had brought down the cancer research establishment. They had thrown the firebombs themselves, set the accelerants, detonated the facility so that little more than an unstable skeleton remained.

"We have to get there first," Lentz said.

The mobile van launched like a killer shark out of the dead-end dirt road and onto the leaf-slick highway, accelerating recklessly up the coast at a speed far from safe.

But a mere traffic accident was not enough to worry Adam Lentz at that moment.

42

Back to the haunted house, Scully thought as she drove up the steep driveway to the gutted, fire-blackened ruins of the DyMar Laboratory.

Behind the clouds the moon spread a pearlescent glow, a shimmering brightness in the soupy sky overhead. On the hills surrounding DyMar, the forest had once been a peaceful, protective barricade—but now Scully thought the trees were ominous, offering cover for the stealthy movement of enemies, perhaps more violent protesters . . . or those other men that Jody feared were after him and his mother.

"Stay in the car, Jody." She walked to the sagging chain-link fence that had been erected to keep trespassers from the dangerous construction site. Nobody manned it now.

The bluff overlooking the sprawling city of Portland was prime business real estate, but she saw only the blackened ruins like the carcass of a dragon sprawled beneath the diluted moonlight. The place was empty, dangerous yet enticing.

As Scully passed through the open and too-inviting chain-link gate, she heard a car door slam. She whirled, expecting to see Mulder and his captor, the big man who had shot Jody—but it was only the boy climbing out of the car and looking around curiously. The black Lab bounded out next to him, anxious to be free, glad that his boy was healthy.

"Be careful, Jody," she called.

"I'm following you," he said. Before she could scold him, he added, "I don't want to be left alone."

Scully didn't want him to go into the burned ruins with her, but she couldn't blame him, either. "All right. Come on, then."

Jody hurried toward her while Vader bounded ahead, frolicking. "Keep the dog next to you," Scully warned.

Small sounds of settling debris came from the unstable site, structural timbers tugged by time and gravity. No damp breeze stirred the ashes, but still the blackened timbers creaked and groaned.

Some of the structural walls remained intact, but looked ready to collapse at any moment. Part of the floor had fallen into the basement levels, but in one section concrete-block walls stood tall, coated with fire-blistered enamel paint and covered with soot.

Bulldozers sat like metal leviathans outside the building perimeter. A steam shovel, Porta Potti outhouses, and construction lockers had been set up by the contractor in charge of erasing the last scar of DyMar's presence.

Scully thought she heard a sound, and proceeded cautiously toward the bulldozer. Fuel tanks sat near the heavy equipment. The demolitions crew had been ready to begin— and she wondered if the unusual rush to level the place had anything to do with the cover-up plans Dorman had talked about.

Then Scully saw a metal locker that had been pried open. A starburst of bright silver showed where a crowbar had ripped off the lock, just below the marking, "Danger: Explosives."

Suddenly the darkness seemed much more oppressive, the silence unnatural. The air was cold and gauzy damp in her nostrils, with a sour poison of old burning.

"Jody, keep close to me," she said.

Her heart pounded, and all of her senses came fully alert. This meeting between the boy and Jeremy Dorman would be tense and dangerous. But she would make sure Jody got through it.

She heard the approach of another engine, a vehicle rattling and laboring up the slope, tires crunching on gravel. Twin headlights swept through the night like bright coins.

"Stay with me." She put a protective hand on Jody's shoulder, and the two stayed at the edge of the burned-out building.

It was an old red pickup truck patched with primer, rusted on the sides. The body groaned and creaked as the driver's door opened and Mulder climbed out.

Of all the unbelievable things she had witnessed with Fox Mulder, seeing her strictly suit-and-tie partner driving a battered old pickup ranked among the most unusual.

"Fancy meeting you here, Scully," Mulder said.

A larger form heaved itself out of the passenger side. Her eyes had adjusted to the dim light, and even the shadows could not hide that something was wrong with the way he moved, the way his limbs seemed to have extra joints, the way weariness and pain seemed ready to crush him.

Jeremy Dorman had looked bad before, and now he appeared even worse.

Scully took a step forward but kept herself in front of Jody. "Are you all right, Mulder?"

"For now," he said.

Dorman took a step closer to Mulder, who edged away in an attempt to keep his distance. The broad-shouldered man held a revolver in his hand . . . but the weapon itself seemed the least threatening aspect about him.

Scully drew her own handgun. She was a good shot and

utterly confident. She pointed the 9mm directly at Jeremy Dorman. "Release Agent Mulder right now," she said. "Mulder, step away from him."

He did so by two or three steps, but he moved slowly, carefully, not wanting to provoke Dorman.

"I'm afraid I can't return your partner's weapon," Dorman said. "I've touched it, you see, and it's no use to anyone anymore."

"And I've also lost my jacket and my cell phone," Mulder said. "Think of all the paperwork I'm going to need to fill out."

Jody came hesitantly forward, standing close behind Scully. "Jeremy, why are you doing this?" he said. "You're as bad as . . . as bad as *them*."

Dorman's shoulders sagged, and Scully was reminded of the pathetic lummox Lenny from *Of Mice and Men*, who hurt things he loved without knowing why or how.

"I'm sorry, Jody," he said, spreading one hand while he gripped the revolver in the other. "You can see how this is affecting me. I had to come here. You can help me. It's the only way I know to survive."

Jody said nothing.

"Other people are after us, Jody," Dorman said. He took a step closer. Scully did not back away, maintaining herself as a barrier between them.

"We're being hunted by government officials, people trying to bury your dad's work so that no other cancer patients will ever be helped. No one else will be cured like you were. These men want to keep that cure for themselves."

He was so emphatic that the skin on his face shifted with his intense emotion. "The protesters that killed your dad, the ones who burned down this whole facility, were not just animal-rights activists. They were staged by the group I'm talking about. It was planned. It's a conspiracy. They're the ones who killed your father."

At that point, as if on cue, other figures appeared, shadowy silhouettes, men in dark suits emerging from the perimeter of the chain-link fence. They came out of the trees and the access road. Another group trudged up the steep driveway with bright flashlights blazing.

"We have evidence that suggests otherwise, Mr. Dorman," said one of the men in the lead. "We're your reinforcements, Agent Mulder. We'll take care of the situation from here."

Dorman looked around wildly and glared at Mulder, as if the agent had betrayed him.

"How did you know our names?" Mulder asked.

Scully backed away until she clutched Jody's wrist. "It's not that simple," she said. "We won't relinquish custody of this boy."

"I'm afraid you have to," the man in the lead said. "I assure you, our jurisdiction in this matter supersedes yours."

The men came closer; their dark suits acted as camouflage in the shadowy overhangs in the burned building.

"Identify yourselves," Scully said.

"These men don't carry business cards, Scully," Mulder said.

Jody looked at the man who had spoken. "What did you mean?" he said, his eyes gleaming. "What did you mean that they weren't the ones who killed my father?"

The man in the lead looked over at Jody like an insect collector assessing a prize specimen. "Mr. Dorman didn't explain to you what really happened to your father?" His voice held a mocking tone.

"Don't you dare, Lentz," Dorman said. His voice seethed. He had raised the revolver in his hand, but Lentz didn't seem at all bothered by the threat.

"Jeremy killed your dad, Jody. Not us."

"You bastard!" Dorman wailed in despair.

Scully was too astonished to respond, but it was clear to her that Dorman realized he would never convince the boy to help him, not now.

With a roar, swinging his too-flexible arms, Jeremy Dorman brought up the revolver in his hand, aiming at Lentz.

The other team members were much faster, though. They snatched their own weapons and opened fire.

43

The hail of small-caliber bullets struck Jeremy Dorman, and he thrashed out his arms in a scream of pain—as his body suddenly went haywire.

Mulder and Scully both dove to one side, reacting according to their training. Jody cried out as Scully dragged him with her, scrambling toward shelter among the large construction equipment.

Mulder moved away, shouting for the men to hold their fire, but no one paid the slightest attention to him.

Dorman himself remained the focus of all the shooting. He had known these men wanted to take him down, though he doubted that they had known he was still alive before now. They did not know what had changed inside of him . . . how he was *different*.

Adam Lentz had betrayed him before: The people in the organization that had promised him his own laboratory, the ability to continue the nanotechnology research, had already attempted to destroy him. Now they were here to finish the job.

As two hot bullets struck him, one high in the shoulder

and the other on the left side of his rib cage, the pain and adrenaline and fury destroyed the last vestiges of his control over his own body. He let slip his hold on the systems that had played havoc with his genetic structure, his muscles and nerves. He roared a wordless howl of outrage.

And his body *changed*.

His skin stretched like a trembling drumhead. Inside, his muscles convulsed and clenched. The wild tumorous growths that had protruded from his ribs, his skin, his neck, came loose, ripping their way through his already mangled shirt.

The mass of protrusions had fought themselves free one time previously, while he had been trapped with Wayne Hykaway in the logging truck. But that loss of control was nothing compared to the unleashed biological chaos he exhibited now, a wild-card reorganization that the nano-critters had found in his most primitive DNA coding.

His shoulders groaned, his biceps bulged, and his arms bent and twisted. Another whipping tumor crawled out of his throat from the base of his tongue. The skin on his face and neck ran like melting plastic.

The men in dark suits continued to fire at him, in alarm and self-defense now, but Dorman's bodily integrity was breaking down, mutating, able to absorb the impacts like soft clay.

From his position at the lead of the team, Adam Lentz reacted quickly, retreating to cover as the gunfire continued.

Dorman charged forward to attack the nearest dark-suited man with one twisted arm while tentacles whipped out in a hideously primeval mass from his body. His mind was a blur, filled with pain and static and conflicting images. The nerve signals he tried to send to his muscles had very little effect. Now his warped and rebellious body broke free, going on the rampage.

The government man's cool professionalism quickly degenerated into a scream as an explosion of fleshy protrusions, tentacled claws, a nightmare of bizarre biological abominations wrapped around his arms, his chest, his neck. Dorman squeezed and strangled, until the man broke like balsa kindling in his grasp.

Another bullet shattered Dorman's femur, but before he could collapse, the nanomachines knitted the bone together again, allowing him to charge forward to snare another victim.

The hot translucent slime covered Dorman's body, providing a vehicle for the seething nanocritters. He needed only to touch the enemy men and the cellular plague would instantly eradicate their systems—but his out-of-control body took great delight in snapping their necks, crushing their windpipes, folding up their rib cages like accordions.

The single tentacle whipped out of his mouth like the long sharp tongue of a serpent, lashing the air. He didn't know how to interpret his own senses anymore. He had no idea how much—or how little—humanity still remained within him.

For now he saw only the enemy, the conspirators, the traitors—and his buzzing, disintegrating brain thought only of killing them.

But even as he continued the struggle, Dorman felt disoriented. His vision blurred and distorted. The surrounding agents brought more weapons to bear. The bullet impacts drove him away, and Dorman stumbled backward.

A dim spark in his mind made him remember the DyMar laboratory, the rooms where Darin and David Kennessy had developed their fantastic work—work that even now had brought them to this threshold of disaster.

Like a wounded animal fleeing into its lair, Jeremy Dorman lurched into the burned wreckage, seeking refuge.

And the men with weapons charged after him.

44

As soon as Lentz and his team conveniently appeared, Mulder knew that these men were no "reinforcements," but a cleanup crew, minor players in the same conspiracy that he and Scully battled constantly. They had tracked Patrice and Jody, they had staged the violent protest that burned the lab down, they had ransacked the Kennessy home, they had confiscated the evidence in the hospital morgue.

Mulder could do without that kind of "reinforcement" any day of the week.

When the shots rang out, he was instantly afraid that he, Scully, and young Jody would all be mowed down in the rain of bullets. He ducked to one side, seeking shelter. Thanks to Dorman, he no longer had a handgun of his own, but Scully was still armed.

"Scully, stay with the boy!" he shouted. He heard the solid wet impact of bullets striking skin, and Dorman roared in pain.

Mulder scuttled along the darkened ground, ducking behind fallen beams and broken walls. He looked up as the ululating sound emanating from the ominous fugitive turned more bestial, less defined.

Jeremy Dorman transformed into a monster before his eyes.

All the horrors of wild cellular growth, the reckless spread of a malignant cancer with a mind of its own, extended like some ill-defined creature that had lain dormant inside Dorman's cells. Now it spread forth, growing without a plan. *Like tract home developments approved by a bribed city council, he thought.*

And this cellular assault was unleashed with a predatory mind bent on attack and destruction.

From her vantage point, Scully couldn't see the details. She shielded Jody with her own body and ran over to the shelter of the nearby bulldozer. With the bright echoing sound of metal upon metal, bullets ricocheted from the armored side of the machine. Scully dove down into the shadows, knocking Jody to safety.

Mulder kept low, racing along the broken bricks and fallen timbers. He ran into the dubious shelter of the gutted structure of the DyMar Laboratory.

Dorman—or what was left of him—managed to grab two more of the attacking agents and kill them, using a combination of hands and tentacles, as well as the incredibly virulent plague that lived in the slime on his skin.

Gunfire continued to ring out, sounding like an out-of-control popcorn popper. Yellow pinpoints of light flew like fireflies in the darkness. Mulder could see that the dark-suited men had scattered to surround the entire perimeter. They closed in, driving Dorman back into the ruins.

As if it was part of a plan.

Mulder ducked beneath an overhanging archway, bristling with teeth of shattered glass, had somehow remained standing even after the fire and the explosion.

Over by the bulldozer, Jody shouted in despair as his dog let out a long and nerve-grating chain of barks and growls. Raising his head, Mulder saw a dark shadow, the black Labrador, racing into the ruins. Vader barked and snapped as he pursued Jeremy Dorman.

Lentz's other agents also crept up to the labyrinthine wreckage, but they were wary now. Dorman had withstood their hail of gunfire, and he had already killed several of them. Two of the men had flashlights, bright white eyes that burned a white lance into the murk. Ash sifted down from where Dorman had stirred the debris. Mulder smelled the tang of soot and burned plastic.

One of the agents pinned Dorman with his flashlight beam, attempting to stun him like a deer facing oncoming headlights. With a grunt, the monstrous man shoved sideways against a support pillar, knocking a charred wooden pole down along with a shower of concrete blocks.

The agent with the flashlight tried to scramble back, but the wreckage fell on his upper leg. Part of the wall collapsed. Mulder heard the hard bamboo sound of a bone breaking. Then the dark-suited man, who had been so calm as he hunted down his victim, yelped in pain; he had a high-pitched bawling voice.

Somewhere inside the burned building, the dog barked.

Mulder tried to stay under cover, but he made plenty of noise as he tripped over fallen bricks and crunched broken glass. He ducked behind a slumped, charred desk as more gunfire rang out.

A bullet struck the office furniture, and Mulder let out a hiss of surprise. He could see Scully outside in the pearly gray of fog-muffled moonlight. She was holding the boy back, clutching his torn shirt. Jody continued to shout after his dog as the gunfire peppered the night with sharp sounds. Scully pushed Jody back down as a barrage of bullets struck the bulldozer again.

Another shot slammed into the desk near where Mulder hid.

He realized that these shots couldn't be accidental

misfires, though they would be excused as such. To the men who had surrounded the DyMar site and tried to kill Dorman and Jody, it might also prove advantageous if Agents Mulder and Scully were also "accidentally" caught in the line of fire.

45

The trap had sprung. Not as neatly as Adam Lentz had hoped, perhaps, but still the results would be the same . . . if a bit messier.

Messes could be cleaned up.

The gunfire crackled in the night with sharp, deadly sounds, but none of the shots caused sufficient damage to take down Jeremy Dorman, their immediate target. Though Lentz's team members had standing instructions to use all the force necessary to capture the boy and the dog as well, Agent Scully had protected young Jody Kennessy. She had sheltered him with all the training and skills she had learned at the FBI Academy at Quantico.

Lentz and his men had undergone more rigorous training, though, in other . . . less accredited schools.

After the initial gunfire, he thought he had seen Agent Mulder also run for cover into the gutted building. No matter. Everything would be taken care of in time.

Jeremy Dorman's horrific transformation had captured the focus of the team members. Seeing several of their comrades slaughtered in the monster's murderous rage, they set out after him, grim-faced and murderous.

Though Lentz himself had ducked out of the way of Dorman and his plague-laced slime, he was still disappointed in how his team's cool efficiency had so quickly shattered into a backwash of vengeance. He'd believed that these men were the best and most professional in the world. If so, the world should offer better.

He heard the shrill cry of another man inside the burned ruins, and more gunshots rang out. The team had trapped Dorman inside the unstable facility. In that respect, at least, everything was going as smoothly as he had hoped.

Lentz stopped at the nearest tactical vehicle, reached into the front seat, and took out the demolition control. But he had to wait for the right moment.

His team had arrived a full twenty-five minutes before Agent Scully and the boy, but Lentz had not moved prematurely. It was so much more efficient to wait for everyone to reach the same rendezvous point.

Lentz's hand-picked demolitions men had used the blasting caps stored at the construction site, as well as other incendiaries and explosives they kept inside their cleanup van. Working in the precarious structure, his men had rigged sealed drums of jellied gasoline in the half-collapsed basement levels. When the drums exploded, flames would shoot up through the remaining floors and incinerate the rest of the DyMar building. No trace would remain.

Lentz didn't particularly want to obliterate his team members who had foolishly followed Dorman inside, chasing him in a cat-and-mouse routine among the falling-down walls. But they were expendable. Each man had been aware of the risks when he signed up.

Agent Mulder had also vanished inside, and Lentz suspected that some of the gunfire was also directed at him. The team members would have taken it upon themselves to eradicate all witnesses.

Lentz had received clear instructions that Mulder was not to be killed. He and his partner Scully were already part of a larger plan, but Lentz had to make on-the-spot decisions. He had to set priorities—and seeing the rampaging *thing* unleashed from within Dorman's body had hardened him to the extreme necessity. If he had to, Lentz would make excuses to his superiors. Later.

Mulder and Scully both knew too much, after all, and this weapon, this breakthrough, this curse of rampant nanotechnology had to be controlled, no matter what the cost. Only certain people could be trusted with so much power.

And the time was now.

One of the other men rushed back to the armored cleanup van. His eyes were glazed; sweat bristled across his forehead. He panted, looking around wildly.

Lentz glanced over at him and snapped, "Control yourself."

The effect was like an electric shock running through the team member. He stopped, reeled for a second, then swallowed hard. He stood straight, his breathing resumed a normal rate almost instantly, and he cleared his throat, waiting for additional orders.

Lentz held up the control in his hand. A small transmitter. "Is everything prepared?"

The man looked down at the controls inside the van. He blinked, then answered quickly. His words were as fast and as crisp as the gunshots that pattered through the darkness.

"That's all you need, sir. It will set off the blasting caps and trigger the remaining explosives. On a parallel circuit, the jellied gasoline will ignite. Just push the red button. That's all you need."

Lentz nodded to him curtly. "Thank you." He took one last look at the blackened skeletal building and pushed the indicated button.

The DyMar Laboratory erupted in fresh flames.

46

The shock wave toppled some of the remaining girders and the once-solid concrete wall. The metal desk sheltered Mulder from the worst of the blast, but still the hammer of heat pressed the heavy piece of furniture against the wall, nearly crushing him.

Flames swept upward, bright yellow and orange, moving rapidly, as if by magic. He'd thought most of the flammables would have been consumed in the first fire two weeks earlier. Shielding his eyes from the glare and the hot wind, Mulder could see from the magnitude of the blaze that someone had rigged the ruins to go up in an instant inferno.

The dark-suited men had planned for this.

Hearing a shriek of terror and pain, Mulder carefully raised his head, blinking his watery eyes against the furnace blast of the inferno. He saw one of the men who had hunted after him stumbling through the wreckage, his suit engulfed in flames. More gunshots rang out, frantic firepower among shouts and screams—and a barking dog.

The fire raced up along the wooden support beams. The

heat was so intense, even the glass and broken stone seemed to have caught fire. The black Labrador had bounded into the building, gotten caught in the explosion, and was thrown against a wall. Vader's fur smoldered, but still he ran, casting about for something.

One of the overhead girders fell with a crash among the debris. Flames licked along the splintered edge.

Mulder stood up from behind the desk, shielding his eyes. "Vader!" he shouted. "Hey, over here!" That black dog was evidence. Vader's bloodstream carried functional nanotechnology that could be studied to save so many people, without the horrendous mutations Jeremy Dorman had suffered.

Mulder waved his hand to get the dog's attention, but instead another man trapped inside the wreckage turned and fired at him. The gunshot spanged against the desk and ricocheted onto one of the broken concrete walls.

Before the man could shoot again, though, the inhuman form of Jeremy Dorman crashed through the debris. The man with the gun tore his attention from Mulder—the easy target—to the monstrous creature. He didn't have time to make an outcry before several of Dorman's new appendages grasped him. With a twisted but powerful arm, Dorman snapped the man's neck, then discarded him.

At the moment, Mulder didn't feel inclined to shower the distorted man with gratitude. Shielding his eyes, barely able to see through the smoke and the blaze, he staggered toward the outside, needing to get away.

The dog was hopelessly lost inside the facility. Mulder couldn't understand why Vader had run into such a dangerous area in the first place.

The unstable floor was on fire. The walls, the debris . . . even the air burned his lungs with each gasping, retching breath he drew.

Mulder didn't know how he was going to get out alive.

● ● ●

Scully clutched Jody's torn shirt, but the fabric ripped and pulled free as he lunged after his dog.

"Jody, no!"

But the boy charged after Vader. The men in the ambush continued shooting, but Dorman was killing them one after another. The black dog plunged directly into the crossfire. The twelve-year-old boy—perhaps a bit too confident in his own immortality, as many twelve-year-olds were—ran after him a few seconds later.

Scully dropped the useless scrap of cloth in her hand. Desperate, she stood up from behind the shelter of the bulldozer. Scully watched the boy run miraculously unharmed toward the charred walls of DyMar. With a loud ricochet, another bullet bounced off the heavy tractor tread; she didn't even bother to duck.

Bits of debris showered Jody, but he lowered his head and kept running. He stood screaming at the edge of the walls, looking at the barrier of flames. He ducked down and tried to get inside. She heard Mulder's voice call out for the dog, then more gunshots. The DyMar facility and all it stood for continued to burn.

So far, no police, no fire engines, no help whatsoever came to investigate the gunfire, the explosion, the flames.

"Mulder!" she shouted. She didn't know where he was or how he could get out. Jody ducked recklessly inside. "Jody!" she shouted. "Come back here!"

She ran to the threshold and squinted through the smoke. A girder tumbled as a ceiling collapsed, showering sparks. Part of the floor showed gaps and holes where the flames and the explosion beneath had weakened it, causing it to crack and tumble down in sections like a house of cards.

Jody stood half-balanced, flailing his hands. "Vader, where are you? Vader!"

Throwing all caution to the wind, needing to save the boy as if it were some measure of her own worthiness to survive, Scully hurried inside. She struggled ahead, taking shallow breaths. Most of the time, she held her eyes closed, blinking them open for a quick glimpse, then staggering along.

"Vader!" Jody called again, out of sight.

Finally Scully reached the boy's side and grabbed his arm. "We have to go, Jody. Out of here! The whole place is going to collapse."

"Scully!" Mulder shouted, his voice raw and ragged with the smoke and heat. She turned to see him making his way across the floor, stepping in flames and racing along. He swatted out a fire that smoldered on his trousers.

She gestured for him to hurry—but then a wall behind her crumbled. Concrete blocks fell to one side in a mound of cinders as a wooden support beam split.

"Hello, Jody . . ." Jeremy Dorman's tortured voice said as he pushed himself through the fire and debris of the wall he had just knocked down. The distorted man stood free, undisturbed by the heat raging around him. Embers pattered on his body, smoking on his skin and leaving black craters that shifted and melted and healed over. His body ran like candle wax. His clothes were fully involved in the fire that blazed around him, but his skin thrashed and writhed, a horror show of tentacles and growths.

Dorman blocked their way out.

"Jody, you wouldn't help me when I asked—and now look what's happened."

Jody bit back a small scream and only glared at the hideously mutated creature. "You killed my dad."

"Now we're all going to die in this fire," Dorman said.

Scully doubted that even the swarming nanomachines could protect the boy from the intense flames. She knew for a fact, though, that she and Mulder had no such protection, mere humans, completely susceptible to the fire's heat and smoke. They were both doomed unless they could get around this man.

Mulder tripped and fell to one knee in the hot broken

glass; he hauled himself up again without an outcry. Scully still had her handgun, but she knew that would offer no real threat against Dorman. He would laugh off her bullets, the way he had ignored the crossfire from the dark-suited men . . . the way he even now didn't seem troubled by the fire that raged around them.

"Jody, come to me," Dorman said, plodding closer. His skin roiled and rippled, glistening with slime that oozed from his every pore.

Jody staggered back toward Scully. She could see burns on his skin, scratches and bleeding cuts where debris had showered him in the explosion, and she wondered briefly why the small injuries weren't magically healing as his gunshot wound had. Was something wrong with his nanocritters? Had they given up, or shut down somehow?

Scully knew she couldn't protect the boy. Dorman lunged closer, reaching out to him with a flame-covered hand.

And then from a wall of burning wreckage to one side, where the light and the smoke made visibility impossible, the black Labrador howled and launched himself at the target.

Dorman spun about, his head twisting and swiveling. His broken, bent hands rose up, thrashing. His tentacles and tumors quivered like a basket of snakes. The dog, a black-furred bulldozer, knocked Dorman backward.

"Vader!" Jody screamed.

The dog drove Dorman staggering into the flames, where bright light and curling fire rose up through ever-growing gaps in the floor, as if the pit of hell itself lay beneath the support platform.

Dorman yelped, and his tentacles wrapped around the dog. The black Lab's fur caught on fire in patches, but Vader didn't seem to notice. Immune to the plague Dorman carried, the dog snapped his jaws, digging his fangs deep into the soft flowing flesh of the nanotech-infected man.

Dorman wrestled with the heavy animal and both tumbled to the creaking, splintering floorboards. Dorman's left foot crashed through one of the flame-filled holes.

He cried out. His tentacles writhed. The dog bit ferociously at his face.

Then the floor collapsed in an avalanche of flaming debris. Sparks and smoke flew upward like a land-mine explosion. With a howl and a scream, both Dorman and Vader fell into the seething basement.

Jody wailed and made as if to run after his dog, but Scully grabbed him fiercely by the arms. She dragged the boy back toward the opening, and safety. Coughing, Mulder followed, stumbling after her.

The flames roared higher, and more girders collapsed. Another concrete wall toppled into shards, then an entire section of the floor fell in, nearly dragging them with it.

They reached the threshold of the collapsing building, and Scully could think of nothing more than to push herself out into the fresh air, into the blessed relief. Safe from the fire.

The cool night seemed impossibly dark and cold as they fought their way from the flames and the wreckage. Her eyes burned, so filled with tears that she could barely see. Scully held the despairing boy, wrapping her arms around him. Mulder touched her shoulder, getting her attention as they stumbled away from the flames.

She looked up to see a group of men waiting for them, staring coldly. The survivors of Lentz's team held their automatic weapons high and pointed at them.

"Give me the boy," Adam Lentz said.

47

X Mulder should have known the men in suits would be waiting for them at the perimeter of the inferno. Some of Lentz's "reinforcements" would have realized there was no need to endanger themselves—better just to hang around and let any survivors come to them.

"Stop right there, Agent Mulder, Agent Scully," the man in the lead said. "There's still a chance we can bring this to a satisfactory resolution."

"We're not interested in your satisfactory resolution," Mulder answered with a raw cough.

Scully's eyes flashed as she placed her arm protectively around the boy. "You're not taking Jody. We know why you want him."

"Then you know the danger," Lentz said. "Our friend Mr. Dorman just showed us all what could go wrong. This technology can't be allowed to be disseminated uncontrolled. We have no other choice." He smiled, but not with his eyes. "Don't make this difficult."

"You're *not* taking him," she said more vehemently.

To emphasize her point, Scully drew herself tall. Her face

261

was smudged with soot; her clothes reeked of smoke and cinder burns. She stood defiantly in front of Jody, a barricade between him and their automatic weapons. Mulder wasn't sure if her body would block a hail of high-powered gunfire, but he thought her sheer determination just might stop them.

"I don't know who you are, Mr. Lentz," Mulder said, taking a step closer to Scully to support her stand, "but this young man is in our protective custody."

"I just want to help him," Lentz said smoothly. "We'll take him to medical care. A special facility where he'll be looked after by people who can . . . understand his condition. You know no normal hospital would be able to help him."

Scully did not budge. "I'm not convinced he would survive your treatment."

From below, finally, Mulder could hear sirens and approaching vehicles. Response crews with flashing red and blue lights raced along the suburb streets toward the base of the hill. The second DyMar fire continued to blaze at the top of the bluff.

Mulder stepped backward, closer to his partner. He kept his eyes nailed on Lentz's, ignoring the other men in suits.

"Now you're sounding like me, Scully," Mulder said.

"Give us the boy now," Lentz said. Below, the sirens were getting louder, closer.

"Not a chance in hell," Scully answered.

Fire engines and police cars raced up the hill, sirens wailing. They would reach the hilltop inferno in seconds. If Lentz meant to do something, it would be now. But Mulder knew if he did shoot them, he wouldn't have time to clean up his mess before the DyMar site became very public.

"Mr. Lentz—" one of the surviving team members said.

Scully took one step, paused a terribly long moment, then began to walk slowly away, one step at a time. Her determination didn't waver.

Lentz stared at her. The other men kept their guns trained.

Rescue workers and firefighters yanked open the chain-link gate, hauling it aside so the fire trucks could drive inside.

"You don't know what you're doing," Lentz said coldly. He eyed the arriving vehicles, as if still gauging whether he could get away with shooting the two agents and eliminating the bodies under the very noses of the rushing emergency crews. Adam Lentz and his men stood angry and defeated, backlit by the raging inferno that burned the remains of DyMar Laboratory to the ground.

But Scully knew she was saving the boy's life. She kept walking, holding Jody's arm. He looked forlornly back at the wall of flames.

As the uniformed men rushed to hook up hoses and rig their fire engine, Lentz's team stepped back, disappearing into the forest shadows.

Somehow the three of them managed to reach the rental car.

"I'll drive, Scully," Mulder said as he popped open the driver's-side door. "You're a bit distracted."

"I'll keep an eye on Jody," she said.

Mulder started the engine, half-expecting that gunshots from the trees would ring out and the windshield would explode with spider-webbed bullet cracks. But instead, he managed to drive off, his tires spitting loose gravel on the steep driveway leading down from DyMar Laboratory. He had to flash his ID several times to get past the converging authorities. He wondered how Lentz would explain himself and his team . . . if they were found at all in the surrounding forest.

48

Mercy Hospital
Portland, Oregon
Saturday, 12:16 P.M.

In the hospital, Scully checked and rechecked Jody Kennessy's lab results, but she remained as baffled after an hour of contemplation as when she had first seen the data.

She sat in the bustling cafeteria at lunchtime, nursing a bitter-tasting cup of coffee. Doctors and nurses came through, chatting about cases the way sports fans talked about football games; patients spent time out of their stuffy rooms with their family members.

Finally, realizing the charts would show her nothing else, Scully got another cup to go, and went to meet Mulder where he sat stationed on guard duty outside the boy's hospital room.

As she walked from the elevator down the hall, she waved the manila folder in her hand. Mulder looked up, eager for confirmation of the technology. He stuffed the magazine he had been reading back into its plain brown envelope. The door to Jody's room stood ajar, with the TV droning inside. So far, no mysterious strangers had come to challenge the boy.

"I don't know whether to be more astonished at the evidence of functional nanotechnology—or at the lack of it." Scully shook her head and pushed the dot matrix printouts of lab scans at Mulder.

He picked them up, glancing down at the numbers, graphs, and tables, but obviously didn't know what he was looking for. "I take it this isn't what you expected?"

"Absolutely no traces of nanotechnology in Jody's blood." She crossed her arms over her chest. "Look at the lab results."

Mulder scratched his dark hair. "How can that be? You saw him heal from a gunshot wound—a mortal wound."

"Maybe I was mistaken," she said, "Perhaps the bullet managed to miss vital organs—"

"But Scully, look at how healthy he is! You saw the picture of him with the leukemia symptoms. He only had a month or two to live. We *know* David Kennessy tested his cure on him."

Scully shrugged. "He's clean, Mulder. Remember the sample of dog's blood at the veterinarian's office? The remnants of nanotechnology were quite obvious. Dr. Quinton said the same thing about the fluid specimen I took during my autopsy of Vernon Ruckman. The traces aren't hard to find if the nanomachines are as ubiquitous in the bloodstream as they should be—and there would have to be millions upon millions of them in order to effect the dramatic cellular repairs that we witnessed."

Her first evidence that something was not as she suspected, though, had been Jody's recent scrapes, scratches, and cuts after the fire. Though not serious, they failed to heal any more quickly than other ordinary scratches. Jody Kennessy now seemed like a normal boy, despite what she knew of his background.

"Then where did the nanocritters go?" Mulder asked. "Did Jody lose them somehow?"

Scully had no idea how to explain it.

Together they entered Jody's room, where the boy sat up in bed, paying little attention to the television that played loudly in the background. Considering all he had been through, the twelve-year-old seemed to be taking the ordeal well enough. He gave Scully a wan smile when he saw her.

A few moments later, the chief oncologist bustled into the room, holding a clipboard in his hand and shaking his head. He looked over at Scully, then at Jody, dismissing Mulder entirely.

"I see no evidence of leukemia, Agent Scully," he said, shaking his head. "Are you sure this is the same boy?"

"Yes, we're sure."

The oncologist sighed. "I've looked at the boy's previous charts and lab results. No blast cells in the blood, and I performed a lumbar puncture to study the cerebrospinal fluid for the presence of blast cells—still nothing. Very standard procedures, and usually very conclusive. In an advanced case such as his is supposed to be, the symptoms should be obvious just by looking at him—lord knows, I've seen enough cases."

Now the oncologist finally looked at Jody. "But this boy's leukemia is completely gone. Not just in remission—it's *gone.*"

Scully hadn't honestly expected anything else.

The oncologist blinked his eyes and let his chart hang by his hip. "I've seen medical miracles happen . . . not often, but given the number of patients through here, occasionally events occur that medicine just can't explain. But this boy, who was facing terminal cancer only a month or two ago, now shows no symptoms whatsoever."

The oncologist raised his eyebrows at Jody, who seemed uninterested in the discussion, as if he knew the answers all along. "Mr. Kennessy, you're cured. Do you understand the magnitude of that diagnosis? You're completely healthy, other than a few scratches and scrapes and minor burns. There's absolutely nothing wrong with you."

"We'll let you know if we have any further questions," Scully said, and the doctor seemed disappointed that she wasn't quite as amazed as he was. A little too brusquely, perhaps, she ushered him out the door of the hospital room.

After the oncologist departed, she and Mulder sat at the end of Jody's bed. "Do you know why there's no trace left of the nanocritters in your bloodstream, Jody? We can't understand it. The nanomachines healed you from the gunshot wound before, they cured you of your cancer—but they're gone now."

"Because I'm cured." Jody looked up at the television, but did not care about the housewives' talk show going on at low volume. "My dad said they would shut down and dissolve when they were done. He made them so they would fix my leukemia cell by cell. He said it would take a long time, but I would get better every day. Then, when they were finished . . . the nanocritters were supposed to shut themselves down."

Mulder raised his eyebrows at Scully. "A fail-safe mechanism. I wonder if his brother Darin even knew about it."

"Mulder, that implies an incredible level of technological sophistication—" she began, but then realized that the entire prospect of self-sustaining biological policemen that worked on the human body, using nothing more than DNA strands as an instruction manual, was also fantastically beyond what she had believed were modern capabilities.

"Jody," she said, leaning closer to the boy, "we intend to release these results as widely as possible. We need to let everyone know that you are no longer carrying any signs of the nanotechnology. If you're clean, there should be no reason why those men will continue to be after you."

"Whatever," he said, sounding glum.

Scully didn't waste her effort in a false cheeriness. The boy would have to deal with his situation in his own way.

Jody Kennessy had carried a miracle cure, not just for cancer but probably for all forms of disease that afflicted humanity. The nanocritters in his blood might even have offered immortality.

But with DyMar Laboratory destroyed, Jeremy Dorman and the black Lab swallowed up in the inferno, and David Kennessy and anyone else involved in the project dead, similar nanotechnology breakthroughs would be a long time coming if they had to be made from scratch.

Scully already had an idea of how the Bureau might keep Jody safe in the long run, where they could take him. It didn't make her feel good, but it was the best option she could think of.

Mulder, meanwhile, would simply write up the case, keep all of his records and his unexplained speculations, add them to his folders full of anecdotal evidence. Once again, he had nothing hard and fast to prove anything to anyone.

Just another X-File.

Before long, Scully figured, Mulder would need to install several more file cabinets in his cramped office, just to keep track of them all.

49

Adam Lentz made his final report verbally and face to face, with no paperwork buffers between them. There would be no written record of this investigation, nothing that could be uncovered and read by the wrong sets of prying eyes. Instead, Lentz had to face down the man and tell him everything directly, in his own words.

It was one of the most terrifying experiences he had ever known.

A curl of acrid cigarette smoke rose from the ashtray, clinging like a deadly shroud around the man. He was gaunt, his eyes haunted, his face unremarkable, his dark brown hair combed back.

He did not look to be a man who held the eggshells of human lives at the mercy of his crushing grip. He didn't look like a man who had seen presidents die, who had engineered the fall of governments and the rise of others, who played with unknowing test groups of people and called them "merchandise."

But still, he played world politics the way other people played the game of Risk.

He took a long drag on his cigarette and exhaled the smoke slowly through parchment-dry lips. So far, he had said nothing.

Lentz stood inside the nondescript office, facing the man squarely. The ashtray on the desk was crowded with stubbed-out cigarette butts.

"How can you be so sure?" the man finally said. His voice was deceptively soft, with a melodious quality.

Though he had never once served in the military, at least not in any official capacity, Lentz stood ramrod straight. "Scully and Mulder have tested the boy's blood extensively. We have complete access to his hospital records. There is absolutely no evidence of a nanotechnology infestation, no microscopic machines, no fragments—nothing. He's clean."

"Then how do you explain his remarkable healing properties? The gunshot wound?"

"No one actually saw that, sir," Lentz said. "At least, no one on record."

The man just looked at him, smoke curling around his face. Lentz knew his answer wasn't acceptable. Not yet. "And the leukemia? The boy shows no sign of further illness, as I understand it."

"Dr. Kennessy knew the potential threat of nanotechnology—he was no fool—and he might have been able to program his nanocritters to shut down once their mission was accomplished, once his son was cured of his cancer. And according to the tests recently run in the hospital, Jody Kennessy is perfectly healthy, no longer suffering from acute lymphoblastic leukemia."

Eyebrows raised. "So he's been cured, but he no longer carries the cure." The man blew out a long breath of cigarette smoke. "We can be happy for that, at least. We certainly wouldn't want anyone else to get their hands on this miracle."

Lentz didn't answer, simply stood watchful and wary. In a secret repository, a building whose address was unknown, in rooms without numbers, drawers without markings, the Cigarette-Smoking Man kept samples and bits of evidence hidden away so that no one else could see. These tangible items would have proven enormously useful to others who sought the truth in all its many forms.

But this man would never share them.

"What about Agents Mulder and Scully?" the smoking man said. "What do they have left?"

"More theories, more hypotheses, but no evidence," Lentz said.

The smoking man inhaled again, then coughed several times, a deep ominous cough that held a taint of much deeper ills. Perhaps he just had a guilty conscience . . . or perhaps something was wrong with him physically.

Lentz fidgeted, waiting to be dismissed or complimented or even reprimanded. The silence was the worst.

"To reiterate," Lentz said, speaking uncomfortably into the man's continued gaze. Languid smoke curled up and around, making a sinuous arabesque dance in the air. "We have destroyed the bodies of all the known plague victims and sterilized every place touched by the nanotechnology. We believe none of these self-reproducing devices has survived."

"Dorman?" the smoking man asked. "And the dog?"

"We sifted through the DyMar wreckage and found an assortment of bones and teeth and a partial skull. We believe these to be the remains of Dorman and the dog."

"Did dental records verify this?"

"Impossible, sir," Lentz answered. "The nanotechnology cellular growths had distorted and changed the bone structure and the teeth, even removing all the fillings from Dorman's mouth. We can't make a positive identification, even as to the species. However, we have eyewitness accounts. We saw the two fall into the flames. We found the bones. There seems to be no question."

"There are always questions," the man said, raising his eyebrows. But then, unconcerned, he lit another cigarette and smoked half of it without saying a word. Lentz waited.

Finally the man stubbed out the butt in the already over-crowded ashtray. He coughed one more time, and finally allowed himself a thin-lipped smile. "Very good, Mr. Lentz. I don't think the world is ready yet for miracle cures . . . at least not anytime soon."

"I agree, sir," Lentz said.

As the man nodded slightly in dismissal, Lentz turned, forcibly stopping himself from running full-tilt out of the office. Behind him, the man coughed again. Louder this time.

50

Survivalist Compound
Oregon Wilderness
One Month Later

 The people were strange here, Jody thought . . . but at least he felt safe. After the ordeal he had recently survived, after his entire world had been destroyed in stages—first the leukemia, then the fire that had killed his father, then the long flight that ended with the death of his mother—he felt he could adapt easily.

Here in the survivalist compound, his Uncle Darin was overly protective but helpful as well. The man refused to talk about his work, his past . . . and that was just fine with Jody. Everyone in this isolated but vehement community fit together like interlocking puzzle pieces.

Just like the puzzle of the Earth rising above the Moon he and his mother had put together one of those last afternoons hidden in the cabin. . . . Jody swallowed hard. He missed her very much.

After Agent Scully had brought him here, the other members of the heavily guarded survivalist compound had taken him under their wing. Jody Kennessy was an icon for them now, something like a mascot for their group—this twelve-year-old boy had taken on the dark and repressive system, and had survived.

Jody's story had only heightened the resolve of the compound members to keep themselves isolated and away from the interfering and destructive government they despised so much.

Jody, his Uncle Darin, and the other survivalists spent their days together in difficult physical work. All the members of the compound shared their own specialties with Jody, instructing him.

Still healing from the stinging wounds in his heart and in his mind, Jody spent much of his time walking the camp's extended perimeter, when he wasn't working in their gardens or fields to help make the colony self-sufficient. The survivalists did a lot of hunting and farming to supplement their enormous stockpile of canned and dried foods.

It was as if this entire community had been ripped up and transplanted here from another time, a self-sufficient time. Jody didn't mind. He was alone now. He didn't feel close even to his Uncle Darin . . . but he would survive. He had overcome terminal cancer, hadn't he?

The other members of the group knew to leave Jody alone when he was in one of his moods, to give him the time and space he needed. Jody wandered the barbed-wire fences, looking at the trees . . . but mainly just being by himself and walking.

A mist clung to the forest, hiding in the hollows, drifting like cottony fog as the day warmed up. Overhead, the clouds remained gray and heavy, barely seen through the tall treetops. He watched his step carefully, though Darin had assured him that there really was no minefield, no booby traps or secret defenses. The survivalists just liked to foster such rumors to maintain the aura of fear and security around their compound. Their main goal was to be left undisturbed by the outside world, and they would use whatever means necessary to accomplish that end.

Jody heard a dog bark in the distance, clear and sharp. The cold damp air seemed to intensify the sound waves.

The survivalists had many dogs in their compound, German shepherds, bloodhounds, rottweilers, Dobermans. But this dog sounded familiar. Jody looked up.

The dog barked again, and now he was more certain. "Come here, boy," he called.

He heard a crashing sound through the underbrush, branches and vines tossed aside as a large black dog bounded toward him, emerging from the mist. The dog barked happily upon seeing him.

"Vader!" Jody called. His heart swelled, but then he dropped his voice, concerned.

The dog looked unharmed, fully healed. Jody had seen Vader vanish into the flames. He had seen the DyMar facility collapse into embers, shards, and twisted girders.

But Jody also knew that his dog was special, just like he'd been before all the nanocritters in his own body had died off. Vader had no such fail-safe system.

The dog bounded toward him, practically knocking Jody over, licking his face, wagging his tail so furiously that it rocked his entire body back and forth. Vader wore no tags, no collar, no way to prove his identity. But Jody knew.

He suspected his uncle might guess the truth, but the story he would have to tell the others was just that he had found another dog, another black Lab like Vader. He would give his new pet the same name. The rest of the survivalists didn't know, and no one else in the outside world would ever need to find out.

He hugged the dog, ruffling his fur and squeezing his neck. He shouldn't have doubted. He should have kept watch, hoping, waiting. His mother had said it herself. The dog would come back to him eventually.

Vader always did.

THE
X-FILES

WHIRLWIND

*A novel by Charles Grant based on
the characters created by Chris Carter.*

Unnatural disasters . . .
Serial killers come in all shapes and sizes. But this one is
particularly puzzling. There's no pattern to the muti-
lated bodies that have been showing up in Phoenix:
both sexes, all races, ages, ethnic groups. There is no
evidence of rape or ritual. Only one thing connects the
victims, the natural disaster that killed them. One of the
most unnatural natural disasters imaginable, leading to
a most painful, most certain and most hideous death . . .

'The series remains one of the most slickly produced
hours on television, notable for its cryptic endings, and
sharp, intelligent writing'   *Variety*

'The most provocative series on TV'
                              Entertainment Weekly

0 00 648205 8

THE
X-FILES

GOBLINS

A novel by Charles Grant
Based on the television series created by Chris Carter.

Opening the X-Files...
Meet Mulder and Scully, FBI. The agency maverick
and the female agent assigned to keep him in line.
Their job: investigate the eeriest unsolved mysteries in
modern America, from pyro-psychics to death row
demonics, from rampaging Sasquatches to alien inva-
sions. The cases the Bureau want handled quietly, but
quickly, before the public finds out what's *really* out
there. And panics.
The cases filed under 'X'.

'*The X-Files* is a true masterpiece. There's no more
challenging series on television and, as a bonus, it's also
brainy fun.'   *Los Angeles Times*

ISBN 0 00 648204 X